Also available from Black Hare Press

DARK DRABBLES ANTHOLOGIES

WORLDS
ANGELS
MONSTERS
UNRAVEL

Twitter: @BlackHarePress
Facebook: BlackHarePress
Website: www.BlackHarePress.com

BEYOND

A DARK DRABBLES ANTHOLOGY

Compiled & Edited by D Kershaw

NATIONAL
LIBRARY
OF AUSTRALIA

A catalogue record for this
book is available from the
National Library of Australia

ISBN978-1-925809-25-1

Cover Design by Dawn Burdett
Book Formatting by Ben Thomas

Dear, beauteous Death! the jewel of the just,
Shining nowhere but in the dark,
What mysteries do lie beyond thy dust,
Could Man outlook that mark!

- Henry Vaughan, "Beyond the Veil"

Table of Contents

Foreword

Have you ever considered what happens to you when you die? Where do you go? Do you actually *go* anywhere, or is it just the end…you merely fade into the nothingness of non-existence?

Or do you float around in purgatory, just beyond the veil…perhaps, you might have a beautiful, angelic (or demonic) existence in the afterlife? Maybe you'll be resurrected to build a new life with ever diminishing memories of the old one; as a new-born infant or an animal?

Whatever you believe, we're going to look at all the possibilities, condensed into tiny, bite-sized chunks of fiction.

Love and kisses
D. Kershaw & Ben Thomas
Black Hare Press

Mine
by Nicola Currie

I always liked being inside her. Stepping into her pretty skin is a bliss I couldn't imagine. She tries to fight, her body convulsing, but it's pointless. She said she would always be mine, despite my objections that a beauty like her could do better than an old guy on the underside of average-looking.

Of course, the pills she crushed into my wine before running me a bath are a pretty big clue that her sweet words were a lie.

I run my hands over the body we share now and think of the things I will make it do.

Nicola Currie is 34, from Cambridge, UK where she works in educational publishing. She has published poetry in literary magazines, including Mslexia and Sarasvati, and has also completed her first novel, which was longlisted for the Bath Children's Novel Award.
Website: writeitandweep.home.blog

A Brush with Death
by Jason Holden

Just once.

Just once, I wish someone would say thank you. Instead, all I get are cries and screams. "Why me? Why me?" Nobody is ever grateful that I ended their pain and suffering. They scream and try to run at the sight of me.

Although I like that part, when the cord of their soul brings them flying back to me like an elastic band before I swing my scythe and free them from their mortal coil.

Anyway, I'd ask how your day was, but since you're talking to me, I think we both know the answer.

Not good.

*After giving up a full-time job as a quarry operator so that his wife could follow her dream career as an academic in the field of chemistry, **Jason Holden** and his family left England and temporarily moved to Spain where they currently reside. While there, he took on the role of full-time parent and began to create stories for his daughter. Now that she is in school, he creates stories for himself and hopes to share those stories with others.*

Ghost Hunter
by Raven Corinn Carluk

Patrizia strode into the house like she owned it. Maggie clutched her children in the breakfast nook, letting Robert handle the paranormal investigators. She wanted to leave, but he wouldn't let her go to her mother's.

Maggie feared the statuesque woman in black, her grey eyes and eerie presence. This ghost hunter was almost scarier than their ghost.

Patrizia grinned when Robert finished. "I've already taken care of your little problem. A sharecropper from before this house was built. Drunkard. Child died of scarlet fever, wife of sorrow. He killed himself when he burnt his place down.

"He was delicious."

Raven Corinn Carluk writes dark fantasy, paranormal romance, and anything else that catches her interest. She's authored five novels, where she explores themes of love and acceptance. Her shorter pieces, usually from her darker side, can be found in Black Hare Press anthologies, at Detritus Online, and through Alban Lake Publishers.
Twitter: @ravencorinn
Website: RavenCorinnCarluk.Blogspot.Com

Out of Body
by R.J. Hunt

I died, once.

My heart stopped on the operating table, for two minutes. It doesn't sound long, but imagine your blood frozen in your veins then count out the seconds. Hold your breath if you really want to feel it. I'll wait. 120 seconds can feel like forever.

I had the classic hallucination; floating above my dead self. Only I wasn't floating. I sank. Through my body, bed, and floor. Through dark earth, plunging deeper. I heard screams, smelt burning. A rank stench. Sulphur. Rot. Blackened pork.

Then I woke up. And I knew I never wanted to die again.

R.J. Hunt is a Civil Engineer from Nottingham who loves creating worlds and writing stories in his spare time. Whilst he has a roughly infinite supply of half-finished stories, he's currently working on the second draft of his debut novel, 'The Final Carnivore' - a story about horrible people being granted immortality and mind-control powers, causing misfits with hidden abilities of their own to rise in an effort stop them.
Twitter: @RJHuntWrites
Reddit: RJHuntWrites

Dad's Songs
by Alanna Robertson-Webb

My dad sings me to sleep each night, his heavy hand gently smoothing back my hair. He's always gone by the time I wake up, but our routine remains constant.

Some nights he croons jazz from the 1920's, sometimes it's pop music from the 1970's, and sometimes it's 2000's RnB. No matter which decade he sings, I still get lulled into deep slumber, and I rarely have nightmares anymore.

We've had this routine for years now, and with each day that passes I dread hearing his voice each night. Why won't he pass on? Why can't he find peace yet?

Alanna Robertson-Webb is a sales support member by day, and a writer and editor by night. She loves VT, and lives in NY. She has been writing since she was five years old, and writing well since she was seventeen years old. She lives with a fiance and a cat, both of whom take up most of her bed space. She loves to L.A.R.P., and one day she aspired to write a horrifyingly fantastic novel. Her short horror stories have been published before, but she still enjoys remaining mysterious.
Reddit: MythologyLovesHorror

Séance
by Liam Hogan

Another seaside town; another séance. His hundredth.

Malcolm preferred the off-season. Audiences of retirees, rather than rowdy tourists.

From the wings he scanned the room, surprised to find the hall full. Some local convention? An odd mix of old-fashioned clothes. But quiet, subdued, respectful.

Easy marks.

He strode purposefully to the middle of the stage as the lights dimmed.

"Is there anyone out there?" he called.

His trademark patter. There would be silence, and then he'd grin: "Not even an audience?"

Instead, a hundred pairs of feet rapped once for yes, and a hundred pairs of hateful eyes glowed yellow.

Liam Hogan is a London based short story writer, the host of Liars' League, and a Ministry of Stories mentor. His story "Ana", appears in Best of British Science Fiction 2016 (NewCon Press) and his twisted fantasy collection, "Happy Ending Not Guaranteed", is published by Arachne Press. Website: happyendingnotguaranteed.blogspot.co.uk Twitter: @LiamJHogan

Until the End
by Crystal L. Kirkham

"Thank you for staying," Jackie croaked.

Cold hands brushed lightly over Jackie's fevered skin. "I'll be here until the end."

Jackie closed her eyes, her energy fading. She'd always feared that her last moments would be lonely ones, but now she had a friend who would wait with her, comfort her as she died.

Spasms wracked her body. Each breath becoming harder than the last until there were no more. The steady beep became a single tone, and the room filled with professionals doing their job.

"Ready to go now?" Death, her friend, asked.

Jackie smiled. "I'm ready. Thank you."

Crystal L. Kirkham *resides in a small hamlet west of Red Deer, Alberta. She's an avid outdoors person, unrepentant coffee addict, part-time foodie, servant to a wonderful feline, and companion to two delightfully hilarious canines. She will neither confirm nor deny the rumours regarding the heart in a jar on her desk and the bottle of reader's tears right next to it. Her paranormal urban fantasy series, Saints and Sinners, is available on Amazon and her YA Fantasy, Feathers and Fae will be released October 11, 2019, from Kyanite Publishing.*
Website: www.crystallkirkham.com

Birthing Poltergeists
by Neen Cohen

He stank of perfume and sex. His dishevelled clothes made her smile.

It's about time!

"I'm so sorry."

Picking up the framed photo, he collapsed on the mattress and sobbed. Her relief turned to anger as he continued clinging to her ghost.

Just let me go!

She heard about their love in his ramblings. Seven years trapped, she now felt nothing but anger and rage.

Mustering what remained of her strength, she slapped the frame from his hands, picked up the biggest shard of shattered glass and slashed.

He sighed in death, instantly released. She screamed, trapped forever by hate.

Neen Cohen lives in Brisbane with her partner, son and fur babies. She is a writer of LGBTQI, dark fantasy and horror short stories and has a Bachelor of Creative Industries from QUT. She can often be found writing while sitting against a tombstone or tree in any number of graveyards.
Facebook: Neen-Cohen-Author-424700821629629
Website: wordbubblessite.wordpress.com

Scared to Death
by Gregg Cunningham

"No way, you do it! I done the last fuckin' question!" Jake demanded as the boys placed their fingers upon the glass again.

Marley sighed, bored with the game already.

"Can you tell us your name?"

Marley turned to Jake with a wink as a cheeky grin cracked his face.

"Don't you dare!" Jake ordered.

The glass began moving, slowly spelling out the word as it jerked across the spirit board.

D...E...A...T...H

Jake rolled his eyes as he watched the two petrified boys run from the room, then turned to Marley's chuckling ghostly figure.

"You ruin the fun every time!"

Gregg Cunningham is a short story writer from Western Australia. He has had several short stories publishing by Zombie Pirate Publishing in Relationship add Vice, Full Metal Horror, Phuket Tattoo, World War four and Flash Fiction Addiction, with GBH due later in the year. Most recently, his work has been accepted into Black Hare Press Drabbles set including Monsters, Angels, Worlds, Unravel, Beyond, and Apocalypse, with his latest short story included in Black Hare Press soon to be released fine Deep Space anthology.
Website: cortlandsdogs.wordpress.com

Brother
by Caitlin Mazur

"Catch me!"

The boy took off from the tree line, sprinting through the tall grass, giggles floating high to the heavens. I followed as fast as my little legs could carry me.

My chase came to an abrupt end as two strong arms engulfed me. "Diana," my father scolded. "Don't run so far this close to dark."

"It was my brother," I whined. My father stiffened, and we walked in silence until we reached the sad place. On his knees, my father wept. The boy popped up from behind the square tombstone and stuck his tongue out at me.

Caitlin Mazur is an author, marketer, wife, and mother to two. By night, she writes primarily science fiction and horror stories with hints of romance. By day, she is a marketing mastermind at a software company.
Twitter: @caitwritesstuff

Banshee
by Cindar Harrell

The wind howled through barren branches, cutting through the night air. In a small house on a hill in the marshlands, a man sat waiting. He heard a shrill cry that was separate from the wind. The sound froze his heart; he knew what that meant. The sound was that of the harbinger of death. A pale woman with white hair appeared before him.

"Am I dead?" the man asked.

"You soon will be."

Before he could reply, a sharp pain ripped through his chest. The breath froze on his lips as he surrendered to death. Silently, the woman disappeared.

Cindar Harrell loves fairy tales, especially ones with a dark twist. Her stories are often fairy tale inspired, but she is also working on a mystery series. Her stories can be found on Amazon and in various anthologies. You can follow her on Facebook and visit her blog, which she promises to try and update more often,
Website: cindarharrell.wordpress.com
Facebook: CindarHarrell

Frank
by Andrew Anderson

There it was again, women giggling, coming from the cellar.

Frank couldn't stand the torment any longer, he snatched the door open.

Two apparitions floated at the foot of the stairs, their wet, black hair obscuring bloated grey faces.

Frank recognised them though; it was Susie and Maria.

He could still see his hand marks around their necks, and the concrete floor was damp where he had buried them three years before.

Maria pushed her dank hair to the side, grinning.

"So nice of you to join us, Frank, it's been a while."

"And rest-assured, you *will* be joining us."

Andrew Anderson is a full-time civil servant, dabbling in writing music, poetry, screenplays and short stories in his limited spare time, when not working on building himself a fort made out of second-hand books. He lives in Bathgate, Scotland with his wife, two children and his dog. Twitter: @soorploom

Gift or Curse?
by Stephen Herczeg

Is it a gift or a curse?

I see them all around me. Departed souls, gentle wisps of lives lived and lost. They pass others who never realise they're there.

But today is different. There's something wrong.

These normally placid spirits are agitated, animated. They know I see them, but instead of ignoring me, they want me to follow. They crowd behind, funnel me towards a doorway of an old house.

Unlocked, it swings open. The stench of death hangs heavy.

A body lies nearby in a pool of blood.

I turn away. The spirits fade, their work is done.

Stephen Herczeg is an IT Geek based in Canberra Australia. He has been writing for over twenty years and has completed a couple of dodgy novels, sixteen feature length screenplays and numerous short stories and scripts. His horror work has featured in Sproutlings, Hells Bells, Below the Stairs, Trickster's Treats #1 and #2, Shades of Santa, Behind the Mask, Beyond the Infinite; The Body Horror Book, Anemone Enemy, Petrified Punks and Beginnings. He has also had numerous Sherlock Holmes stories published through the Belanger Books - Sherlock Holmes anthologies.

Boomer
by G. Allen Wilbanks

"Do you believe in psychic gifts?" I asked into my cellphone.

I picked up the box of cat treats from the kitchen floor. My orange tabby, Boomer, munched contentedly on a few stray treats still on the ground.

"Like E.S.P?" my friend asked. "No idea. Never thought about it."

"Do you think animals could have…abilities?" I said, stretching an arm to place the box on the highest shelf of the cabinet.

"I suppose if people can have them, animals could, too," he replied. "Why?"

"No reason."

I watched as Boomer pawed open the treat box on the floor again.

G. Allen Wilbanks is a member of the Horror Writers Association (HWA) and has published over 50 short stories in various magazines and on-line venues. He is the author of two short story collections, and the novel, When Darkness Comes.
Website: www.gallenwilbanks.com
Blog: DeepDarkThoughts.com

Moving On
by Amber M. Simpson

She looks so peaceful lying there, long limbs spread across the sheets, light hair a halo on the pillow around her head. Her lashes seem to flutter with movement against her cheeks as I hover over her in the dark.

You'd never know she was dead, if not for the bullet hole and spattered blood.

It's funny, I can't remember why I pulled the trigger now. Part of me longs to cut her open and slither back inside. Against my will, floating, I rise higher towards the ceiling. And with one last look at my former body, off I fly.

Amber M. Simpson *is a chronic nighttime writer with a penchant for dark fiction and fantasy. When she's not editing for Fantasia Divinity Magazine, she divides her creative time (when she's not procrastinating) between writing a mystery/horror novel, working on a medieval fantasy series, and coming up with new ideas for short stories. Above all, she enjoys being a mom to her two greatest creations, Max and Liam, who keep her feet on the ground even while her head is in the clouds.*
Website: www.ambermsimpson.com

Premonition
by Dawn DeBraal

Daria was a precocious child. As a toddler, she came to her mother to comfort her.

"Don't cry mommy, it's alright. It was an accident." Moments after their hug, her mother bumped and shattered grandmother's vase while vacuuming.

Riding to school as a teenager, Daria screamed,

"Mom, stop!" Panicked, her mother slammed on the brakes narrowly avoiding the pickup that ran the red light.

When the neighbour man went missing. Daria's mother asked her if she "knew" anything about Mr. Wright's disappearance. Daria said coldly,

"He died. He was going to do bad things to people, so I stopped him."

Dawn DeBraal lives in rural Wisconsin with her husband, two rat terriers, and a cat. She successfully raised two children (meaning they didn't return to the nest!) After many years serving the government at the Federal and County level, she recently retired. Having extra time on her hands she started to write after a paralyzed vocal cord took her ability to speak for two months. Not finding her voice, she discovered that her love of telling a good story could be written. Her works have been published in Palm-sized press, Spillwords, Mercurial Stories, Potato Soup Journal, and Blood Song Books.

Contact
by Joel R. Hunt

"Spirits are anchored to our world," explained Madam Za, "Their secrets, their desires, their broken dreams – these weigh down their souls, prevent their passage. Spirits crave contact with the living in order to unburden themselves and pass on."

Madam Za's visitor tapped his fingers on his knee and shot a look over his shoulder.

"What if their message is harmful?" he asked, "What if it shouldn't be shared? Is there a way to stop a spirit from getting in contact?"

"With you?"

"With anyone."

A red-throated woman leant down, hissed into Madam Za's ear: "He's the one who strangled me."

Joel R. Hunt is a writer from the UK who dabbles in the darker aspects of life, particularly through horror, science fiction and the supernatural. He has been published here and there (though likely nowhere you've heard of) and hopes to have released his first anthology of short stories later this year.
Twitter: @JoelRHunt1
Reddit: JRHEvilInc

Child of the 80s
by Cameron Marcoux

My first sleepover. I'm excited. I never get invited to these things.

I vote for Jenga. But my friends want to play with Oscar's dad's spirit board that he keeps hidden in the closet.

"Jenga's for babies!"

"Yeah! Don't be such a pussy!"

Lights are off, except for a flashlight.

Fingers press against the planchette. Mine last. They tingle. Probably just nerves. Oscar asks a question to an empty room. Oscar asks a question to a spirit. "Hello, Spirit. Will anything bad happen tonight?"

Planchette moves: YES

Was it Oscar? Jeff? I'm nervous.

"What will happen, Spirit?"

J

A

C

K

W

I

L

L

D

I

E.

Cameron Marcoux is a writer of stories, which, considering where you are reading this, makes a lot of sense. He also teaches English to the lovely and terrifying creatures we call teenagers. He lives in the quiet, northern reaches of New England in the U.S. with his girlfriend and scaredy dog.

Spirit
by Umair Mirxa

Steve spun on the spot, frantically considering his options. Desperate, he took the plunge.

For a moment, everything was pitch black.

Wake up! RUN! he screamed.

His wife's eyes flew open, even as the intruder barged his way into the bedroom.

The knife missed her by a hair's breadth. She scrambled out of bed, ran into the Jack and Jill bathroom. Out the door, down the hall, and into the backyard through the kitchen. *She would make it.*

Steve heard the gunshot before he felt the pain. His wife crumpled onto the grass as his spirit fled her lifeless body.

Umair Mirxa lives in Karachi, Pakistan. His first published story, 'Awareness', appeared on Spillwords Press. He has also had stories accepted for anthologies from Zombie Pirate Publishing, Blood Song Books, Fantasia Divinity Magazine and Publishing, and Iron Faerie Publishing. He is a massive J.R.R. Tolkien fan, and loves everything to do with fantasy and mythology. He enjoys football, history, music, movies, TV shows, and comic books, and wishes with all his heart that dragons were real.
Website: www.umairmirxa.com
Facebook: UMirxa12

Guilty Call
by R.J. Hunt

After she died, the phone would not stop ringing.

I clamped my hands over my ears. Tried to distract myself with idle things.

But still the phone kept ringing.

I unplugged it. Removed it. Burnt it.

The phone would not stop ringing.

I moved away to sea, on a rickety boat, screaming into the wind.

The phone would not STOP RINGING.

"I killed her, okay? It was my fault. Is that what you want to hear?" I howled.

It. Would. Not. Stop. Ringing.

I rammed a steel rod down my ears until I could hear nothing.

Except the ringing phone.

R.J. Hunt is a Civil Engineer from Nottingham who loves creating worlds and writing stories in his spare time. Whilst he has a roughly infinite supply of half-finished stories, he's currently working on the second draft of his debut novel, 'The Final Carnivore' - a story about horrible people being granted immortality and mind-control powers, causing misfits with hidden abilities of their own to rise in an effort stop them.
Twitter: @RJHuntWrites
Reddit: RJHuntWrites

The Anniversary
by Isabella Fox

Henry scrambled out of the hole and staggered off into the night. He did this on the same date every year, an anniversary thing.

Outside the pub, people mingled in groups laughing and drinking. One guy saw Henry and said, "Great costume, mate! How did you get the flesh to look like it's falling off you? And where's your other eyeball?"

Henry ignored him and muttered, "Why did I have to die on Halloween?"

He continued down the road to his old home to watch his family toast his memory. Contented, he wandered back to his grave until next year.

Isabella Fox teaches primary aged students to love writing by making it challenging. In her spare time she reads, goes for long walks with her husband and works hard on her farm.

Forever and Ever
by K.T. Tate

She looks hurt, betrayed, as I plunge the dagger into her heart. Waking bound in a circle of mystical symbols isn't common in most relationships, I get that. But she'd said she'd love me forever, and I'd believed her.

Eldritch chants come easy, well-rehearsed. She starts to glow. I love to watch the soul as it leaves. A strange ethereal jellyfish, floating deliciously until I capture it. It squirms, resists, but my enchantments are strong. No light for you, you promised me eternity.

Housed in a doll of perfect likeness, I place her on the shelf with all the others.

K.T. Tate lives in Cambridgeshire in the UK. She writes mainly weird fiction, cosmic horror and strange monster stories.
Website: eldritchhollow.wordpress.com
Tumblr: eldritch-hollow.tumblr.com

Never Again
by Gabriella Balcom

"You call yourself *God*?" Hetty raged. Beating her chest with her fists, she shook them at the sky. Tears streamed from her red, puffy eyes. Her runny nose and chapped lips could've been another woman's for all the attention she paid them.

"I lost everyone I loved but you still let my baby die."

When her infant son reappeared alive, Hetty gasped and grabbed him but still fumed. "Is this a game to you? *Never* again will I praise you. May oblivion consume you. I hope you lose your power and fade from memory. I wish you nothing but misery."

Gabriella Balcom lives in Texas with her family, loves reading and writing, and thinks she was born with a book in her hands. She works in a mental health field, and writes fantasy, horror/thriller, romance, children's stories, and sci-fi. She likes travelling, music, good shows, photography, history, interesting tales, and animals. Gabriella says she's a sucker for a great story and loves forests, mountains, and back roads which might lead who knows where. She has a weakness for lasagne, garlic bread, tacos, cheese, and chocolate, but not necessarily in that order.
Facebook: GabriellaBalcom.lonestarauthor

The Cat
by Stephen Herczeg

I snap awake. It's 3AM. Pitch black.

I stagger into the bathroom and sit down. Too dark to aim. Can't bear the clean-up in the morning.

Brain is groggy from too many wines.

I hear the familiar footfalls padding across the floor, then feel the touch of soft fur against my legs.

I stroke her head and run my hand down her back.

She rubs back and forth against my legs and I hear the sound of her deep contented purr.

Back in bed, I search for sleep.

My eyes snap open. Heart thumping.

The cat died a month ago.

Stephen Herczeg is an IT Geek based in Canberra Australia. He has been writing for over twenty years and has completed a couple of dodgy novels, sixteen feature length screenplays and numerous short stories and scripts. His horror work has featured in Sproutlings, Hells Bells, Below the Stairs, Trickster's Treats #1 and #2, Shades of Santa, Behind the Mask, Beyond the Infinite; The Body Horror Book, Anemone Enemy, Petrified Punks and Beginnings. He has also had numerous Sherlock Holmes stories published through the Belanger Books - Sherlock Holmes anthologies.

Kaidan
by Patrick Winters

Yoshi awoke suddenly, unable to move, unable to scream. And scream he would've, for his wife hung above him—pale, moaning, and dripping wet.

She glared at him in mournful loathing, her mouth gaping, a choked gurgle coming out of her bloated throat. A torrent of frigid water came raging out of it, shooting across his face, down his nose, into his mouth.

Yoshi could not get out from under the horrid flow.

He died, drowned in the same waters that he had forced Akari under a month before, leaving her body to sink into the pond beside their hut.

*Patrick Winters is a graduate of Illinois College in Jacksonville, IL, where he earned a Bachelor of Arts degree in English Literature and Creative Writing and achieved membership into Sigma Tau Delta, an international English honors society. Winters is now a proud member of the Horror Writers Association, and his work has been published in the likes of Sanitarium Magazine, Deadman's Tome, Trysts of Fate, and other such titles. A full list of his previous publications may be found at his author's site.
Website: wintersauthor.azurewebsites.net/Publications/List*

Never Alone
by Eddie D. Moore

The lights flickered, and Cynthia stepped away from the autopsy table. She placed her scalpel on the tray beside her and let out a sigh before asking the empty room, "How am I supposed to get any work done under these conditions?"

The air conditioning abruptly stopped working with a metallic clink, and the lights went completely out. Her laptop in the other room switched to battery power and provided a dim light. She looked into the face of the large burly man on the table and said, "At least I'm never alone here."

A deep voice whispered, "Never alone."

Eddie D. Moore travels hundreds of hours a year, and he fills that time by listening to audiobooks. When he isn't playing with his grandchildren, he writes his own stories. You can find a list of his publications on his blog or by visiting his Amazon Author Page. While you're there, be sure to pick up a copy of his mini-anthology Misfits & Oddities. Website: eddiedmoore.wordpress.com Amazon: amazon.com/author/eddiedmoore

Sandman
by Sinister Sweetheart

The sand was golden; the sky a myriad of pastels as the sun set. Desolate Pomar Beach was ours that day.

My friends and I were having a blast. But too many libations led to stupid ideas. One of which involved burying me in sand.

Once buried, I fell into a seemingly endless tunnel of black. Upon landing, I found myself in a room of black. Emptiness found me at every corner.

A window appeared in the distance. My lifeless body was being pulled from the sand. My friends sobbed as the EMTs zipped up the black bag around me.

*Since **Sinister Sweetheart** made her first post to a popular Internet forum, she's taken the horror community by storm. Her ability to create, terrify, and drive home her stories is insurmountable. Sinister Sweetheart's published works can be found in multiple anthologies for all to read, but be forewarned, if you do... you may want to call your therapist after, her stories are terrifying, disturbing and devilishly unsettling. She is not only a fright visually, but also has a creepy tentacle in horror podcasting as well. Sinister Sweetheart writes, voice acts and is the media director of the Scarecrow Tales podcast.*
Website: Sinistersweetheart.wixsite.com/sinistersweetheart
Facebook: NMBrownStories

Trinity
by Jem McCusker

Cold, damp and suffocating. Sweat pools and beads, oozing fear. The cloaked figures call out, the voices in chorus reverberate off the walls.

Faces twist and contort. The stained-glass window hovers above, its colours flickering across the room as the soft candlelight creates an ominous glow.

A man lies chained to the bed posts as his body ceases. The dark shadow claws from his shell, blood streaks across his chest.

"We cast you out," the chorus of voices shout.

"In the name of the father, the son, the—" They fall as blood trickles from their noses.

The beast is free.

Jem McCusker is a middle grade fiction author, living near Brisbane with her two sons and husband. Her first book Stone Guardians the Rise of Eden was released in 2018 and she is working on the sequel. She is releasing a Novella for the Four Quills writing group, A Storm of Wind and Rain series in July, 2019. She longs to be a full-time author, won't wear yellow and loves rabbits. Follow Jem on Twitter, Facebook and Instagram. Details on her website.
Website: www.jemmccusker.com

The Narrow Ledge Between Heaven and Hell
by Shelly Jarvis

The light is brighter than expected. Blinding, really. TV and movies say to walk into it, to go through, move beyond. They don't mention how hot it is.

The heat is surprising. I wasn't sure you could still feel physical pain after death. Now I know. I wish I didn't.

I hear voices in the distance and wonder if it's my parents. Do dogs go to heaven? Maybe Duke will be with them, wagging his tail. The thought makes me smile.

I'm nearly touching the light now. I take a deep breath and step into it and feel myself burn.

Shelly Jarvis is a speculative fiction author from West Virginia, US. She found a life-long love of sci-fi and fantasy in the 3rd grade when she found Madeleine L'Engle's "A Wrinkle in Time." Shelly is an avid reader, a Whovian, the ideal viewer of dog rescue videos, and undoubtedly Ravenclaw. She currently has two YA sci-fi books available for purchase on Amazon.
Website: www.ShellyJarvis.com

The Reaper
by J. Farrington

A year ago today, I almost died.

Out on the highway, a drunk driver ploughed into the side of my car, throwing me from the vehicle. The impact with the road below should have killed me.

I wish it had.

When people almost die, they profess to seeing a bright light and loved ones passed. That couldn't be further from the truth. You're thrown into complete blackness, a large desolate room with no escape. But you're not alone.

The Reaper is there, to claim your soul.

And if you get revived, pulled from the blackness?

The Reaper follows you back.

J. Farrington is an aspiring author from the West Midlands, UK. His genre of choice is horror; whether that be psychological, suspense, supernatural or straight up weird, he'll give it a shot! He has loved writing from a young age but has only publicly been spreading his darker thoughts and sinister imagination via social platforms since 2018. If you would like to view his previous work, or merely lurk in the shadows...watching, you can keep up to date with future projects by spirit board or alternatively, the following;
Twitter: @SurvivorTrench
Reddit: TrenchChronicles

The Ferryman
by Stuart Conover

Humans loved their stories of angels and demons and grim reapers.

Yet these were not who cared for the dead.

Not who judged them.

The truth was buried in history.

The Ferryman had guided souls across the River since humanity was born.

However, few were able to still make it into the afterlife.

None were prepared any longer for the judgement which awaited them.

Too busy destroying the paradise they had been given.

Sighing, the Ferryman picked up more souls.

Begging for a way out, an explanation.

Silence was their only answer.

Their fates were up to the Gods now.

Stuart Conover is a father, husband, rescue dog owner, published author, blogger, journalist, horror enthusiast, comic book geek, science fiction junkie, and IT professional. With all of that to cram in daily, we have no idea if or when he sleeps or how he gets writing done! (We suspect it has to do with having evil clones.) Stuart is a Chicago native and runs the author resource Horror Tree.

Slumber Party Seance
by Crystal L. Kirkham

"Who should we summon?" Cassie asked. All of us at the slumber party shouted out answers, but we couldn't agree on anything.

"How about we just chant and see what happens?" Cassie giggled as she placed the spirit board in the middle of the circle. We all placed our hands on the planchette and it moved immediately. A shiver ran down my spine.

"No," I pulled my hands away, "what if we summon something evil?"

"Too late," a voice growled from a dark corner.

I wanted to run, but I was frozen. We all were. There would be no escape.

Crystal L. Kirkham resides in a small hamlet west of Red Deer, Alberta. She's an avid outdoors person, unrepentant coffee addict, part-time foodie, servant to a wonderful feline, and companion to two delightfully hilarious canines. She will neither confirm nor deny the rumours regarding the heart in a jar on her desk and the bottle of reader's tears right next to it. Her paranormal urban fantasy series, Saints and Sinners, is available on Amazon and her YA Fantasy, Feathers and Fae will be released October 11, 2019, from Kyanite Publishing.
Website: www.crystallkirkham.com

Beyond Love
by Gregg Cunningham

"I'm sorry, but he's gone to a better place now."

The diener stood by the trolley with the white sheet raised from my face, just enough so that my angry fiancé could nod and weep one last time for her terrible loss.

The truth was, I'm actually still here, in the same place.

Only now I'm debt free.

So what if she was the one that fed me my last supper, laced with the rat poison, on the false understanding I had life insurance.

So what if I refinanced our house to pay for the hookers.

It's her problem now.

Gregg Cunningham is a short story writer from Western Australia. He has had several short stories publishing by Zombie Pirate Publishing in Relationship add Vice, Full Metal Horror, Phuket Tattoo, World War four and Flash Fiction Addiction, with GBH due later in the year. Most recently, his work has been accepted into Black Hare Press Drabbles set including Monsters, Angels, Worlds, Unravel, Beyond, and Apocalypse, with his latest short story included in Black Hare Press soon to be released fine Deep Space anthology.
Website: cortlandsdogs.wordpress.com

The Medium is the Message
by Shawn M. Klimek

Rubbing his aching temples, Noel explained, "From birth, my identical twin and I could share sensations across any distance. That's how I know he must be in Hell."

The spirit medium exhaled a mélange of sardines and tobacco smoke. Indifferent to his cringe, she countered, "Leon's Hell is self-imposed. He lingers only to punish you for his murder."

"But I repented!" Noel pleaded. "Will he haunt me forever?"

Caressing his hands with her clammy palms, the hag replied, "No. Your brother is tired of pain and ready to reconcile. Now, he only wishes to feel you make love to me."

Shawn M. Klimek is the middle child of seven creative siblings, a globetrotting, U.S. military spouse, an internationally best-selling short-story writer, a poet, and butler to a Maltese. Almost one hundred of his stories or poems have been published in digital magazines or anthologies, including BHP's Deep Space and the first six books in the Dark Drabbles series.
Website: jotinthedark.blogspot.com
Facebook: shawnmklimekauthor

The Death of Future's Past
by Hari Navarro

"Why are you so scared?" asks the assassin to her mark as she watches the wetness spread from his crotch to his leg.

"I do not wish to die."

"You've nothing to fear. I've been there and, behold, see that I have returned."

"You're mad..."

"Then we're all lunatics, for you have been there too. Albeit, you won't remember until my blade does tongue the veins at your neck. It is the ink dark hollow, the cradle which held you before you fell to the canal and unfurled from the grip of your mother. I am but sending you home."

Hari Navarro has had work published at the very fine online flash fiction portal 365tomorrows.com, BREACH - a bi-monthly online zine for SF, horror and dark fantasy short fiction and AntipodeanSF - Australia's longest running online speculative fiction magazine. Hari was the Winner of the Australasian Horror Writers' Association [AHWA] Flash Fiction Award 2018 and has, also, succeeded in being a New Zealander who now lives in Northern Italy with no cats.
Facebook: HariDarkFiction
Twitter: @HariFiction

Madam Zora
by Vonnie Winslow Crist

Another sucker, thought Madam Zora as a well-dressed man entered her shop. *He's an accountant or lawyer*, she decided.

She'd never communicated with the dead but was so adept at reading customers that they believed she did.

"May I help you?"

"I'm waiting for my wife," he explained.

Annoyed she'd wasted time studying him, Zora frowned.

Suddenly, a woman strode in, walked over, sat in the chair opposite Zora. "I want to contact my deceased husband."

As the medium watched, the businessman, whom she now recognised as a ghost, drifted near.

Bloodlines matter, Zora realised, *I do have the Gift!*

Vonnie Winslow Crist is author of *The Enchanted Dagger, Owl Light, The Greener Forest, Murder on Marawa Prime*, and other award-winning books. Her fiction is included in "Amazing Stories," "Cast of Wonders," "Outposts of Beyond," *Killing It Softly 2, Defending the Future - Dogs of War, Midnight Masquerade, Chaos of Hard Clay*, and elsewhere. A cloverhand who has found so many four-leafed clovers she keeps them in jars, Vonnie strives to celebrate the power of myth in her writing.
Website: www.vonniewinslowcrist.com

Dreams and Awareness
by Pamela Jeffs

Sleep is akin to death—the stillness, the slowing of the heart. But with any loss of consciousness, dreams awaken.

An awareness past *awareness*.

And that is where my grandmother dwells. She sits in her oak rocking chair on a dream-wrought veranda. A teapot sits on the side table, steam rising from the spout. Her gnarled fingers encircle a favoured teacup; another sits empty next to her. That one is mine. She rocks the chair, watching the sunlight wane. Waiting for nightfall. Waiting for me to sleep. It's dangerous for me to go, but I do. Her call is insistent.

Pamela Jeffs is a speculative fiction author living in Queensland, Australia with her husband and two daughters. She is a member of the Queensland Writers' Centre and has had numerous short fiction pieces published in recent national and international anthologies. In 2017 and again in 2018, Pamela was nominated for an Australian Aurealis Award in the category of 'Best Science Fiction Short Story'. Her debut collection titled 'Red Hour and Other Strange Tales' was released in March 2018.
Website: www.pamelajeffs.com
Facebook: pamelajeffsauthor

Obsession
by John Saxton

"Is there anybody there...?"

McShane believed, deep down in his heart, that he could break through the spirit veil: commune with his parents on the other side. It had become an obsession.

The surrounding shadows aided perfect concentration. He focussed his mind, his emotions, his *will*, as fully as he could muster. Despite the darkness, he detected their presence. Hell, he could *see them!*

But as yet, he had raised no response. His fellow inmates ridiculed him.

He ignored their derision—tonight was Halloween, the ideal night for breaching the spectral barrier; for escaping the mausoleum.

And contacting the living.

John Saxton hails from Yorkshire, UK, where he is happily married, with two sons. He has had over 50 short horror stories published in the independent press, including his own collection: 'Bloodshot'. He writes mainly after dark...
Twitter: @jsaxtonwriter

Calm
by G. Allen Wilbanks

"Start playlist B," I called out. The virtual assistant reacted immediately. The first heavy beats of Cum on Feel the Noize rumbled through the air.

Lawrence covered his ears in mock distress. "Why do you play such loud music?" he complained.

"It calms the ghosts," I explained. "For some reason, they really like heavy metal music."

"Stop music!" shouted Lawrence. Then, when silence filled the room, "I don't believe in ghosts. You're being an idiot."

I waited a moment in the quiet.

Lawrence's eyes grew wide at something he saw over my right shoulder.

"Playlist B!" he screamed. "Playlist B!"

G. Allen Wilbanks is a member of the Horror Writers Association (HWA) and has published over 50 short stories in various magazines and on-line venues. He is the author of two short story collections, and the novel, When Darkness Comes.
Website: www.gallenwilbanks.com
Blog: DeepDarkThoughts.com

The Time Keeper
by Jasmine Jarvis

If the clock stops, he will get you. You need to keep the clock wound and ticking. That ticking is your heart, taken from you at birth and placed within the clock. You are bound to the time keeper. You listen to it ticking, and when it slows down, so do you. Then he appears, ready to claim you, as the deal was made when you were born, a deal he made with your mother. Wind the clock back up and he sinks back into the shadows.

Waiting for you.

Always waiting.

When the clock stops, he will get you.

Jasmine Jarvis is a teller of tales and scribbler of scribbles. She lives in Brisbane, Australia with her husband Michael, their two children, Tilly and Mish; Ripley, their German Shepherd; indoor fat cat, Dwight K. Shrute; and grumpy old guinea pig, Doctor Who.

The Darkness
by Zoey Xolton

Down the stairs she ran, the malingering darkness not far behind. It flowed down the staircase, inevitable, formless, horrifying. No matter which corridor she turned down, which door she opened, or which direction she chose—they all led back to the same place; the heart of the house, where the *Darkness* dwelled. There was no escape, no hope of survival. She was the last of the twelve that had entered. A billion dollars had seemed worth a night in a haunted hotel. She'd dreamed of holidays and designer labels. Now, all she wanted was to wake up from this nightmare…

Zoey Xolton is an Australian Speculative Fiction writer, primarily of Dark Fantasy, Paranormal Romance and Horror. She is also a proud mother of two and is married to her soul mate. Outside of her family, writing is her greatest passion. She is especially fond of short fiction and is working on releasing her own themed collections in future.
Website: www.zoeyxolton.com

Nana

by Alanna Robertson-Webb

My grandmother, who I called Nana, was never anything but kind and loving towards me. She passed away from cancer when I was eleven, and my mom taught me that death was final.

Now that I'm older, I don't quite believe my mom. Nana's body is long gone, but I'm sure it's her who turns her favourite radio station on late at night, and her who makes sure my blanket keeps me warm.

But, if that *is* her, then who else is at my apartment, slamming doors, scaring my cat, and smashing my breakables?

I think someone else found me.

Alanna Robertson-Webb is a sales support member by day, and a writer and editor by night. She loves VT, and lives in NY. She has been writing since she was five years old, and writing well since she was seventeen years old. She lives with a fiance and a cat, both of whom take up most of her bed space. She loves to L.A.R.P., and one day she aspired to write a horrifyingly fantastic novel. Her short horror stories have been published before, but she still enjoys remaining mysterious.
Reddit: MythologyLovesHorror

Possessed
by Nancy Brewka-Clark

I draw no breath, yet I live because I nurture a hatred stronger than the power of death. Thanks to you, I have no flesh, no blood, no beating heart.

But I am no longer your victim.

I will drive you mad each minute that you live. You took your fiendish pleasure. I had none. You beg for mercy now, but I've none to give. I'll come to you each night and lie beside you, bone to fleshless bone, until you howl with terror, not lust.

This bed's your coffin now.

You'll never escape the hellish consequences of my rape.

Nancy Brewka-Clark's dark, mystery, horror and speculative fiction have appeared in Yellow Mama, Mysterical-E, Eastern Iowa Review, Every Day Fiction, Close2theBone and a number of anthologies including four by FunDead Publications of Salem, Massachusetts. She lives in the city of Beverly which until 1668 was part of Salem and is married to a direct descendant of one of the witchcraft victims of 1692, which might have happened yesterday for all the intense interest it still stirs.
Website: nancybrewkaclark.com

Fool's Gold
by Dawn DeBraal

The ring appeared on a bookshelf one day. Scrolled initials, so ornate no one could decipher them. Axel brought the ring to a jeweller.

"Very nice! Twenty-four karat gold!" the jeweller commented.

"The diamonds?" asked Axel

"Real," confirmed the jeweller.

"Initials?" Axel's interest was piqued.

"J.S.T. Very old script," said the jeweller. "Are you selling it?"

"John Stephen Traylor," whispered Axel. He was the man who had built Axel's house. Turning down the $8,000 offer, Axel took the ring home, putting it back on the bookshelf. The next day the gold ring was gone as mysteriously as it had appeared.

Dawn DeBraal lives in rural Wisconsin with her husband, two rat terriers, and a cat. She successfully raised two children (meaning they didn't return to the nest!) After many years serving the government at the Federal and County level, she recently retired. Having extra time on her hands she started to write after a paralyzed vocal cord took her ability to speak for two months. Not finding her voice, she discovered that her love of telling a good story could be written. Her works have been published in Palm-sized press, Spillwords, Mercurial Stories, Potato Soup Journal, and Blood Song Books.

Hans Rising
by Sue Marie St. Lee

A glowing fog hovered over the cemetery. The tall, robed figure gestured for me to follow him. His large, bare feet led the way. With no idea of the destination, or why I was following this stranger, I felt no fear.

We stopped where a violet fog rumbled from the ground. The figure pointed to where I stood; I was to stop. A few steps beyond, the figure turned to face me. The ground between began to open. I saw a bright light from the opening, and someone was ascending the stairs from within. It was Hans, he was smiling.

Sue Marie St. Lee is a retired Finance Manager who has been freelancing, researching, writing content, designing corporate websites and brochures over the past fifteen years. She also started a small business specializing in digital photo restoration. Born and raised in Chicago, she moved to Canada where she and her husband raised their sons until her husband's untimely death. As a young widow, Sue Marie employed her skills, tenacity, strengths and wisdom to support her young family. Currently, Sue Marie contributes to several blogs, is a ghostwriter for numerous online publishers and corporate websites. Her sons are grown, productive adults.

Quick Fade In
by Beth W. Patterson

You always did have a rational, scientific explanation for everything, including how I died.

Of course, she's consoling you now. It's quite touching, really, considering that she's the one you almost married instead of me. But her proclamation that only she ever understood you is in pretty poor taste. Not that I'm surprised, since she told me as much to my face when I was alive.

If only you two could have seen the expressions on your faces just now when the jar on the shelf smashed as you were about to kiss! Here comes another!

Suspend your disbelief, motherfuckers!

Beth W. Patterson was a full-time musician for over two decades before diving into the world of writing, a process she describes as "fleeing the circus to join the zoo". She is the author of the books Mongrels and Misfits, and The Wild Harmonic, and a contributing writer to thirty anthologies. Patterson has performed in eighteen countries, expanding her perspective as she goes. Her playing appears on over a hundred and seventy albums, soundtracks, videos, commercials, and voice-overs (including seven solo albums of her own). She lives in New Orleans, Louisiana with her husband Josh Paxton, jazz pianist extraordinaire.
Website: www.bethpattersonmusic.com
Facebook: bethodist

The Devil's House
by E.L. Giles

Standing at the edge of a cliff was a dilapidated house, towering over a forest into which none but the bravest of men dared adventure, for it was known to be inhabited by ghosts and evil spirits.

"Beware, the forest is damned, and the Devil himself inhabits the house," warned locals, their voices full of dread.

With their words, they stoked the fires of the old, gloomy legends and fairy tales.

As long as anyone could remember, no one had ever occupied the Devil's house, yet every night, strange voices came from within, and from its chimney expelled blood-red smoke.

E.L. Giles is a dreamer, passionate about art, a restless worker and a bit of a weird human. He started his artistic journey as a music composer until the need to put his thoughts and stories down on paper grew too strong for him to resist it any longer. He lives in the French Province of Quebec, Canada, with his girlfriend and two boys.
Facebook: elgilesauthor
Website: www.elgilesauthor.com

Little Brother
by Raven Corinn Carluk

Let me out, Sammie.

Sammie huddled beneath her covers, trying to drown out the voice of her brother.

I'm so cold. I just want to be warm again.

She knew it couldn't be Wally, because Wally had died in July. Drowned in the lake. Mommy had made her go to the funeral, so Wally couldn't have been here for the last week.

Don't you miss me?

Sammie bit her lip and cried. If she told Mommy about Wally, she'd have to see that doctor with all the toys again, and she didn't want to do that.

I love you, Sammie.

Raven Corinn Carluk writes dark fantasy, paranormal romance, and anything else that catches her interest. She's authored five novels, where she explores themes of love and acceptance. Her shorter pieces, usually from her darker side, can be found in Black Hare Press anthologies, at Detritus Online, and through Alban Lake Publishers.
Twitter: @ravencorinn
Website: RavenCorinnCarluk.Blogspot.Com

Wings
by Annie Percik

I swoop in on wings of fire at the moment of transition. Their faces show a mixture of awe and terror. The occasional hint of gratitude flavours the experience. I see them at their worst, stripped bare of all bravado, naked and alone as they were at the beginning. I envelop them in a fiery embrace and lift them from all their cares. But I do not take them to horror or to peace, whatever they expect. I eject them into oblivion, then turn back for the next in line. An endless round of separation. My eternal task to perform.

Annie Percik lives in London with her husband, Dave, where she is revising her first novel, whilst working as a University Complaints Officer. She writes a blog about writing and posts short fiction on her website. She also publishes a photo-story blog, recording the adventures of her teddy bear. He is much more popular online than she is. She likes to run away from zombies in her spare time.
Website: www.alobear.co.uk
Website: aloysius-bear.dreamwidth.org

The Séance
by Tracy Davidson

This séance is lame. Full of cheap tricks and mumbo jumbo. Time to liven it up a little. Show this fake medium what spirits can really do...

I may have gone too far. Only meant to breathe down necks, squeeze a few of the more fulsome breasts, whisper in ears. But, somehow, the room is now full of broken bodies. Blood and brain matter on the walls, limbs scattered in all corners.

Only the medium lives; she sits hugging herself on the floor, rocking back and forth, mumbling prayers.

Much good they did her. She will not cheapen us again.

Tracy Davidson lives in Warwickshire, England, and writes poetry and flash fiction. Her work has appeared in various publications and anthologies, including: Poet's Market, Writers Digest, Mslexia, Modern Haiku, Atlas Poetica, The Binnacle, Artificium, Journey to Crone, The Great Gatsby Anthology, WAR and In Protest: 150 Poems for Human Rights.

Goodbyes
by A.R. Johnston

I creep out of my bed because I just heard something. Rubbing my eyes with the fist of my hand. I'm barely five years old and not supposed to be out of bed yet. A big yawn catches me but then I see her. Clear as day, she stands before me.

"Grandma."

"Hello love. I'm going to miss you so much."

"Where are you going? Do you have to go?"

"Yes, love. It's time for me to go."

"I'm going to miss you so much." I start to cry.

"No tears. I love you too."

"Goodbye, Grandma, I love you."

A.R. Johnston is a small-town girl from Nova Scotia, Canada. Her style of writing is considered Urban Fantasy. Her first major publication is part of an anthology called First Love and she has several more titles lined up. She is a lover of coffee, good tv shows, horror flicks, and reader of books. She pretends to be a writer when real life doesn't get in the way. Pesky full-time job and adulting!

What Hides in Shadows?
by Jason Holden

There's a dark shadow that follows her. It creeps behind her with malicious intent, hiding in plain sight.

Her time is near, and she walks on unaware, the music pumping into her headphones as she waits for a break in the traffic to cross the busy road. The hairs on the back of her neck prickle, just as the dark thing prickles with excitement.

It's almost time.

She gets ready to step out. The shadow swoops away from her and into the path of an oncoming car, causing the driver to swerve unexpectedly and mount the pavement where she stands.

*After giving up a full-time job as a quarry operator so that his wife could follow her dream career as an academic in the field of chemistry, **Jason Holden** and his family left England and temporarily moved to Spain where they currently reside. While there, he took on the role of full-time parent and began to create stories for his daughter. Now that she is in school, he creates stories for himself and hopes to share those stories with others.*

For Want of a Crow
by Jonathan Ficke

Death was supposed to be a transition. What once was alive moved along into an unknowable existence beyond. I had faith in life after death, but not the pride to predict what came next. I didn't expect stasis.

I spent a lifetime tending the grounds of All Saints Cemetery. Not a singular crow slipped my watch. Little did I know that it was the crows that escort souls along their transition. So I, along with countless others damned by a dedication to the illusion of clean death, rage atop our graves, tethered to the earth.

Perhaps my purgatory was well-earned.

Jonathan Ficke lives outside of Milwaukee, WI with his beautiful wife. His fiction has appeared in "Writers of the Future, Vol 34" and he muses online at;
Website: jonficke.com
Twitter: @jonficke

Nardis
by D.J. Elton

Nardis calls.

There is a world where the light is constantly golden red. Humans have tried to encounter this place over centuries, even poking slabs of wood into their foreheads to accelerate the process, but it is impossible. No man can reach Nardis. It is timeless and spaceless.

Even in death man cannot reach Nardis.

It is not forbidden, just hidden.

"Wo! Some rave." Ian shuddered. Slapped the dusty book shut.

Mala, always cool, eyed her cousin. "Of course—it's inner space." She paced the room. "Beyond matter." Looked out the window into cacophony, five stories below. "Let's go."

D.J. Elton *writes fiction and poetry, and is currently studying writing and literature which is improving her work in unexpected ways. She spends a lot of time in northern India and should probably live there, however there is much to be done in Melbourne, so this is the home base. She has meditated daily for the past 35 years and has worked in healthcare for equally as long, so she's very happy to be writing, zoning in and out of all things literary.*
Twitter: @DJEltonwrites

Honourable Discharge
by Jonathan Inbody

He wakes each morning to the sound of screams from long-dead children. He sees a decapitated woman standing in the produce aisle, dripping invisible blood onto the tiled floor. As he drives, he passes one-hundred and twenty-nine souls that would still be alive if not for his actions. No matter what orders he was given, it was his hands that carried them out, and his hands were covered in phantom stains that could never be clean.

It was true, what the dying old shaman in the desert had said. He could leave the war, but it would never leave him.

Jonathan Inbody is a filmmaker, author, and podcaster from Buffalo, New York. He enjoys B-movies, pen and paper RPGs, and New Wave Science Fiction novels. His short story "Dying Feels Like Slowly Sinking" is due to be published in the anthology Deteriorate from Whimsically Dark Publishing. Jon can be heard every other week on his improvisational movie pitch podcast X Meets Y.
Website: xmeetsy.libsyn.com

Dust in the Soul
by Jo Seysener

He battled webs sweeping his face as he passed along the corridors of death. Wisps adhered to his hair and teeth. A pair of tunnels split the path before him and he stood, considering.

Should he choose the left path, as he had so many times? Or maybe a new path, just to make things exciting. He eyed the right-hand tunnel. Only darkness lay within. An icy finger of breeze stroked his cheek and he shivered.

Left. Always left.

After a lifetime as a special forces soldier, trail blazing on campaigns, he couldn't believe he was lost in the afterlife.

Jo Seysener is a mum of three crazies, a scatter of chickens, a decrepit kelpie and a rambunctious GSD. She lives with her husband near Brisbane, Australia. When she is not exposing her kids to cult story books from her childhood, she can be found in the kitchen experimenting with new flavours and pairings. She adores alpacas.
Facebook: joseysener
Website: www.joseysener.com

The Summoning
by J.M. Meyer

The spirit board and gentle finger tips sandwiched the planchette. Dressed in their Halloween costumes, the four friends—gathered to summon spirits—took turns asking questions.

"Do we know you?" asked Sam.

The planchette moved to "YES."

"Are you angry?" asked Jordan.

"YES."

"Will you hurt us?" asked Avery.

"YES."

"What's your name?" asked Kennedy.

"S-A-T-A..."

"OK. Stop. This isn't funny. Who is pushing this thing around?" Avery had the sense to say.

They removed their fingers to argue but then silently watched the planchette moved itself to "N". Then they were thrown about like eggs hitting houses on Halloween.

J.M. Meyer *is writer, artist and small business owner living in New York., where she received her master's degree from Teacher's College, Columbia University. Jacqueline loves the science fiction and horror genres. Reading Ray Bradbury was a mind-blowing experience for her in 8th grade. Alfred Hitchcock and Rod Serling were the horror heroes of her youth. Mercedes M. Yardley is her current horror writing hero. Jacqueline also enjoys the company of her husband Bruce and their three children, Julia, Emma and Lauren. Jacqueline's mantra: The only time it's too late to try something new is when you are dead.*

Website: jmoranmeyer.net
Twitter: @moran_meyer

Playing with Fire
by David Bowmore

"Are you late for a wedding?"

"No, officer."

"Perhaps there's a fire?"

"There is no fire, officer."

"Then would you mind explaining why you're in such a hurry, miss?"

"Sorry. Do you want there to be a fire?"

"No, of course not."

"I can make it happen."

"What?"

"In your car, perhaps."

"Look, miss, tell me why you were doing fifty in a thirty, so I can issue you with a ticket. Do you have a license for this vehicle?"

"I think you had better look at your car, officer."

"But... It's burning. Wait there. No wait, don't go."

David Bowmore has lived here, there and everywhere, but now lives in Yorkshire with his wonderful wife and a small white poodle. He has worn many hats in his time; head chef, teacher and landscape gardener. His first collection of short stories 'The Magic of Deben Market' is available from Clarendon House.
Website: davidbowmore.co.uk
Facebook: davidbowmoreauthor

A New House
by C.L. Williams

The Wendell family moved into their new home. The house was large enough for all six family members and affordable. Ian Wendell was warned about the house but did not listen because he needed something large. At first, it was only the occasional sound, then it became worse. One night, Ian Jr. claimed to be the spirit of the previous owner. Before the Wendell family knew any better, their house was possessed by a family of ghosts telling them to get out before it's too late. Now the house is for sale again with six new ghosts inside the house.

C.L. Williams is an independent author from central Virginia. He has written eight poetry books, four novellas, one novel, and a contributor to multiple anthologies, with the most recent appearance being an all-ages anthology titled Temoli from Thazbook. His most recent poetry book, The Paradox Complex, features the poem "Sad Crying Clown" that is now a video on YouTube directed by Matthew Mark Hunter of MMH Productions. C.L. Williams is currently working on his first sci-fi book, an all-ages book titled Novo: Away from Earth. When not writing, C.L. Williams is reading and sharing the work of other independent authors.
Facebook: writer434
Twitter: @writer_434

Wasted Souls
by Brandy Bonifas

I tried to tell Chester about the shadow people, but he'd have none of it.

"Crazy, old woman," he said. "Seein' things. Talkin' nonsense."

More showed up, but I didn't bother Chester with it. They weren't interested in me. I woke one night to find them crowding around Chester's side of the bed, blacker than the darkness around them. I tried to warn Chester. He just cursed at me for waking him.

Coroner said he went peacefully in his sleep…but I saw different. He's one of those shadow folk now, gone off to harvest others like himself…wasted souls.

Brandy Bonifas lives in Ohio with her husband and son. Her work has appeared or is forthcoming in anthologies by Clarendon House Publications, Pixie Forest Publishing, Zombie Pirate Publishing, and Blood Song Books, as well as the online publications CafeLit and Spillwords Press. Website: www.brandybonifas.com Facebook: brandybonifasauthor

Hanging Tree
by Elizabeth Montague

He had to do it—all the other boys did—bring a bit of bark to school to prove his bravery.

The Hanging Tree was feared, the place his father sent those charged with witchcraft. The last woman he'd sentenced had cursed it, they said, cursed the tree to take her revenge.

He ignored the vines hanging down like rope and the roaring shriek of the wind through the leaves that sounded like a warning. The vine was round his neck in a second, choking, lifting him to hang next to the ghostly figure of the last witch to die.

Elizabeth Montague is a multi-genre author from Hertfordshire, England. Her short story collection, Dust and Glitter, was released by Clarendon House Publications in May 2019. She has previously featured in nine anthologies from the same publisher alongside publications from Scout Media, Black Hare Press and Iron Faerie Publishing. She is currently working on her first novel alongside continuing to produce short stories in several genres.
Website: elizabethmontagueauthor.wordpress.com
Facebook: elizabethmontaguewrites

Twenty-Four Hour Scour
by C.L. Steele

"Don't touch the teapot!"

"Why?"

"My grandma lives in there. If you touch it, she will come out and eat you alive a bite at a time."

"Seriously, Kendra, you don't believe that." Malicious intent filled Michelle's eyes.

One touch later, grandma's ghost materialised. Her craggy voice screamed and echoed off the kitchen walls. "You call this place clean? You've been lazy too long." Both girls clutched their hearts.

"It feels like she's eating my soul."

"Bite by bite—gets worse."

"Sorry."

"Yeah…thanks."

Grandma's cold touch made them both scream. "Enough talk. Clean. Bring me tea and my switches."

BEYOND

C.L. Steele creates new worlds and mystical places filled with complex characters on exciting journeys. Her typical genre is Sci-Fi/Fantasy, where she concentrates on writing in the sub-genres of Magical Realism, Near Future, and Futuristic worlds. Published in numerous anthologies, she looks forward to the release of her debut novel. In the interim, she works on other novels and continues to write short stories, novellas, and poetry. She is featured as one of five international authors in ICWG Magazine through Clarendon Publishing House and is a contributing author to Blood Puddles Literary Journal.
Facebook: author.CLSteele
Instagram: @clsteele.author

Sleep Paralysis
by Nerisha Kemraj

Joan heard him whisper.

Goosebumps rose, and the hair on her body stood on ends.

"Joan, undress. Don't make me do it."

She knew it was just a dream but she couldn't move.

His body hovered over her, slowly pressing down—the bed creaked from their combined weight. Paralysed, her screams were muffled as her throat was somehow constricted. Her heart threatened to explode.

He lifted her with him. Tears streaked her face as her eyes bulged in terror.

What did he want?

He'd been dead more than a week.

Why was he still tormenting her even in death?

*Multi-genre (short-fiction) author, and poet, **Nerisha Kemraj**, resides in South Africa with her husband and two, mischievous daughters. She has work traditionally published/accepted in 30 publications, thus far, both print and online. She holds a BA in Communication Science from UNISA and is currently busy with a Post-Graduate Certificate in Education.*
Facebook: Nerishakemrajwriter

Windy Paris
by A.L. Paradiso

"She twirled across this bridge, full of joy. We danced to this very post. I let whirlwinds take my gossamer top and skirt away. Kneeling before me, she kissed me, foot to lips. She made me dizzy and, remarkably, I knew I was in love. I removed all her clothes and let the airstream take them. So beautiful. I spent fifty-seven years with Ali, wonderful years. This teal urn contains her. Now, naked as that day, je dit, 'Adieux Paris,' and release her."

The ashes became a laughing vortex; swirled into her face and she fell on her naked ass.

A.L. Paradiso was born in Europe. English is his second language, Italian was first—followed by Latin, Pig Latin, French and assorted computer languages. In college he took a dislike to writing of any kind and swore never to try that again. Well, some years later, influenced by Babylon 5's creator and his own pressure to write about two traumatic events, he turned to creative writing. As of 2018, he has published 126 stories.
Website: books2read.com/ap/RWjj5e/AL-Paradiso
Amazon: www.amazon.com/A-L-Paradiso/e/B07QVZ5NDN

Never Leaving
by Alexander Pyles

I thought this would be easier. Slipping the bounds of my body was excruciating, but here I was, floating. And still, I stared at my loved ones, who had kept to my bedside for weeks. I didn't deserve them, yet resentment festered.

They only cared because of their own selfish wants.

Their regrets were fresh, not old and grudgingly accepted. They blamed themselves. Where would that guilt go? Internalised. Hurled at others. They would clutch it for months if not years, maybe never letting it go.

I had to stay. I'd help, and if I could not help…I would haunt.

Alexander Pyles resides in IL with his wife and children. He holds an MA in Philosophy and an MFA in Writing Popular Fiction. His short story chapbook titled, "Milo (01001101 01101001 01101100 01101111)," from Radix Media, is due out fall 2019. His other short fiction has appeared on 101fiction.org, River and South Review, and other venues.
Website: www.pylesofbooks.com
Twitter: @Pylesofbooks

Can You Escape the Chateau in Time?

by Carole de Monclin

Some invitations can't be ignored. We'd already beaten all the escape rooms in town. An indie game in an abandoned mansion proved too enticing to miss. Especially when the last clue would reveal the identity of our host.

With real cobwebs for décor, creaking hardwood floors for soundtrack, our small group solved every clue, meandering from foyer to cellars, sitting rooms, and bedchambers, until only one door remained, one last lock requiring a five-letter combination.

The ridiculously easy riddle read, "Everyone's final fate."

Once I set the dials to spell DEATH, I hesitated.

But the door opened on its own.

Carole de Monclin has lived in France and Australia, but for the moment the USA is home. She finds inspiration from her travels. She loves Science Fiction because it explores the human mind in a way no other genre can. Plus, who doesn't love spaceships and lasers? Her stories appear in the Exoplanet Magazine and Angels - A Dark Drabbles Anthology.
Website: CaroledeMonclin.com
Twitter: @CaroledeMonclin

Both Sides of the Veil
by John H. Dromey

Ebenezer Scrooge IV awoke to a cacophonous sound emanating from his kitchen. Had he dreamed it? He opened his eyes. A wispy wraith stood beside his bed.

"Who are you? What are you doing here?"

"I've been designated your Ghost of Christmas Past. I'm here to remind you to pay your overdue bills from last Yuletide."

"Did you break my dishes?"

"Not me."

"Who then?"

"My poltergeist assistant. His job was to get your attention."

"Well, he succeeded. Why are you doing this? You're despicable!"

"You think I'm bad? You should see the conniving vultures in pursuit of my legacy."

John H. Dromey was born in northeast Missouri, USA. He enjoys reading—mysteries in particular—and writing in a variety of genres. He's had short fiction published in Alfred Hitchcock's Mystery Magazine, Martian Magazine, Stupefying Stories Showcase, Thriller Magazine, Unfit Magazine, and elsewhere, as well as in a number of anthologies, including Chilling Horror Short Stories (Flame Tree Publishing, 2015).

The Hand
by Jem McCusker

I wake to the pressure, the nagging need to go; the glass of water. I tell myself to just hold on. My body disagrees.

No shadows fill the room. I blink into the dark. I toss the sheets and leap from the bed, hitting the light at a run. Relieved at last, I keep the light on and go to bed. I stop to adjust the sheet and that's when it happens, the paralysing fear, the hand I thought lived in the dark found me in the light. The burn of carpet as I'm pulled below, no chance to flee.

Jem McCusker is a middle grade fiction author, living near Brisbane with her two sons and husband. Her first book Stone Guardians the Rise of Eden was released in 2018 and she is working on the sequel. She is releasing a Novella for the Four Quills writing group, A Storm of Wind and Rain series in July, 2019. She longs to be a full-time author, won't wear yellow and loves rabbits. Follow Jem on Twitter, Facebook and Instagram. Details on her website.
Website: www.jemmccusker.com

Invisible
by Terry Miller

When Kelly died, not a person in the room wept. Each went their separate ways while the hospital staff performed their duties.

Kelly lived a sad life, just kind of there. She felt as though she was no one's priority, not even her own.

Her gravestone bore her name, birth, and death, nothing more. She was gone, forgotten. Her name would be remembered only in carved stone to be eroded in time.

Kelly's steps led her to the cemetery gates, the leaves unmoved by her path. A ghost, she would be as invisible in death as she was in life.

Terry Miller is an author and 2017 Rhysling Award-nominated poet residing in Portsmouth, OH, USA. He has self-published a dark poetry collection on Amazon and one short story to date. His work has also appeared in Sanitarium, Devolution Z, Jitter Press, Poetry Quarterly, O Unholy Night in Deathlehem, and the 2017 Rhysling Anthology from the Science Fiction and Fantasy Poetry Association.
Facebook: tmiller2015

Tell Me a Story
by Joshua D. Taylor

In an uncharacteristic fit of whimsy Jim typed, 'Tell me a story' on the dusty old typewriter. The keys made a mechanical *clack* when pressed. The ink ribbon had dried out decades ago, so no words appeared on the paper.

Jim turned away then heard the *clack clack* of the typewriter. When he turned back, there were words on the paper.

'Soon you will die' was typed in dark black ink. The *clanking* resumed. More unnatural words appeared but his fear gripped him, and he fled the room, terrified. The harsh keystrokes followed him as he ran out the door.

***Joshua D. Taylor** is an amateur writer who started writing a few years ago when he realised he was too old to play make-believe. He lives in southeastern Pennsylvania with his wife and a one-eared cat. He enjoys gardening, comic books, ska-punk music, Disney World, and travelling with his wife. Raised during weirdness that was the late 20th century Josh's eclectic interests produce eclectic works. He loves to mix-n-match things from different genres and stories elements to achieve a madcap hodgepodge of the truly unexpected. His short story 'the Obelisk' appears in Salty Tales by Stormy Island Publishing.*
Facebook: authorjoshuadtaylor

Death is an Angel
by Monica Schultz

Sweat. Dripping from her brow. Condensing on palms of nervous hands. Trickling down the midwife's back. Death is rarely greeted in a roomful of sweat.

Death stretches their wings, dropping shadowy feathers to the disinfected floor. They are expecting Death elsewhere. In the room with the frail grandparent. At the bedside of cancer's next victim. Yet Death lingers in this room full of life.

The final cry. Her womb empties, and breaths are held waiting for an unmistakable wail. Silence.

Death cradles another stillborn child. Skeletal arms become tender, softened by mother's heartbreak. *Hush.* Death comforts those departed too early.

Monica Schultz writes young adult fantasy novels for anyone who needs an escape from reality. She can often be found reading novels, with a cat curled on her lap, to hide from her own mundane life.
Twitter: @MonicaSchultz_
Instagram: @miss.schultz

The Moon Pool
by R.J. Meldrum

The pond was nicknamed the Moon Pool. When the moon was full, the still water shimmered like silver. Locals avoided it; the place had an evil reputation. Dead animals were often found near the water's edge after the full moon. William, not caring about local gossip, decided to visit. He stared into the shimmering water. It was beautiful; he felt elevated. He was hypnotised.

Shaking his head, he looked away. He'd had enough, the sensation had become unpleasant. He stepped away from the water's edge and walked away. He wasn't aware that behind him, on the bank, lay his body.

*R. J. Meldrum is an author and academic. Born in Scotland, he moved to Ontario, Canada in 2010. He has had stories published by Horrified Press, the Infernal Clock, Trembling with Fear, Darkhouse Books, Smoking Pen Press, and James Ward Kirk Fiction. He also has had stories published in The Sirens Call e-zine, the Horror Zine and Drabblez Magazine. He is an Affiliate Member of the Horror Writers Association.
Twitter: @RichardJMeldru1
Facebook: richard.meldrum.79*

A Cold Reading
by Steven Holding

It's not a gift. It wasn't given. It just *is*.

Two voices. One spoken. Another inside.

I hear both.

Imagining the miraculous, there's no thought of consequence; dreaming of flight, never contemplating crashing.

Superpowers don't make a Superman.

Taking cheques from widows. Listening to what's on their mind. Telling them whatever they need. They get happy. I don't go hungry.

So, why nothing greater? Why not heal the world?

Simple.

We are unique. But no matter what, there's only one true thought.

Pauper to prince, from cradle to grave.

I AM AFRAID.

And it makes me feel so terribly afraid.

BEYOND

Steven Holding lives with his family in the United Kingdom. His stories have been published by TREMBLING WITH FEAR, FRIDAY FLASH FICTION, THEATRE CLOUD, AD HOC FICTION and MASSACRE MAGAZINE. Most recently, his story THREE CHORDS AND THE TRUTH received first place in the INKTEARS 2018 FLASH FICTION COMPETITION, while another of his pieces WALK WITH ME THROUGH THE LONG GRASS AND I SHALL HOLD YOUR HAND was runner up in the annual WRITING MAGAZINE 500 WORD SHORT STORY COMPETITION. He is currently working upon further short fiction and a novel.
Website: www.stevenholding.co.uk

Afterglow
by Sam M. Phillips

The lightning cracks as I duck into the inn, shaking rain from my shoulders, the door slamming in the wind behind me.

Inside, there is silence, darkness.

I take a tentative step forward, strike a match. It illuminates old furniture hanging with cobwebs.

The match fades, leaving an afterglow on my retinas. To my surprise, the glow persists and takes shape, ghostly figures moving about the room.

My stomach clenches in fear.

"Come and take your seat, boy," says a man in a fine coat.

"Am I dead?"

The man points. I look down, my body glowing in the dark.

Sam M. Phillips is the co-founder of Zombie Pirate Publishing, producing short story anthologies and helping emerging writers. His own work has appeared in dozens of anthologies and magazines such as Full Moon Slaughter 2, 13 Bites Volumes IV and V, Rejected for Content 6, and Dastaan World Magazine. He lives in the green valleys of northern New South Wales, Australia, and enjoys reading, walking, and playing drums in the death metal band Decryptus.
Website: zombiepiratepublishing.com
Blog: bigconfusingwords.wordpress.com

Estekene
by James Turnbow

Our dog's howls echoed in the forest as we followed them into the darkness.

I smelled our prize before I saw it. Organs scattered about on limbs high in the air.

"When they leave their bodies, they can't carry it," my father said as he took a stick and knocked the foul smelling mush to the ground. Our dogs happily slopped it up.

The Estekene returned and fell from the sky in screeches of desperation. Each horned owl carried inside it the consciousness of a man.

"Wander for eternity in this form!" my father commanded. "The tribe has passed judgment."

James Turnbow is a graduate from the University of Central Oklahoma with a degree in Strategic Communications. He is a proud member of the Seminole Nation of Oklahoma and works with tribal youth to empower them to pursue higher education as an Education Advisor for the Muscogee Creek Nation. He is a curator of Seminole culture and language and works to preserve the stories and words of his ancestors.

Icy Revenge
by Crystal L. Kirkham

BANG!

John jumped as an icy wind rushed in through the open door. He ran over, slammed it closed and turned the bolt to be sure it would stay that way before heading back to watch TV.

BANG!

John whipped around. The door was open again. Snow billowed in, outlining a familiar shape.

"A-Annie?" He stammered the name of his recently deceased wife.

An icy grip took hold of his heart and squeezed.

"I told you that you'd never get away with murder," she said as the ice of her deadly grip turned to the burning flames of his destination.

Crystal L. Kirkham resides in a small hamlet west of Red Deer, Alberta. She's an avid outdoors person, unrepentant coffee addict, part-time foodie, servant to a wonderful feline, and companion to two delightfully hilarious canines. She will neither confirm nor deny the rumours regarding the heart in a jar on her desk and the bottle of reader's tears right next to it. Her paranormal urban fantasy series, Saints and Sinners, is available on Amazon and her YA Fantasy, Feathers and Fae will be released October 11, 2019, from Kyanite Publishing.
Website: www.crystallkirkham.com

A Quieter Sound
by Joel R. Hunt

If you listen closely enough, you can hear the sounds of the dead.

Storms whisper the last breaths of lost hikers. Pipes in old houses rattle with the cries of murdered wives. These are the fortunate souls. Bound to their places of death, they wander the surface. They still see the sky.

Beneath them is a quieter sound, almost beyond detection. It belongs to those who perish underground, bound to a world of soil, stone and eternal suffocation.

You might hear it as you lie in bed at night.

Their desperate scraping. Their ceaseless choking.

Listen closely.

Do you *hear*?

Joel R. Hunt is a writer from the UK who dabbles in the darker aspects of life, particularly through horror, science fiction and the supernatural. He has been published here and there (though likely nowhere you've heard of) and hopes to have released his first anthology of short stories later this year.
Twitter: @JoelRHunt1
Reddit: JRHEvilInc

When Dusk Comes Creeping
by Rowanne S. Carberry

Walking through the hallways my torch flickers.

"No," I groan, shaking it in desperation. But the light goes.

Fumbling in my pocket, I reach for my phone when a floorboard creaks behind me.

I knew I shouldn't have come to this fucking haunted house.

Another creak, I turn.

"Matt! Thank God!"

I go to grab him, but my hands go through him.

"Run," he screams at me, trying to push me.

Finally, my feet move, I run. I reach the door, but it won't open.

Floorboards creak, my heart stops.

Pale faces stare at me.

Hands reach out.

"Join us."

Rowanne S. Carberry *was born in England in 1990, where she stills lives now with her cat Wolverine. Rowanne has always loved writing, and her first poem was published at the age of 15, but her ambition has always been to help people. Rowanne studied at the University of Sunderland where she completed combined honours of Psychology with Drama. Rowanne writes to offer others an escape. Although Rowanne writes in varied genres each story or poem she writes will often have a darkness to it, which helped coin her brand, Poisoned Quill Writing – Wicked words from a poisoned quill.*

Facebook: PoisonedQuillWriting
Instagram: @poisoned_quill_writing

Smile
by Tim Boiteau

During a high school trip to France, I meet Her for the first time in her climate-controlled chamber. Afterwards, a boy packing some hashish leads me to Parc des Buttes-Chaumont where we smoke. Then he lies on top of me while I gaze up at the shivering canopy, thinking about how disappointing seeing the painting had been.

Several millennia later, as a phantom wandering the ashes, an urgency to encounter Her overcomes me.

I ghost through every underground vault on Earth, searching.

I find Her at last, mouth now drawn into a corpse's rictus.

Time has robbed Her of ambiguity.

Tim Boiteau lives in the Detroit area with his wife and son. Find his fiction in places such as Deep Magic, LampLight, Kasma SF, and The Colored Lens. He is currently working on his second novel while finding a home for his first. Twitter: @timboiteau

When the Pain is Gone
by Neen Cohen

The dark shadow sits in the corner of the room with legs crossed and black cloak hiding the paleness beneath.

"Do you want the pain to end?"

"Yes!" The word is a mere rattled whisper from the bed.

The shadow smiles and picks up the scythe from the floor.

"Come on, then."

"The pain is gone." She smiles and takes a deep breath. No pain. She heads toward the door. From the corner of her eye she sees the truth. The bedcovers are still intact.

"No!"

She screams as the shadow laughs.

"You asked for the pain to be gone."

Neen Cohen lives in Brisbane with her partner, son and fur babies. She is a writer of LGBTQI, dark fantasy and horror short stories and has a Bachelor of Creative Industries from QUT. She can often be found writing while sitting against a tombstone or tree in any number of graveyards.
Facebook: Neen-Cohen-Author-424700821629629
Website: wordbubblessite.wordpress.com

Death Isn't Fair to the Dead
by Rennie St. James

Death doesn't treat the dead and living equally. Mourners grieve with laughter and love. Death smooths the rough edges to make a bad life look good. It blurs the past to allow the living to live.

The dead like me aren't treated so well.

That earthly shell offers more protection than the living know. Ripping away the distraction of living leaves you even more vulnerable. There's nothing left but memories of a life squandered and lost. The painful, inner darkness you could ignore when alive devours you long after you die.

No, death isn't fair at all to the dead.

Rennie St. James *shares several similarities with her fictional characters (heroes and villains alike) including a love of chocolate, horror movies, martial arts, history, yoga, and travel. She doesn't have a pet mountain lion but is proudly owned by three rescue kitties. They live in relative harmony in beautiful southwestern Virginia (United States). The first three books of Rennie's urban fantasy series, The Rahki Chronicles, are available now. A new series and several standalone stories are already in the works as future releases.*
Website: writerRSJ.com

Magic Ian's Box
by Gregg Cunningham

"I need a fearless volunteer from the audience," Magic Ian bellowed.

I was up out of my seat and onto the stage in no time, the crowd gasping as the creaky wooden door closed me inside the coffin-like box.

The Magician said the incantation as the audience clapped, sending me on my way into the *Beyond*.

After a moments silence, I was actually contemplating not returning to my seat and instead just finding the nearest pub, when the creaky door opened and the empty theatre faced me.

"Magic Ian, my arse!" I scoffed, frowning at the rows of empty seats.

Gregg Cunningham is a short story writer from Western Australia. He has had several short stories publishing by Zombie Pirate Publishing in Relationship add Vice, Full Metal Horror, Phuket Tattoo, World War four and Flash Fiction Addiction, with GBH due later in the year. Most recently, his work has been accepted into Black Hare Press Drabbles set including Monsters, Angels, Worlds, Unravel, Beyond, and Apocalypse, with his latest short story included in Black Hare Press soon to be released fine Deep Space anthology.
Website: cortlandsdogs.wordpress.com

No Graduation
by Melissa Neubert

They sat on top of the bleachers at the fifty-yard line. She wore her cheerleading sweater, he was in his football jersey. They held hands as they watched the game. The team was on fire and they were winning big.

During half time, the band played. Then there was a moment of silence and they looked down and watched their parents being honoured. Pictures of them were on the track, draped with flowers.

They climbed down the bleachers and walked down to the field. They gave their parents kisses they never felt, then headed toward the light waiting for them.

Melissa Neubert was born in the Pacific Northwest and currently lives in Illinois with her husband, three children and two dogs. Melissa has been a daycare provider, veterinary assistant, teacher/library aide, and administrative assistant. Melissa travels extensively both domestically and internationally where she finds inspiration for her writing in beautiful and unique locations. When she is not writing she enjoys music, reading, concert and wildlife photography, football and camping. Although Melissa has been writing since grade school, she has only recently begun pursuing the craft seriously. She writes mostly in the genres of Suspense/Thriller and Adult Paranormal Romance.

The Night We Died
by Ximena Escobar

"You know death's a seamstress?"

"Huh?"

"She's right there, behind the night sky." Carlos pointed at the stars—we were lying flat on our backs, on the sand. "She pricks it each time she takes one of us."

We looked at each other one last time.

"Grandma told me about her, but I remembered her from another life... She's right...here..." He touched his third eye with his fingertip.

I grasped the cool sand, letting it slide away like time.

"It's time," he said.

Our fingers interlocked as gravity released us. We plunged vertiginously into space.

Two stars were born.

Ximena Escobar is an emerging author of literary fiction and poetry. Originally from Chile, she is the author of a translation into Spanish of the Broadway Musical "The Wizard of Oz", and of an original adaptation of the same, "Navidad en Oz". Clarendon House Publications published her first short story in the UK, "The Persistence of Memory", and Literally Stories her first online publication with "The Green Light". She has since had several acceptances from other publishers and is working very hard exploring new exciting avenues in her writing.
She lives in Nottingham with her family.
Facebook: Ximenautora

Beyond Insanity
by Olivia Arieti

Spencer, the asylum's head doctor, noticed that some residents' perceptions went beyond mortal parameters; insanity provided them with an unknown portal to the supernatural.

Lewis's case confirmed his suppositions. The insane bloke charged with his wife's murder, had always claimed the killer was a neighbour whose spirit was still roaming around.

One night, Spencer followed the patient into the park; a ghastly presence was waiting for him.

"Confess the murder or you'll never rest in peace," shouted Lewis.

"That's why I'm here," the spirit replied.

Instantly, the psycho stabbed the criminal that with a hollow cry vanished before his eyes.

Olivia Arieti *has a degree from the University of Pisa and lives in Torre del Lago Puccini, Italy, with her family. Besides being a published playwright, she loves writing retellings of fairy tales, and at the same time is intrigued by supernatural and horror themes. Her stories appeared in several magazines and anthologies like Enchanted Conversations, Enchanted Tales Literary Magazine, Fantasia Divinity Magazine, Cliterature, Medieval Nightmares, Static Movement, 100 Doors To Madness Forgotten Tomb Press, Black Cats Horrified Press, Bloody Ghost Stories Full Moon Books, Death And Decorations Thirteen O'Clock Press, Infective Ink, Pandemonium Press, Pussy Magic Magazine.*

Hallowed Lands
by Chris Bannor

The Old Ones swarmed like death upon the land, leaving nothing more than smouldering ruins and shivering animus in their wake. There was no heaven or hell to hold the spirits any longer, only the soft pitch of dirt and the hot winds that raked over shrieking memories.

The strong fell, as did the mighty, next to the weak and impoverished. Fools and scholars and the everyman did no better. In the end, all fell to the vast array of horrors in the Old One's fists. The earth was filled with the torment of the masses.

The lucky remained dead.

Chris Bannor *is a science fiction and fantasy writer who lives in Southern California. Chris learned her love of genre stories from her mother at an early age and has never veered far from that path. She also enjoys musical theater and road trips with her family, but is a general homebody otherwise. Twitter: @BannorChris*

Sibling Rivalry
by Stuart Conover

Stupid Kyle had to go and sin before dying.

Lisa fumed.

There was no way he'd repented.

They had unfinished business from childhood.

Now she'd never have closure.

He had damned himself to the Abyss.

She spent years mastering the mystical arts.

Nearly twice that to learn to summon the dead without damning her soul.

Finally, Lisa was ready.

She called to her brother from beyond!

Standing before her, Kyle looked broken but smiled when he saw her.

For a perfect moment, they held one another.

"Tag! You're it," she exclaimed before pushing away and banishing him back to Hell.

Stuart Conover is a father, husband, rescue dog owner, published author, blogger, journalist, horror enthusiast, comic book geek, science fiction junkie, and IT professional. With all of that to cram in daily, we have no idea if or when he sleeps or how he gets writing done! (We suspect it has to do with having evil clones.) Stuart is a Chicago native and runs the author resource Horror Tree.

A Voice in the Dark
by E.L. Giles

"Sit down," said the old man, inviting the two boys to be seated by the candle in the middle of the dark room.

The man then raised his arm high, as if he were venerating some obscure deity, before opening his worn grimoire. He had recited only a few lines when the oldest boy spoke.

"Dad won't come," he said. "He's dead. This man's a charlatan."

His brother looked at him, his eyes glassy. He didn't reply.

A sudden breeze swept through the room, bringing an eerie, inexplicable chill.

"My sons," a strange voice suddenly whispered, "what have you done?"

E.L. Giles is a dreamer, passionate about art, a restless worker and a bit of a weird human. He started his artistic journey as a music composer until the need to put his thoughts and stories down on paper grew too strong for him to resist it any longer. He lives in the French Province of Quebec, Canada, with his girlfriend and two boys.
Facebook: elgilesauthor
Website: www.elgilesauthor.com

I'm Afraid of the Dark
by Lynne Lumsden Green

Beyond life lies the great Unknown. Chaos. Darkness. Heaven? Hell?

Religion is the wall you build to put between yourself and death. The wall can seem so strong, but death is the earthquake that throws the illusion to the ground.

Life is just a chemical process. Intelligence was a fortuitous accident. When you are dead, you are dead. It is said that everyone dies alone, no matter who is holding their hand.

I so don't want to die.

I will miss you.

I'm afraid of the dark.

I don't want to go alone.

Will you follow me into the dark?

Lynne Lumsden Green has twin bachelor's degrees in both Science and the Arts, giving her the balance between rationality and creativity. She spent fifteen years as the Science Queen for HarperCollins Voyager Online and has written science articles for other online magazines. Currently, she captains the Writing Race for the Australian Writers Marketplace on Facebook. She has had speculative fiction flash fiction and short stories published in anthologies and websites.
Website: cogpunksteamscribe.wordpress.com

Revolutionary Vision
by Matthew M. Montelione

Timothy Callahan, curator of the historic Manor of St. George, was tired after a successful festival in celebration of Mastic's rich American Revolution history. He walked over to his colleague Daniel Harding. "I'm heading into the manor to do some work. Thanks for your help today."

Timothy spotted a British soldier re-enactor near the bay. "Cool! I didn't know we hired Crown re-enactors!" Timothy excitedly said.

Daniel gave him a strange look. "We didn't."

"What? He's over there." Timothy pointed but realised that nobody was there.

"You alright, Tim?"

Timothy shook his head. "Been a long day. I'm going inside."

Matthew M. Montelione *is a horror writer born and raised on Long Island in New York. His stories have been published in Quoth the Raven: A Contemporary Reimagining of the Works of Edgar Allan Poe, Thuggish Itch: Devilish, MONSTERS: A Horror Microfiction Anthology, Eerie Christmas, and other titles. Matthew is also an American Revolution historian who focuses on the local experiences of Loyalists on Long Island. His work on the subject has been published in Long Island History Journal and Journal of the American Revolution. Matthew lives with his wife in New York.*
Website: maybeevils.com
Twitter: @maybeevils

Victoria's Song
by Terry Miller

In the hallowed halls, music played. So eloquently did her fingers glide over the keys, only she had been dead many moons; her body buried.

Victoria's song roamed the night, knowing no boundaries of walls nor doors. Its notes lulled the visitors to sleep in their private chambers. In dreams, she led them down darkening corridors; deeper, darker still. She led them until complete darkness overtook them. The voices of the others were so near, but they could not touch; could not find one another in the infinite blackness.

Victoria's song echoed between the walls, the castle was hers alone.

Terry Miller is an author and 2017 Rhysling Award-nominated poet residing in Portsmouth, OH, USA. He has self-published a dark poetry collection on Amazon and one short story to date. His work has also appeared in Sanitarium, Devolution Z, Jitter Press, Poetry Quarterly, O Unholy Night in Deathlehem, and the 2017 Rhysling Anthology from the Science Fiction and Fantasy Poetry Association.
Facebook: tmiller2015

The March
by Stephen Herczeg

Dad never missed the march. We paraded with his unit. I'd wear Grandad's medals and a smile. Dad treated me like one of his mates, but once it finished, we wouldn't see him until morning.

Then his unit shipped out to Iraq.

Dad didn't come home.

It's the first parade since. Now I've got Grandad's and Dad's medals. There aren't as many soldiers marching, Dad wasn't the only one.

As we head off, a hand claps me on the shoulder. I look up.

It's Dad. He salutes me. Grandad stands next to him.

I smile. Dad never missed the march.

Stephen Herczeg is an IT Geek based in Canberra Australia. He has been writing for over twenty years and has completed a couple of dodgy novels, sixteen feature length screenplays and numerous short stories and scripts. His horror work has featured in Sproutlings, Hells Bells, Below the Stairs, Trickster's Treats #1 and #2, Shades of Santa, Behind the Mask, Beyond the Infinite; The Body Horror Book, Anemone Enemy, Petrified Punks and Beginnings. He has also had numerous Sherlock Holmes stories published through the Belanger Books - Sherlock Holmes anthologies.

He Watched
by David Bowmore

He said he would wait an eternity.

While he waited, he watched.

Every night he watched his wife as she put the child to bed. After showering, she would rub her body with fragrant oils. He ached for one more hit of her scent.

When the time came, and she had put the book down, he would watch over her dreams.

Sometimes, he sat on the edge of the bed and tried to touch her as he used to when he had still been warm.

After years of this torture, she met someone new and he could watch no longer.

David Bowmore has lived here, there and everywhere, but now lives in Yorkshire with his wonderful wife and a small white poodle. He has worn many hats in his time; head chef, teacher and landscape gardener. His first collection of short stories 'The Magic of Deben Market' is available from Clarendon House.
Website: davidbowmore.co.uk
Facebook: davidbowmoreauthor

The Sceptic
by Isabella Fox

"This house is haunted," explained the guide.

"Yeh, sure," Rodney sneered. "Let's see you prove it."

The guide ignored him, and the believers moved forward, following her single torch beam.

Rodney had moved to the back of the group, intent on scaring them, when he felt a bony hand grip his shoulder.

"Very funny," he said as icy breath brushed the nape of his neck.

Cold hands clasped his throat and squeezed hard.

Rodney tried frantically to call for help as the spectre crushed his larynx and broke his neck.

The ghost whispered in his ear, "Is that enough proof?"

Isabella Fox teaches primary aged students to love writing by making it challenging. In her spare time she reads, goes for long walks with her husband and works hard on her farm.

125

Two of Clubs
by G. Allen Wilbanks

"He's holding the two of clubs," says Louis.

"Is your card the two of clubs?" I ask. The audience member holds the card out so everyone can see. They are all properly amazed at my psychic abilities.

"This is all crap," mutters Louis. "Self-indulgent, egotistical crap."

"Hush," I tell him as the volunteer walks off the stage.

"Why can't you just tell the truth?" Louis continues. "That you see and talk to ghosts."

"Are you kidding?" I ask him through clenched teeth. "People would think I was nuts. Now, shut up before someone starts wondering why I'm talking to myself."

G. Allen Wilbanks is a member of the Horror Writers Association (HWA) and has published over 50 short stories in various magazines and on-line venues. He is the author of two short story collections, and the novel, When Darkness Comes.
Website: www.gallenwilbanks.com
Blog: DeepDarkThoughts.com

Don't Fear the Reaper
by Shelly Jarvis

Marissa appears like smoke, moves in and out of focus until she's solid beside me. "Boss said there was trouble. Gimme the rundown."

I wince but get down to it. "Eleanor Deacon, 97, heart failure."

"Time of death?"

"4:07 am."

Marissa checks her watch, turns to me and says, "That was six minutes ago."

I squirm under her gaze, words tumbling out without thought. "She looks sweet, her hair in curlers. Seems a shame to kill her."

"You've got a good heart. Unusual for a reaper." Marissa sighs, shoots a finger-gun at Eleanor, and we watch her life melt away.

Shelly Jarvis is a speculative fiction author from West Virginia, US. She found a life-long love of sci-fi and fantasy in the 3rd grade when she found Madeleine L'Engle's "A Wrinkle in Time." Shelly is an avid reader, a Whovian, the ideal viewer of dog rescue videos, and undoubtedly Ravenclaw. She currently has two YA sci-fi books available for purchase on Amazon.
Website: www.ShellyJarvis.com

Séance
by Rickey Rivers Jr.

"Hold hands, everyone."

"This is so dumb."

"Quiet!"

In the darkness they held on to each other, the glowing orb lay before them.

"Oh, great afterlife, is anyone there?"

No answer, only a chill from the orb.

"Oh, great afterlife, are there any spirits here with us?"

No answer.

"This is stupid!"

"No, I heard something!"

They quieted. From beyond the stare of the orb came a faint cry.

"Who's there?"

"Sounds like a baby."

They began rocking in their chairs.

"Stop moving."

"I can't help it!"

Instantly, each one was pulled into the orb and the cry became many.

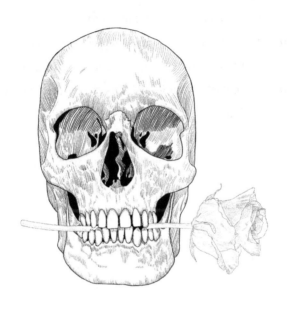

Rickey Rivers Jr. was born and raised in Alabama. He is a writer and cancer survivor. He likes a lot of stuff. You don't care about the details. He has been previously published in Fabula Argentea, ARTPOST magazine, the anthology Chronos, Enchanted Conversations Magazine, (among other publications).
Twitter: @storiesyoumight

Born Dead
by Zoey Xolton

The reaper lay down his scythe, leaning in to observe the newest addition to his shelf. From inside a jar made of immortal star-glass, a sad-eyed girl stared back at him.

For twelve thousand years, each night that he retired from a day of reaping, she was there, tear-rimmed eyes unblinking.

The reaper sighed from within his cowl. "I'm sorry," he said finally. "Your mother didn't want you."

"I never even took my first breath," she said.

"No child of mine can be born living, I'm afraid."

"You should not have loved her."

"If only it had been a choice."

Zoey Xolton is an Australian Speculative Fiction writer, primarily of Dark Fantasy, Paranormal Romance and Horror. She is also a proud mother of two and is married to her soul mate. Outside of her family, writing is her greatest passion. She is especially fond of short fiction and is working on releasing her own themed collections in future.
Website: www.zoeyxolton.com

Visit
by Annie Percik

She throws stones at my window. She climbs the tree to sit just inches from the glass, smiling and laughing, inviting me to go outside and play. She beckons and she pouts, disappointed when I draw the curtains. But I know she's still out there, waiting for me. Just like she used to be when I was as small as she remains. I have grown old, lived a life and followed my dreams. She never got the chance and she won't let me forget it. Her laugh is always on the breeze, reminding me of my failure to protect her.

Annie Percik lives in London with her husband, Dave, where she is revising her first novel, whilst working as a University Complaints Officer. She writes a blog about writing and posts short fiction on her website. She also publishes a photo-story blog, recording the adventures of her teddy bear. He is much more popular online than she is. She likes to run away from zombies in her spare time.
Website: www.alobear.co.uk
Website: aloysius-bear.dreamwidth.org

Four Things Come Not Back : #1 The Spoken Word
by Aiki Flinthart

Dad: *Jess?*

Me: *You don't normally text me. What? Still pissed at you.*

Dad: *I'm sorry we argued.*

Me: *You yelled, you mean? You wouldn't listen.*

Dad: *Please? I need to—*

Me: *It's always about you. Stop trying to control me.*

Dad: *I just want—*

Me: *Mum's calling. We'll talk later.*

"Mum?" I answered, irritable. "I'll call you back. I'm busy, now."

There was a long silence, then a broken sob. "The police called. Your father had a car crash…th-three hours ago."

"Oh, shit! He didn't say."

"He's dead, Jess. He died an hour ago."

Me: *Dad? Dad? DAD!*

Aiki Flinthart has had short stories shortlisted in the Aurealis awards and top-8 listed in the USA Writers of the Future competition, as well as published in various anthologies and e-mags. She has 11 published spec fic novels and has edited 2 short story anthologies. She regularly gives workshops on writing fight scenes at conventions. Lives in Brisbane. Does martial arts, archery, knife throwing and lute-playing.
Website: www.aikiflinthart.com

Four Things Come Not Back : #2 The Sped Arrow
by Aiki Flinthart

Five bullets end his life. And the power of his fists.

But the torment continues. A tile falls from the roof to smash my shoulder. A glass vase slips from the shelf to slice my arm. The gas left on when I know I turned it off.

I move house. He comes with me, an incurable disease.

Now I sit in darkness, trembling, holding gun to temple. His insubstantial fingers curl over mine. I resist.

He'll never let me go. I should have known when he removed *until death do us part* from our wedding vows.

We pull the trigger.

Aiki Flinthart has had short stories shortlisted in the *Aurealis awards* and top-8 listed in the USA *Writers of the Future competition*, as well as published in various anthologies and e-mags. She has 11 published spec fic novels and has edited 2 short story anthologies. She regularly gives workshops on writing fight scenes at conventions. Lives in Brisbane. Does martial arts, archery, knife throwing and lute-playing.
Website: www.aikiflinthart.com

Four Things Come Not Back : #3 Past Lives
by Aiki Flinthart

The fifth time around was the worst. By then I'd had ample opportunities for regret, but none for redemption. Just repetition. I remembered each one, no matter how small, pathetic, short, or brutal. And the knowledge that dozens more lay ahead made me want to rail against the gods.

But I didn't.

Because I also remembered the crimes for which I was being punished. The thefts, the lies. And, finally, the murder. Her terrified face haunted every waking moment.

So, on my fifth life, when I was taken to the butcher, I lay my goat-head on the block willingly.

Again.

Aiki Flinthart has had short stories shortlisted in the *Aurealis awards* and top-8 listed in the *USA Writers of the Future* competition, as well as published in various anthologies and e-mags. She has 11 published spec fic novels and has edited 2 short story anthologies. She regularly gives workshops on writing fight scenes at conventions. Lives in Brisbane. Does martial arts, archery, knife throwing and lute-playing.
Website: www.aikiflinthart.com

Four Things Come Not Back : #4 The Missed Opportunity
by Aiki Flinthart

Had I but driven a blade through my treacherous brother's heart that morning, my son, my wife, my friends…might still live. My country might not have fallen to Norway's ambition.

I suspected Claudius's black intent. But I, in my arrogance, slept peacefully beneath the whispering apple trees. And never awoke. Poison. Dripped into my ear.

Then, without last rites, I lingered, ghostly. But could not convince my son my death was murder. Something made him think me a demon, not his father's unshriven soul. And so, he chose that mad play. And so, they all perished.

Ah, my Hamlet.

Aiki Flinthart *has had short stories shortlisted in the Aurealis awards and top-8 listed in the USA Writers of the Future competition, as well as published in various anthologies and e-mags. She has 11 published spec fic novels and has edited 2 short story anthologies. She regularly gives workshops on writing fight scenes at conventions. Lives in Brisbane. Does martial arts, archery, knife throwing and lute-playing.*
Website: www.aikiflinthart.com

Poltergeist
by K.T. Tate

You can't let it out. Can't tell them how you feel. I know. I've watched you push your anger down, not knowing what to do with all that pain. But don't worry, I'm here now. No child should suffer.

I start by blowing the bulbs. I rattle the windows and tip over mugs. The more they fear the stronger I get. I throw things, break mirrors, and cause bruises. My haunting undeniable.

It's working. Soon your life will be under scrutiny of press and public. Soon someone will discover what you can't say.

I won't let him hurt you anymore.

K.T. Tate lives in Cambridgeshire in the UK. She writes mainly weird fiction, cosmic horror and strange monster stories.
Website: eldritchhollow.wordpress.com
Tumblr: eldritch-hollow.tumblr.com

Bell Ringer
by Cecilia Dockins

The house had once been lavish, built in the image of an English manor, on suffering land by suffering hands. Many of the original details had been stripped, though not the five bells attached to the dining room, to the bedrooms, to the cook's kitchen.

Pritchard thought it marvellous and purchased the ailing house against his wife's wishes. During dinner, before the first slice of pizza could be consumed, the bells began to ring.

Tinkling.

Soft as whispers.

Then insistent.

A door groaned from below. The heavy trudge of feet leading toward the family.

Land built with blood always remembers.

Cecilia Dockins grew up fishing in the creeks and rivers deep in the backwoods of Tennessee. She earned her B.A. in English from Middle Tennessee State University in 2010 and is a graduate of the Odyssey Writing Workshop. She has passed instruments in surgical suites and slung drinks in bars. When not writing, she spends her free time digging through decaying boxes at local bookstores or the occasional barn for the forgotten, the lost, and the bizarre. Cecilia lives with her husband, two parrots, and boxer pup in a lovely subdivision. On rainy nights, she can hear the river calling.

In the Back of Beyond
by Chitra Gopalakrishnan

I, Titu Singh, began telling my family in Delhi about my other life in Agra, 200 kilometres away from home, in 1989.

I was two years old.

I said I was Suresh Batra, had a wife Uma and two children, and was shot in the head in 1983.

When my parents took me to Agra in 1999, I sat next to my stunned widow and recounted specific and very intimate details of our lives.

I then guided her to the pit where we had buried a body to dig him out.

Measure for measure!

How many lives more, I wonder?

Chitra Gopalakrishnan is a journalist by training, a social development communications consultant by profession and a creative writer by choice. Chitra's focus is on issues of gender, environment and health. Chitra dabbles in poetry on the sly and literary creations openly on the web using social media.
Website: unpublishedplatform.weebly.com/chitra-gopalakrishnan

One in Darkness, One in Light
by Aiki Flinthart

Brave, he journeys to the underworld. My darling Orpheus. His exquisite music moves even dour Hades, who grants my return to life. My love gazes into my face and swears.

He will not look back until we reach the light.

He turns away. I follow, staying close. We cross the soul-drowned Styx. Orpheus stares resolutely forward, I hard on his heels. Just a few more steps and I'll see his beloved face once more.

The sun, the sky, the wind. I can almost taste them.

He emerges into the light. And turns back, eager.

But I still stand in darkness.

Aiki Flinthart has had short stories shortlisted in the Aurealis awards and top-8 listed in the USA Writers of the Future competition, as well as published in various anthologies and e-mags. She has 11 published spec fic novels and has edited 2 short story anthologies. She regularly gives workshops on writing fight scenes at conventions. Lives in Brisbane. Does martial arts, archery, knife throwing and lute-playing.
Website: www.aikiflinthart.com

Wendy
by C.L. Williams

Wendy sees what looks like her dead husband in the distance. She has missed her husband and just wants to run to him and be held in his arms. She runs towards him while he stands still. Something feels odd for Wendy. As Wendy gets closer, his figure changes. She finally reaches her husband, "Spencer, I have missed you!" she says as tears roll down her face. She looks up and no longer sees her husband, she sees the agent of death himself, the Grim Reaper.

"Don't worry Wendy, you will see him soon." He says as he touches her.

*C.L. Williams is an independent author from central Virginia. He has written eight poetry books, four novellas, one novel, and a contributor to multiple anthologies, with the most recent appearance being an all-ages anthology titled Temoli from Thazbook. His most recent poetry book, The Paradox Complex, features the poem "Sad Crying Clown" that is now a video on YouTube directed by Matthew Mark Hunter of MMH Productions. C.L. Williams is currently working on his first sci-fi book, an all-ages book titled Novo: Away from Earth. When not writing, C.L. Williams is reading and sharing the work of other independent authors.
Facebook: writer434
Twitter: @writer_434*

They Move Inside the Walls
by Jacek Wilkos

"So, this is it? The haunted house?"

"Yup."

"OK, it looks kinda creepy. Dirty windows, paint peeling off the walls, scraps of old newspapers on the floor. But it's not enough."

"Don't worry, when you see them, you'll be really scared."

"Did you really see ghosts here?"

"Yes."

"Why haven't they shown up yet?"

"They live scattered throughout the house. Lured by human presence, they move inside the walls to the place where they sense life. Then they crawl out through the cracks in the walls and reveal themselves. They'll come."

"Why so confident?"

"I promised them something."

"What?"

"You."

Jacek Wilkos is an engineer from Poland. He lives with his wife and daughter in a beautiful city of Cracow. He is addicted to buying books, he loves coffee, dark ambient music and riding his bike. He writes mostly horror drabbles. His fiction in Polish can be read on Szortal, Niedobre literki, Horror Online. In English his work was published in Drablr, Rune Bear, Sirens Call eZine.
Facebook: Jacek.W.Wilkos

Nona
by Sinister Sweetheart

My Nona Rose and Papa Maurice left a church luncheon early one Sunday, due to him not feeling well. Papa laid down for a nap and never woke up.

The whole family was devastated, but none more so than Nona. My family moved in with her so she wouldn't be alone in the empty house Papa had built for her. She sat silent in her chair, forever waiting for Papa.

He showed up today. As my Nona took her last breath, his figure appeared in the hallway; a pitchforked tail poking from beneath his coat. That was *not* my Papa.

*Since **Sinister Sweetheart** made her first post to a popular Internet forum, she's taken the horror community by storm. Her ability to create, terrify, and drive home her stories is insurmountable. Sinister Sweetheart's published works can be found in multiple anthologies for all to read, but be forewarned, if you do... you may want to call your therapist after, her stories are terrifying, disturbing and devilishly unsettling. She is not only a fright visually, but also has a creepy tentacle in horror podcasting as well. Sinister Sweetheart writes, voice acts and is the media director of the Scarecrow Tales podcast.*
Website: Sinistersweetheart.wixsite.com/sinistersweetheart
Facebook: NMBrownStories

Where Lilies Bloom
by Shelly Jarvis

I stroll with Eliza along the lily road. It's been her favourite for three hundred years. Every day we pass the flowers, blooming in every colour you could imagine, and a few you couldn't. Every day she plucks a single white blossom as pale as her bloodless skin.

She puts the flower in her hair. I smile, but my heart aches at the action. I've seen this so many times, and still it hurts.

We reach the gate and an angel waves me towards them. They refuse Eliza and she returns to lose herself on the flower paths of purgatory.

Shelly Jarvis is a speculative fiction author from West Virginia, US. She found a life-long love of sci-fi and fantasy in the 3rd grade when she found Madeleine L'Engle's "A Wrinkle in Time." Shelly is an avid reader, a Whovian, the ideal viewer of dog rescue videos, and undoubtedly Ravenclaw. She currently has two YA sci-fi books available for purchase on Amazon.
Website: www.ShellyJarvis.com

Double Vision
by Gabriella Balcom

Brittany blinked but nothing changed. Two suns blazed overhead, one slightly in front of the other. "Weird," she muttered. Glancing down at herself, she flinched to see two bodies complete with torsos, arms, legs, and feet, even though that was impossible. In fact, she saw double of everything regardless of the direction she turned.

Then things went back to normal. Brittany rubbed her eyes, surveyed her surroundings again, but only saw one of each thing now.

"I must be losing it," she murmured, then entered her home.

Outside, a voice whispered, "Think she suspects anything?"

"No," a second voice replied.

Gabriella Balcom lives in Texas with her family, loves reading and writing, and thinks she was born with a book in her hands. She works in a mental health field, and writes fantasy, horror/thriller, romance, children's stories, and sci-fi. She likes travelling, music, good shows, photography, history, interesting tales, and animals. Gabriella says she's a sucker for a great story and loves forests, mountains, and back roads which might lead who knows where. She has a weakness for lasagne, garlic bread, tacos, cheese, and chocolate, but not necessarily in that order.
Facebook: GabriellaBalcom.lonestarauthor

Get Out!
by Elizabeth Montague

Get Out!

"Doubt the new owners are going to want that on display," he says as the wallpaper comes off in his hands revealing writing beneath.

"Creepy. You left the spare room door open, it lets a chill through."

"I've not been up there. Red paint…guess it's meant to be blood."

"It looks like blood. No need to breathe so hard, don't panic."

"I'm not breathing hard."

The glint of the knife and blood spattered clothes, centuries old, accompany their last moments and a guttural voice speaks the words he had written when the others wouldn't leave.

"Get out."

Elizabeth Montague is a multi-genre author from Hertfordshire, England. Her short story collection, Dust and Glitter, was released by Clarendon House Publications in May 2019. She has previously featured in nine anthologies from the same publisher alongside publications from Scout Media, Black Hare Press and Iron Faerie Publishing. She is currently working on her first novel alongside continuing to produce short stories in several genres.
Website: elizabethmontagueauthor.wordpress.com
Facebook: elizabethmontaguewrites

Sorry
by D.M. Burdett

The punches, the slaps, the hospital stays—you always regretted them later.

"I'm sorry."

The kicks, the spat slurs, the black eyes—always the same words once sober.

"I'm sorry."

The torment, the harassment, your crocodile tears for the lenient judge.

"I'm sorry."

The last cut, the last bruise, the last shovel of dirt on my shallow grave.

"I'm sorry."

My hatred, my anger, my rage—it follows you in your dreams, your waking moments. Infests your mind, your consciousness, torments and tortures.

As you press the knife to your pulse and the crimson flows, I whisper;

I'm not sorry.

D.M. Burdett *initially roamed as an army brat, but now lives in Australia where she spends her days avoiding drop bears and killer spiders. She has published a Sci-Fi series, has short stories in various anthologies, and has published two children's series. She is currently working on the first book in a dystopian series.*
Website: www.dmburdett.com
Facebook: DMBurdett

Visiting
by Vonnie Winslow Crist

While Granny and Mom wandered the cemetery, checking the condition of the gravesites of relatives, Victoria sat with Uncle Horton.

"I'm sorry it's been so long since I visited," she said as she held her great-uncle's hand.

He smiled, squeezed her hand.

Victoria told him about the third grade, her friends, and dreams.

"Time to leave," called Granny from the graveyard's entrance.

"Do we have to go?" asked Victoria. "I've barely gotten to talk with Uncle Horton."

"Don't be silly," scolded Granny. "Horton's been dead for twenty years."

Victoria looked at her great-uncle sitting beside her.

He winked, then disappeared.

Vonnie Winslow Crist is author of The Enchanted Dagger, Owl Light, The Greener Forest, Murder on Marawa Prime, and other award-winning books. Her fiction is included in "Amazing Stories," "Cast of Wonders," "Outposts of Beyond," Killing It Softly 2, Defending the Future - Dogs of War, Midnight Masquerade, Chaos of Hard Clay, and elsewhere. A cloverhand who has found so many four-leafed clovers she keeps them in jars, Vonnie strives to celebrate the power of myth in her writing.
Website: www.vonniewinslowcrist.com

The Lights in the Night
by S. John Davis

The lights won't stop flickering.

There's a voice in the distance, more than one. They're trying to communicate, trying to let me know something from their deep otherness.

I recoil from them, I'm scared. I'm supposed to be home—supposed to be safe—but the spectres won't leave me. I scream, the sound rolls through the air and pierces the night. They return with a volley of words, sounds and lights. They won't leave me in peace.

The lights flicker. Red and blue. A force from underneath, I'm lifted up. They place me in a bag and let me sleep.

S. John Davis is an author based in Gippsland, Victoria, Australia.
Facebook: sjohndavis

Only a Brief Sleep
by Alexander Pyles

You gather around the plot. The soil undisturbed, freshly packed down. Your cheeks now dry.

The chanting begins and all of you join in. Your thoughts on the past. Memories that you wish to become real again.

The wind picks up from a breeze to a gale, but you stay still. Your clothes flap and billow. The gusts begin to whistle in your ear and your whispers are lost to you.

The air stills. It is quiet.

You stare at the turned earth and wait, holding your breath.

A hand breaks the loose dirt, bony and gaunt.

You breathe again.

Alexander Pyles resides in IL with his wife and children. He holds an MA in Philosophy and an MFA in Writing Popular Fiction. His short story chapbook titled, "Milo (01001101 01101001 01101100 01101111)," from Radix Media, is due out fall 2019. His other short fiction has appeared on 101fiction.org, River and South Review, and other venues. Website: www.pylesofbooks.com Twitter: @Pylesofbooks

Red Earth and Bulldust
by Pamela Jeffs

There is supposed to be light, a tunnel to lead the dead to eternity. But not for me. I'm given a road travelling from East to West, from the sunrise to the sunset. Its length is carved from corrugated red earth and bulldust.

Termite mounds, twice as tall as a man, line the verges like sentinels. Their blind stares follow me, press down and pass judgment on my naked soul. There is no solace in the bright, fierce glare of the sun overhead either. So which way to go? East or West? Somehow, I suspect the outcome will be same.

Pamela Jeffs is a speculative fiction author living in Queensland, Australia with her husband and two daughters. She is a member of the Queensland Writers' Centre and has had numerous short fiction pieces published in recent national and international anthologies. In 2017 and again in 2018, Pamela was nominated for an Australian Aurealis Award in the category of 'Best Science Fiction Short Story'. Her debut collection titled 'Red Hour and Other Strange Tales' was released in March 2018.
Website: www.pamelajeffs.com
Facebook: pamelajeffsauthor

The Belltower
by R.J. Hunt

The priest was old, and the steps were high. It was midnight when he tumbled, and noon when he was found. Concrete edges are not forgiving on old flesh and bone, and he left twelve blood splattered steps on his grisly descent.

Each year on the day he died, at the stroke of midnight, they sound the bells. Not to remember him, but to mask the other sounds. Old pipes, they say. But there's no plumbing in the belltower. As the bells ring, they all pretend not to hear. Twelve slow crunches that seem to come from the steps themselves.

R.J. Hunt is a Civil Engineer from Nottingham who loves creating worlds and writing stories in his spare time. Whilst he has a roughly infinite supply of half-finished stories, he's currently working on the second draft of his debut novel, 'The Final Carnivore' - a story about horrible people being granted immortality and mind-control powers, causing misfits with hidden abilities of their own to rise in an effort stop them.
Twitter: @RJHuntWrites
Reddit: RJHuntWrites

The Craftsman
by Peter J. Foote

When the Craftsman heard the old Gallows Tree had killed that pervert Dickie Misner, he knew he'd found his material.

If anyone noticed when the bloodstained limb from the old oak tree disappeared, the Craftsman never heard, because he was busy milling and drying the lumber.

After countless hours cutting, shaping, and carving the ancient piece of oak, the Craftsman could see the end in sight. The last piece to carve was the planchette, and for this he used a piece still stained with blood, for the Craftsman knew only wood that has killed can make a true spirit board.

Peter J. Foote is a bestselling speculative fiction writer from Nova Scotia. Outside of writing, he runs a used bookstore specialising in fantasy & sci-fi, cosplays, and alternates between red wine and coffee as the mood demands. His short stories can be found in both print and in ebook form, with his story "Sea Monkeys" winning the inaugural "Engen Books/Kit Sora, Flash Fiction/Flash Photography" contest in March of 2018. As the founder of the group "Genre Writers of Atlantic Canada", Peter believes that the writing community is stronger when it works together.
Twitter: @PeterJFoote1
Website: peterjfooteauthor.wordpress.com

Retribution
by Stephanie Scissom

Ted Bundy woke shivering, facedown on a familiar trail. He'd been here many times, with many girls.

The last thing he remembered was the strap biting into his chin. The hood over his face.

Was he dead? He felt sluggish but solid. Alive. Instead of hell, he'd awakened in his favourite place. He'd even requested his ashes be scattered here.

Ted smiled.

Then, a woman emerged from the fog, her face a mask of grinning decomposition.

"Hello, Ted," she said. "We've been waiting."

Others followed. Some he remembered, some he did not.

They didn't look scared anymore. They looked…

Eager.

Stephanie Scissom *hails from Tennessee, where she lives with her two children, inspects tires by night and plots murder by day. She has four full-length romantic suspense titles and is published in both flash and short story anthologies. Her story, Dandelions, garnered her a Sweek Star recognition and placed first in the international short story competition. Her current project and obsession is an apocalyptic trilogy starring Lucifer, his insane wife, and his deadly, power-hungry siblings*
Facebook: Stephanie Scissom, Author
Twitter: @chell22_7

Mother's Day
by Andrew Anderson

Clara shouted up the stairs to her absent daughter again. "Abigail, for the last time! Your dinner is getting cold."

A rosy-faced girl raced into the kitchen and crashed into her seat. "Sorry, Mom. I was just talking to Grandma."

Clara sighed; it had been six weeks since her mother's death. Abigail was close to her grandma, so close that Clara had been almost envious.

Tactfully, she said, "Oh sweetie, you know Grandma isn't with us anymore."

"But, Mom, she was in my room just now."

"Now Abi—"

"And she says she knows exactly what you did with her money."

Andrew Anderson is a full-time civil servant, dabbling in writing music, poetry, screenplays and short stories in his limited spare time, when not working on building himself a fort made out of second-hand books. He lives in Bathgate, Scotland with his wife, two children and his dog.
Twitter: @soorploom

Insurance Money
by Jacob Baugher

"Everyone would be happier if I were dead."

My wife cries on our bed. "No. We love you."

Later, I lie in the dark. The vodka whispers in my ear. It's hidden in the water softener.

Just one drink.

The basement is a festering litterbox. Sweating in the summer heat, I remove the softener's lid; drink two bottles. Darkness fades to light. The Gatekeeper's there.

"Am I dead?"

Peter beckons. I follow.

My wife opens the insurance envelope. A check falls out. She throws it in the fire. My children hold her. White flames burn me. Heaven swallows the smoke.

Jacob Baugher teaches Creative Writing at Franciscan University of Steubenville. When he's not teaching or coaching the track team, he can be found in the Cuyahoga Valley hiking with his wife and son or brewing beer on his front porch. He's received honourable mentions for his work in the Writers of the Future contest and he co-edits a series of Fantasy and Science Fiction anthologies titled Continuum.

Things That Play in the Dark
by Jacob Baugher

Lucy was afraid of the dark because the ghosts came out to play. They hung, oily in her closet doorway. Every night, she made sure her toy sword was next to her nightstand. Her beagle, Hallie, slept on her bed.

The ghosts spoke with voices like liquified meat. They said the meanest things.

"Your mommy's going to hell."

"Your daddy hates you."

Lucy cried. Hallie whined. Then, she thought about Star Wars and said the words she wasn't supposed to say: "Screw this."

She threw the covers back, drew her sword. She screamed, Hallie snarled. Together, they faced the darkness.

Jacob Baugher teaches Creative Writing at Franciscan University of Steubenville. When he's not teaching or coaching the track team, he can be found in the Cuyahoga Valley hiking with his wife and son or brewing beer on his front porch. He's received honourable mentions for his work in the Writers of the Future contest and he co-edits a series of Fantasy and Science Fiction anthologies titled Continuum.

Through a Filter
by Rhiannon Bird

The world looked grey and murky. It moved in and out of focus. Sometimes the sun was out and sometimes it was just the stars. I could never tell anymore. Everything tasted like ash and smelt of smoke. Sounds wobbled as if they were passing through broken glass and the burning in my chest never left. It has been this way for so long I almost couldn't remember what it was like before. Before my car wrapped around a tree. Before the electric shock to my chest was enough to keep me near the world but not part of it.

Rhiannon Bird is a young aspiring author. She has a passion for words and storytelling. Rhiannon has her own quotes blog; Thoughts of a Writer. She has had 4 works published. This includes 3 short stories and 2 poems. These are published on Eskimo pie, Literary yard, Down in the Dirt Magazine and Short break fiction. She can be found on Facebook, Instagram, and Pinterest.

Lost at Sea
by John H. Dromey

Henry became separated from the other pirates of the boarding party. When they completed their raid—organized for recreation, rather than actually obtaining booty—the other swashbucklers left without him.

Bad news. In the vast expanse of the high seas, there could be an exceedingly long delay before Henry was once again within hailing distance of the eighteenth-century ghost ship he called home.

Good news. The buccaneer needn't be bored. If Henry haunted a different passenger stateroom every night, he'd require over five and a half years to complete his spectral rounds on the modern cruise ship he now occupied.

John H. Dromey was born in northeast Missouri, USA. He enjoys reading—mysteries in particular—and writing in a variety of genres. He's had short fiction published in Alfred Hitchcock's Mystery Magazine, Martian Magazine, Stupefying Stories Showcase, Thriller Magazine, Unfit Magazine, and elsewhere, as well as in a number of anthologies, including Chilling Horror Short Stories (Flame Tree Publishing, 2015).

Words Beyond
by A.R. Johnston

The hand-carved spirit board sat on the floor between them. It had been handed down through their family for generations. It was a gorgeous piece of artwork, with the deep carved sun, moon, stars, the hand painted alphabet, yes, no, hello and goodbye.

Fingertips to the planchette, it was warm to the touch. A zing went up the spine to make them gasp and chuckle.

"Say hello if you're here."

Hello.

"Is that you, Jack?"

Yes. How are you girls tonight?

"We miss you. You need to visit again."

I will, things will change soon.

"You promise?"

I promise.

A.R. Johnston is a small-town girl from Nova Scotia, Canada. Her style of writing is considered Urban Fantasy. Her first major publication is part of an anthology called First Love and she has several more titles lined up. She is a lover of coffee, good tv shows, horror flicks, and reader of books. She pretends to be a writer when real life doesn't get in the way. Pesky full-time job and adulting!

The Voices
by Eddie D. Moore

Lighting flashed behind the blinds and tiny pellets of hail tapped the office window. Sylvia folded her arms. Her eyes flicked nervously. "You hear them?"

"I only hear the storm." Dr. Williams made a notation. "I can guarantee you the hospital isn't haunted. You're simply hallucinating again."

Sylvia shook her head and drew herself into a ball on the couch. "They're screaming that they'll kill you, like my last doctor."

"That was just a heart attack. The voic—" Cold unseen fingers tightened around Dr. Williams' throat and his eyes bulged.

Tears ran down Sylvia's cheeks. "I tried to tell you."

Eddie D. Moore travels hundreds of hours a year, and he fills that time by listening to audiobooks. When he isn't playing with his grandchildren, he writes his own stories. You can find a list of his publications on his blog or by visiting his Amazon Author Page. While you're there, be sure to pick up a copy of his mini-anthology Misfits & Oddities. Website: eddiedmoore.wordpress.com Amazon: amazon.com/author/eddiedmoore

No
by Elizabeth Montague

The rustling woke her. She froze in the dark then tried to sit up, but her limbs felt heavy, pinned beneath the sheets by the weight on her.

The moon emerged from behind the cloud, illuminating the room and the creature staring down at her. Wide red eyes smirked, and wicked teeth dripped as it licked its lips and reached a claw towards her.

"No," she squeaked.

The thing grinned, turning its gaze to the other bed where her little brother slept peacefully.

"No," she said again, but the meaning was different as the creature grinned at her once more.

Elizabeth Montague is a multi-genre author from Hertfordshire, England. Her short story collection, Dust and Glitter, was released by Clarendon House Publications in May 2019. She has previously featured in nine anthologies from the same publisher alongside publications from Scout Media, Black Hare Press and Iron Faerie Publishing. She is currently working on her first novel alongside continuing to produce short stories in several genres.
Website: elizabethmontagueauthor.wordpress.com
Facebook: elizabethmontaguewrites

Two Minutes and Seventeen Seconds

by Joel R. Hunt

Before Sylvia was resuscitated, she had been dead for two minutes and seventeen seconds. Whenever people became aware of that fact, their next question was always the same:

"What did you see?"

Sylvia had answered that so many times she didn't need to think about it anymore. She would explain that she had floated above herself, looking down. It was a satisfactory, though predictable, response.

It was also a lie.

Sylvia couldn't bring herself to admit what she had really seen. The memory haunted her.

While her body died, her soul had walked through Heaven.

And it was completely deserted.

Joel R. Hunt is a writer from the UK who dabbles in the darker aspects of life, particularly through horror, science fiction and the supernatural. He has been published here and there (though likely nowhere you've heard of) and hopes to have released his first anthology of short stories later this year.
Twitter: @JoelRHunt1
Reddit: JRHEvilInc

Cries for Help
by Archit Joshi

They started during his afternoon nap. Insistent, unintelligible whispers. Driven crazy, he scrambled madly around his house, hunting for the source.

Nothing. Nowhere. Nobody.

They rose, both in intensity and their frantic urgency. Soon, he could discern the pitch and the words.

"Save me!" a little boy moaned. Moments later, they dissipated.

By the next morning, he'd forgotten the bizarre events.

***

Years thereafter, he waited outside a delivery room. The doctor emerged, ashen-faced.

"Miscarriage," he said.

Perched up on the ceiling of the hospital corridor, Jimmy looked woefully at his would-be father. Shaking his head, he walked towards the light.

Archit Joshi is a published short-story author who loves writing character-driven stories. Besides writing, he studies Computer Science and occasionally lends his hand to Social Services. He has also flirted with Entrepreneurship and had been running a startup in the food sector, before deciding to give his passion for writing a professional platform. Currently, Archit is studying for a Masters degree in Computers along with his pursuit of Creative Writing.

Facebook: authorarchitjoshi

Instagram: @architrjoshi

167

Phantoms at Sea
by Zoey Xolton

Sinead ascended the staircase to the top of the lighthouse with nothing but a small oil burning lantern to light her way. Holding her shawl together across her bust with one hand, she braced herself against the bitter cold.

Duty demanded she check the flame that saved lives every few hours. Looking out at the dark expanse of the raging ocean she gasped. A ship bore down upon the lighthouse.

She raced for the bell, ringing it frantically; a final warning. Sinead watched in horror as the ship breached the rocks and vanished into thin air.

The veteran watchwoman fainted.

Zoey Xolton is an Australian Speculative Fiction writer, primarily of Dark Fantasy, Paranormal Romance and Horror. She is also a proud mother of two and is married to her soul mate. Outside of her family, writing is her greatest passion. She is especially fond of short fiction and is working on releasing her own themed collections in future.
Website: www.zoeyxolton.com

Late and Prompt
by Beth W. Patterson

She hated my music and didn't care for me as a person either. But she begrudgingly hired me to play at her pub because my songs sold beer.

Sometimes, at the end of the night, she'd talk to me if no one else was around. Her late husband George was always hovering at the end of the stage, she said.

Last night I forget the lyrics to her request, but the disembodied voice in my ear reminded me: "*You'll come and find the place where I am lying...*"

Those unseen cold fingers helped me find the chords.

Beth W. Patterson was a full-time musician for over two decades before diving into the world of writing, a process she describes as "fleeing the circus to join the zoo". She is the author of the books Mongrels and Misfits, and The Wild Harmonic, and a contributing writer to thirty anthologies. Patterson has performed in eighteen countries, expanding her perspective as she goes. Her playing appears on over a hundred and seventy albums, soundtracks, videos, commercials, and voice-overs (including seven solo albums of her own). She lives in New Orleans, Louisiana with her husband Josh Paxton, jazz pianist extraordinaire.
Website: www.bethpattersonmusic.com
Facebook: bethodist

The Haunting
by Rowanne S. Carberry

"Do it, you owe me."

Vicky circles Michelle.

"You killed me, I told you not to use your phone."

Vicky passes ghostly fingers through Michelle's hair, giving a wicked laugh when she shudders.

"You wouldn't listen to me. Now. I'm. Dead."

Tears fall from Michelle's eyes.

"Please, Vicky, please." Michelle chokes on her own tears. "I'm sorry. I did everything else. I can't do this."

Michelle's hands wrap around Vicky's throat, wishing she could really squeeze.

"Do it."

Sobs wrenching her chest, Michelle takes the gun and shoots her cat, vomiting over the floor as her friend laughs in glee.

Rowanne S. Carberry was born in England in 1990, where she stills lives now with her cat Wolverine. Rowanne has always loved writing, and her first poem was published at the age of 15, but her ambition has always been to help people. Rowanne studied at the University of Sunderland where she completed combined honours of Psychology with Drama. Rowanne writes to offer others an escape. Although Rowanne writes in varied genres each story or poem she writes will often have a darkness to it, which helped coin her brand, Poisoned Quill Writing – Wicked words from a poisoned quill.
Facebook: PoisonedQuillWriting
Instagram: @poisoned_quill_writing

Death on a Winged Horse
by Cindar Harrell

"You fought bravely, but your battle is over." The woman offered her hand.

"Are you the angel of death?" the soldier asked.

"You could consider me such."

He mounted the winged horse with his remaining arm. Seeing her armour and helm, realisation dawned as they soared through the realms.

"You're a valkyrie!" He smiled as he pictured the warrior's hall from legend, but his smile soon faded as the world around him grew dark and cold.

Dropped in a hall of cold stone, another woman stood above him. "Only those who are whole make it to Valhalla. Welcome to Helheim."

Cindar Harrell loves fairy tales, especially ones with a dark twist. Her stories are often fairy tale inspired, but she is also working on a mystery series. Her stories can be found on Amazon and in various anthologies. You can follow her on Facebook and visit her blog, which she promises to try and update more often,
Website: cindarharrell.wordpress.com
Facebook: CindarHarrell

Christmas Truce
by Eric Lewis

John and Heinrich looked across fields of overgrown trenches and mortar holes. "Here we are again. Another year's passed."

"We never left," said his old enemy, "not really."

"I know. The battlefield's almost unchanged."

"It's no memorial," Heinrich insisted, "quite the opposite! They want to leave it be, forget entirely."

"Can't blame them. So do I. Except Christmas. Our truce. Remember, we played football, traded cigarettes?"

"I remember. Officers were furious. Next day, right back to it."

"The last day."

At sunrise, two dead soldiers disappeared into the air for another year, though never to leave the place. Not really.

Eric Lewis is a research scientist weathering the latest rounds of layoffs and trying to remember how to be a person again after surviving grad school. His short fiction has been published in Nature, Electric Spec, Allegory, Bards and Sages Quarterly, the anthologies Into Darkness Peering, Best Indie Speculative Fiction Vol. 1, Chronos and Crash Code, as well as other venues detailed on his website. His debut novel The Heron Kings is due out in early 2020. Website: ericlewis.ink

Follow Me
by Jo Seysener

The soul shrank back. A smile curved the angel's lips. He could be cruel with the living—it was no big stretch to do it to the dead, too.

The desperate soul had no choice but to follow him, really. Or remain lost, watching those he loved wither, rot in their graves. Never to be reunited in, well...the angel coughed, concealing his smirk.

"I am but a messenger for the great I AM." He intoned with reverence. He bowed low, the hem of his skirts rising. He smoothed them. T'was all put on; the souls ate it every time.

Jo Seysener is a mum of three crazies, a scatter of chickens, a decrepit kelpie and a rambunctious GSD. She lives with her husband near Brisbane, Australia. When she is not exposing her kids to cult story books from her childhood, she can be found in the kitchen experimenting with new flavours and pairings. She adores alpacas.
Facebook: joseysener
Website: www.joseysener.com

Ghost Hunt
by J. Farrington

Panting heavily, panic stricken, I make my way through the brambles and bushes. I push on deeper into the forest. I must get off the track, I need to get my distance from them.

In the distance I can hear galloping horses; it's too late, I need to hide.

Climbing the nearest tree, I sit still on a branch, hand on mouth, peering down at the forest floor below. Four horses with riders come to a stop below. The lead rider headless, the three following with similar life ending injuries.

How did I become part of this year's Ghost Hunt?

J. Farrington is an aspiring author from the West Midlands, UK. His genre of choice is horror; whether that be psychological, suspense, supernatural or straight up weird, he'll give it a shot! He has loved writing from a young age but has only publicly been spreading his darker thoughts and sinister imagination via social platforms since 2018. If you would like to view his previous work, or merely lurk in the shadows...watching, you can keep up to date with future projects by spirit board or alternatively, the following;
Twitter: @SurvivorTrench
Reddit: TrenchChronicles

Margaret Speaks
by Dawn DeBraal

The music played, essential oil filled the air. Debra lay on the bed with her eyes closed relaxing while the Reiki Master channelled energy of healing into her body. Debra was emotionally and physically spent. In vitro fertilisation treatments had done a number on her body. The healer spoke quietly to her, hovering over spots in her body where Debra still held tension.

"Who is Margaret?" the Master asked.

"My grandmother," Debra responded.

"Is that what you are going to name your daughter?" she questioned.

"I don't have any children," Debra said sadly.

"Yes, you do." Smiled the Reiki Master.

Dawn DeBraal lives in rural Wisconsin with her husband, two rat terriers, and a cat. She successfully raised two children (meaning they didn't return to the nest!) After many years serving the government at the Federal and County level, she recently retired. Having extra time on her hands she started to write after a paralyzed vocal cord took her ability to speak for two months. Not finding her voice, she discovered that her love of telling a good story could be written. Her works have been published in Palm-sized press, Spillwords, Mercurial Stories, Potato Soup Journal, and Blood Song Books.

The Collector
by Belinda Brady

Sitting on the bench, I sigh wearily.

I'd lost my job and had answered a newspaper advertisement looking for debt collectors, and even when I was told the unique debt I would be collecting, I signed up anyway. I was desperate and the money was too good to refuse.

That was ten years ago and I've been sighing in this changing room nightly ever since.

A dark figure appears before me, his scythe glistening in the moonlight, black hooded cloak lining his face.

Bill, my co-worker, smiles grimly as he gives handover.

My shift as the Grim Reaper has begun.

Belinda Brady is passionate about stories and after years of procrastinating, has finally turned her hand to writing them, with a preference for supernatural and thriller themes; her love of both often competing for her attention. She has had several stories published in a variety of publications, both online and in anthologies. Belinda lives in Australia with her family and has been known to enjoy the company of cats over people.

The Painting of Void
by Aditya Deshmukh

Cecilia stormed into the room, pinching her nose. She grabbed the pile of stale pizzas and beer bottles and dumped them into the bin. She dragged her brother out of bed. "Dude, get your shit together."

John looked at her, but he didn't see her. He watched his wife's final painting hanging on the wall. A gate to the void.

Cecilia blocked his view. "Enough of this! She's dead. Accept it and move on."

"Dead, not gone," John said, staring right through her. "I've to go."

"Where?"

John pushed her out of his way. He ran towards the void. "Beyond."

Aditya Deshmukh is a mechanical engineering student who likes exploring the mechanics of writing as much as he likes tinkering with machines. He writes dark fiction and poetry. He is published in over three dozen anthologies and has a poetry book "Opium Hearts" and a collection of drabbles coming out soon. He likes chatting with people who share similar interests, so feel free to check him out.
Facebook: adityadeshmukhwrites
Website: www.adityadeshmukh.com

An Eternity
by Kaustubh Nadkarni

I see my wife and daughter at the dinner table. With red eyes and tear-stained faces, they stare at their plates. Two days have passed since I died, but they haven't moved.

I want them to know that I'm fine and miss them dearly. I feel utterly helpless. So finally, I struck a deal with Him. My family will live forever if I slog daily in his dreadful and forsaken place.

Every passing moment, I regret my decision. Their faces are losing lustre, and eyes are sinking deeper into sockets. I want to be alive while they yearn for death.

Kaustubh Nadkarni is an Indian medical practitioner. He loves to unwind, with a mystery novel and a cup of steaming hot chai. Exploring hidden worlds within pages makes him happy. He dabbles in drabbles, short stories, and poetry. When he's not scribbling words, Kaustubh enjoys football and photography. His works have appeared in: Dark Drabbles 4, Sea Glass Hearts and Elemental Drabbles Vol. 1. Twitter: @kaustofsuccess Instagram: @kaustofsuccess

Quaint
by Umair Mirxa

Qasim looked at the quaint little cottage and back at his friends.

"You're telling me he lives here?"

"Yes," said little Sarah. "Go on."

The stranger who answered the door in response to Qasim's timid knock didn't look the part. Still, it couldn't hurt to ask.

"Excuse me, sir," he said. "We were told you could help us."

"Ah yes," said the stranger, looking at the kids with sad, blue eyes. "Come."

They followed him into the tiny kitchen.

"You will find your parents just beyond the light," said the Angel of Death, pointing to a passage behind the sink.

Umair Mirxa lives in Karachi, Pakistan. His first published story, 'Awareness', appeared on Spillwords Press. He has also had stories accepted for anthologies from Zombie Pirate Publishing, Blood Song Books, Fantasia Divinity Magazine and Publishing, and Iron Faerie Publishing. He is a massive J.R.R. Tolkien fan, and loves everything to do with fantasy and mythology. He enjoys football, history, music, movies, TV shows, and comic books, and wishes with all his heart that dragons were real.
Website: www.umairmirxa.com
Facebook: UMirxa12

Dog Food
by Jonathan Inbody

He died asleep in his easy chair, like an old man should. His dog was confused at first, but after enough pangs of hunger Scraps understood that his master was not just dead, but almost entirely edible. Scraps started with the soft tissue; the lips, the ears, the fatty stomach. It felt wrong, reverting to his primal nature, but somehow he felt that his master would understand. His master's ghost, tethered to his rapidly-decaying vessel of flesh, sighed as his dog continued to eat.

Oh, well. At least his dog would have enough food… and plenty of bones to fetch.

Jonathan Inbody is a filmmaker, author, and podcaster from Buffalo, New York. He enjoys B-movies, pen and paper RPGs, and New Wave Science Fiction novels. His short story "Dying Feels Like Slowly Sinking" is due to be published in the anthology Deteriorate from Whimsically Dark Publishing. Jon can be heard every other week on his improvisational movie pitch podcast X Meets Y. Website: xmeetsy.libsyn.com

Veils
by Jonathan Ficke

Some veils were never meant to be pierced. Death was one.

My wife lay in the ground, stolen from me by a disease with no 'cure.' Allegedly, ethics and risks barred the research that might have saved her. Given no other choice, I unchained myself from the strictures that bound the physicians. I rent the veil. I slipped the chains of death from my wife's wrists.

"I'm so hungry," she said through desiccated lips.

I wondered if I would have done anything differently as her teeth met my flesh. I screamed my answer— "No"—til I passed beyond the veil.

Jonathan Ficke lives outside of Milwaukee, WI with his beautiful wife. His fiction has appeared in "Writers of the Future, Vol 34" and he muses online at;
Website: jonficke.com
Twitter: @jonficke

The Other Side
by E.L. Giles

People hustled and bustled down the street. A strange, ghostly mist permeated the air. It was dark and cold and silent—so silent!

I ducked two passers-by, coming directly into the path of a young woman whose eyes were riveted on her phone. We didn't collide. Instead, I simply passed through her, like I was made of smoke, like I was part of the mist surrounding us.

I panicked and screamed, but no one seemed to hear me. When I turned around, I noticed a gathering of people, staring down. I approached and saw myself, lying on the ground. Dead.

E.L. Giles is a dreamer, passionate about art, a restless worker and a bit of a weird human. He started his artistic journey as a music composer until the need to put his thoughts and stories down on paper grew too strong for him to resist it any longer. He lives in the French Province of Quebec, Canada, with his girlfriend and two boys.
Facebook: elgilesauthor
Website: www.elgilesauthor.com

Goodnight
by Jem McCusker

"Who's going to tell my bed time story?" I asked to the sea of faces crowding my room.

The grey haired and grey faced woman in the rocker next to my brother's crib lifted her hand. "I will. But first, what will you give me?"

I sat up, propped against my pillows. "What do you want?"

She threw back her head and laughed. "I want to feel alive again, the beating pulse of a heart."

"Uhh..."

"I'm sure your brother wouldn't mind. Just a light touch on his chest."

"Yeah, sure. Ok, but don't wake him."

"He will not wake."

*Jem McCusker is a middle grade fiction author, living near Brisbane with her two sons and husband. Her first book Stone Guardians the Rise of Eden was released in 2018 and she is working on the sequel. She is releasing a Novella for the Four Quills writing group, A Storm of Wind and Rain series in July, 2019. She longs to be a full-time author, won't wear yellow and loves rabbits. Follow Jem on Twitter, Facebook and Instagram. Details on her website.
Website: www.jemmccusker.com*

The Devil is in the Number
by Carole de Monclin

"Why do you want to change?" the city clerk asked.

"People always look at me sideways when I give the address. Contractors sometimes refuse to work at our house. But the worse is when parents won't bring their kids to playdates. We also get pranks on Halloween. Lots of them."

"What's your address?"

"666 Nightshade Cove. 668 would do, if possible."

"I'll see what I can do."

"Thank you."

Mary desperately hoped the number change would solve her problems. Those she'd listed, and those she couldn't mention; like the bleeding walls, or the sardonic laugh resonating deep into the night.

Carole de Monclin has lived in France and Australia, but for the moment the USA is home. She finds inspiration from her travels. She loves Science Fiction because it explores the human mind in a way no other genre can. Plus, who doesn't love spaceships and lasers? Her stories appear in the Exoplanet Magazine and Angels - A Dark Drabbles Anthology.
Website: CaroledeMonclin.com
Twitter: @CaroledeMonclin

The Unwelcome Test
by Shawn M. Klimek

Reaching Kendra's door, the parapsychologist turned to the child's mother. "I know we agreed to no testing…"

"Not without permission," said Jane Bosch, sternly. "It angers her."

"No one likes to feel like a lab monkey," the doctor sympathised. "Don't worry. I left my kit at home."

Mrs. Bosch nodded with satisfaction.

"What if I just left my phone in recording mode?"

"Don't even think it!" said Jane emphatically. "She would know."

"You're right. Deception would test her telepathy," said the doctor, smiling regretfully. He opened the door.

"You fool!" said Mrs. Bosch, shielding her face from the brain splatter.

Shawn M. Klimek is the middle child of seven creative siblings, a globetrotting, U.S. military spouse, an internationally best-selling short-story writer, a poet, and butler to a Maltese. Almost one hundred of his stories or poems have been published in digital magazines or anthologies, including BHP's Deep Space and the first six books in the Dark Drabbles series.
Website: jotinthedark.blogspot.com
Facebook: shawnmklimekauthor

New Friends
by G. Allen Wilbanks

The four of us sat around the spirit board, one at each corner. With only the light of a few candles to see by, the room was dim and eerie. I don't remember whose idea it was to play this game, but I was eager to see what would happen.

The boy named Theo cleared his throat to speak.

"Are there any spirits here? Do you want to talk to us?"

I reached out my hand, focusing my thoughts on my fingers and willing strength into them. I pushed with everything I had, trying to move the planchette to 'yes.'

G. Allen Wilbanks is a member of the Horror Writers Association (HWA) and has published over 50 short stories in various magazines and on-line venues. He is the author of two short story collections, and the novel, When Darkness Comes.
Website: www.gallenwilbanks.com
Blog: DeepDarkThoughts.com

Ghost Father
by Henry Herz

"Hamlet..."

"Angels and ministers of grace defend me!

Be thou a caring father or helicopter parent,

Bring with thee airs from heaven or blasts from hell?"

"It is time..."

"Why have thy sleeping limbs, clad in complete corduroy,

Risen from thy BarcaLounger; why the recliner,

Wherein thou peacefully dozed,

Hath opened its false leather jaws

To cast thee up again? What may this mean,

That thou, old man, appear whilst I game,

Resurrecting thus our arguments of the past,

Thwarting my plans of Grand Theft Auto night.

What should I do?"

"It is time for you to get a job."

Henry Herz *edited the dark fantasy anthology, BEYOND THE PALE, featuring stories by Saladin Ahmed, Peter Beagle, Heather Brewer, Jim Butcher, Rachel Caine, Kami Garcia, Nancy Holder, and Jane Yolen. His horror story, Gluttony, will appear in the anthology, CLASSICS REMIXED. He authored the children's books: MONSTER GOOSE NURSERY RHYMES, WHEN YOU GIVE AN IMP A PENNY, MABEL & THE QUEEN OF DREAMS, LITTLE RED CUTTLEFISH, CAP'N REX & HIS CLEVER CREW, HOW THE SQUID GOT TWO LONG ARMS, ALICE'S MAGIC GARDEN, GOOD EGG AND BAD APPLE, TWO PIRATES + ONE ROBOT, THE MAGIC SPATULA, and I AM SMOKE.*
Website: www.henryherz.com

Scales
by Annie Percik

The scales of Osiris weigh my guilt. More than a feather is not a surprise. The scales fall from my eyes, revealing the truth of my punishment. Shining darkly, they gather to form a shoal of black fish. They surround me, swimming through air, sinuous and slippery. A fitting sentence for my crime of maternal negligence at the beach that day long ago. Cold flesh presses against my skin, enveloping me. The fish exude the water that gives them life and seals my doom. I fall with the fish, eyes dimming, lungs filling. They draw me down into the deep.

Annie Percik lives in London with her husband, Dave, where she is revising her first novel, whilst working as a University Complaints Officer. She writes a blog about writing and posts short fiction on her website. She also publishes a photo-story blog, recording the adventures of her teddy bear. He is much more popular online than she is. She likes to run away from zombies in her spare time.
Website: www.alobear.co.uk
Website: aloysius-bear.dreamwidth.org

Last Farm
by Vonnie Winslow Crist

"Azaleas: Last Farm at End of Lane," proclaimed a faded placard.

Turning into the driveway, Lynn thought, *Mother's Day is tomorrow. I'd love to have something for Mom.*

Two miles later, Lynn spotted azaleas. She parked, exited her car.

"Howdy," said an elderly man.

"How much?" She prayed they were inexpensive— she was broke.

"Free—just want them to find a home."

"I'll take one for my Mom."

"Here you go." He smiled, then loaded four fresh-dug azaleas into her trunk.

Lynn turned to thank him, but no one was there— only a crumbling farmhouse, "For Sale" sign, and azaleas.

Vonnie Winslow Crist is author of The Enchanted Dagger, Owl Light, The Greener Forest, Murder on Marawa Prime, and other award-winning books. Her fiction is included in "Amazing Stories," "Cast of Wonders," "Outposts of Beyond," Killing It Softly 2, Defending the Future - Dogs of War, Midnight Masquerade, Chaos of Hard Clay, and elsewhere. A cloverhand who has found so many four-leafed clovers she keeps them in jars, Vonnie strives to celebrate the power of myth in her writing.
Website: www.vonniewinslowcrist.com

The Intruder
by Brian Rosenberger

Her murderer as beautiful as when they first exchanged pleasantries at the neighbourhood bar.

Clad in a red, silk nightie, the killer sleeps. Not so peacefully.

The intruder was smitten by her high cheekbones and dark-as-shadows shoulder length hair, her come hither cleavage. She had boobs and knew how to use them.

After a few margaritas, it was easy to ask her back to her townhouse. She was easy to agree.

Then the knife. The evening had been going so well.

She was so beautiful, still is.

She visits her murderer every night. Keeps her from sleeping.

A ghost's revenge.

Brian Rosenberger lives in a cellar in Marietta, GA (USA) and writes by the light of captured fireflies. He is the author of As the Worms Turns and three poetry collections. He is also a featured contributor to the Pro-Wrestling literary collection, Three-Way Dance, available from Gimmick Press.
Facebook: HeWhoSuffers

Silence, Darkness, Light
by S. John Davis

Silence. Darkness. Then light. God, what light, vast and overwhelming. I tried to lift my head from the ground but could not move. I looked out through the light and everything suddenly came into focus after a lifetime of haze.

Shapes and colours then came to me, faces of an unquestionable connection saw me, saw into me and I into them before racing past without ever leaving. Fear departed. Sickness, weakness fled from me as I shed my mortality. Then there in that void did I espy an apex of Gold. His look of distaste. Life's misdeed. Silence. Darkness. Light.

S. John Davis is an author based in Gippsland, Victoria, Australia.
Facebook: sjohndavis

Levitation
by Dawn DeBraal

Jeffrey concentrated harder at the urging of the scientist standing next to him.

"Bend the spoon, Jeff. You can do it."

Jeff concentrated harder, his nose dripping blood. He wiped it away. The spoon started to wiggle ever so slightly.

"Good Jeffrey, keep going! You are so close. You can't go home until you move that spoon!" coaxed the scientist. Jeffrey's headache was about to split him wide open. He couldn't do this anymore. He was so angry he sent the spoon flying across the room where it sunk itself into the scientists' temple.

"I'm leaving now!" Jeff said firmly.

Dawn DeBraal lives in rural Wisconsin with her husband, two rat terriers, and a cat. She successfully raised two children (meaning they didn't return to the nest!) After many years serving the government at the Federal and County level, she recently retired. Having extra time on her hands she started to write after a paralyzed vocal cord took her ability to speak for two months. Not finding her voice, she discovered that her love of telling a good story could be written. Her works have been published in Palm-sized press, Spillwords, Mercurial Stories, Potato Soup Journal, and Blood Song Books.

Bell

by Elizabeth Montague

He'd tended the graveyard for years. Overgrown and underused, no one got buried there any more, and no one visited those who were. The graves pre-dated his grandfather, ancient monuments that were preserved for the art rather than the bones beneath. Victorian oddities. The weeping statues, the eloquent epitaphs, the bells that hung above the graves with their strings long since rotted away.

He chased off graffiti artists and moody teenagers with nothing to do, until there was no one but him in the graveyard.

He wished for a friend though, as the bell above the grave began to ring.

Elizabeth Montague is a multi-genre author from Hertfordshire, England. Her short story collection, Dust and Glitter, was released by Clarendon House Publications in May 2019. She has previously featured in nine anthologies from the same publisher alongside publications from Scout Media, Black Hare Press and Iron Faerie Publishing. She is currently working on her first novel alongside continuing to produce short stories in several genres.
Website: elizabethmontagueauthor.wordpress.com
Facebook: elizabethmontaguewrites

Poppets
by Matt Booth

The urchins shiver under rags, hoping for someone kind to notice them. The streetlamp above them flickers. Then every light on the block goes dark. They whimper as one. The sound of wet footsteps approach. They huddle closer together.

"Hop in the bag, poppets, I have places to be," he said.

His too big grin shined in a night with no moon. With his outstretched arm and too long fingers, he scooped them all into his bag. He threw it over his shoulder and strolled down the street, whistling an ancient tune. The lights flickered back on an empty street.

Matt Booth is a writer who lives in New York.

Grandma's Spirit Board
by Angela Zimmerman

Jason was spending the summer helping his grandfather repair their family home. As he busted the last of the brick in the wall, he saw something. There, hidden behind the closed up fireplace, was a rectangular board covered in enough dirt and webs that the black letters were hardly visible. Dropping his hammer to the floor, he called his grandfather over.

"Grandpa, why is this here?"

Grandpa came over and looked over his shoulder, a forlorn sigh escaping his body.

"For the same damn reason your grandma's buried under the oak tree out back, boy. It ain't nothing but trouble."

Angela Zimmerman is a writer living in the Southern United States. She has been published in Unnvering Magazine and Coffin Bell. You can find her personal writings at Conjure and Coffee.
Website: conjureandcoffee.com

A Kiss at the Sea
by A.S. Charly

Mike was cleaning the beach when he noticed a shadow in the water. Red waves rolled over it, glowing in the setting sun, their hypnotising music filling the air. It rose above the surface, forming the silhouette of a woman against the lilac sky.

Enchanted, Mike waded into the ocean.

She turned towards him, smiling. Water drops glittered between her pearls and jewels. The girl reached out for him.

Spellbound, he surrendered, and she kissed him. Embracing each other, they sunk into the flood.

When he was out of air, he tried to free himself, but she dragged him deeper.

A.S. Charly loves to lose herself in fantastical worlds far away between the stars, filled with magic and wonder. She also writes and draws when she is not roaming through the park with her children. Her stories have been published in various anthologies and online publications.
Facebook: A.S.Charlydreams

Death is Vengeful
by Monica Schultz

Hunger. Death can feel it pulsing in the air. Desperate desire to right unspeakable wrongs. An empty pit in one's stomach until spilt blood brings justice.

The father waits in the alleyway. Thumping music from the club erases all sound. Erases all thought. Death whisper's encouragement. *Kill.*

Midnight. He's right on time. A new girl stumbling in his grip. Her eyes glazed. The father's blood boils. He's seen enough. Death doesn't have to wait for this monster to unzip his pants again.

The father leaps from the shadows. Only Death saw him coming.

"This is for my daughter."

Death grins.

Monica Schultz writes young adult fantasy novels for anyone who needs an escape from reality. She can often be found reading novels, with a cat curled on her lap, to hide from her own mundane life.
*Twitter: @MonicaSchultz_*
Instagram: @miss.schultz

A Hole in the Wall
by A.L. King

I was eight-years-old when I found a block from the basement wall on the floor. No dirt had joined it, so I grabbed a flashlight and peeked inside to see a hallway with several offshoots.

My family moved shortly thereafter.

Turns out an old cemetery was buried by mudslide hundreds of years ago. The house was built— unknowingly—next to it. A mausoleum had shifted slowly through the dirt, cosied up to the basement wall, as if it were part of the structure.

I guess that explains all the imaginary friends who kept wanting me to play in the basement.

A.L. King is an author of horror, fantasy, science fiction, and poetry. As an avid fan of dark subjects from an early age, his first influences included R.L. Stine, Edgar Allan Poe, and Stephen King. Later stylistic inspirations came from foreign horror films and media, particularly Japanese. He is a graduate of West Liberty University, has dabbled in journalism, and is actively involved in his community. Although his creativity leans toward darker genres, he has even written a children's book titled "Leif's First Fall." He was raised in the town of Sistersville, West Virginia, which he still proudly calls home.

Familiar Haunts
by John H. Dromey

As a multigenerational colonisation starship hurtled through space toward a distant Earth-like planet, one of the team leaders felt vaguely uneasy.

She sought an interview with the expedition's organiser.

"When I compare the individuals I recruited with other ethnic groups, I have a sense we're lacking something. Perhaps something essential was left behind. Any idea what it could be? I know this sounds counterintuitive, Director. Especially, since you generously supply us with all critically-needed cultural artefacts."

"Not all! Apparently, your group overlooked an important clause in the fine print of our charter."

"What does it say?"

"Bring your own ghosts."

John H. Dromey was born in northeast Missouri, USA. He enjoys reading—mysteries in particular—and writing in a variety of genres. He's had short fiction published in Alfred Hitchcock's Mystery Magazine, Martian Magazine, Stupefying Stories Showcase, Thriller Magazine, Unfit Magazine, and elsewhere, as well as in a number of anthologies, including Chilling Horror Short Stories (Flame Tree Publishing, 2015).

Answering Prayers
by Raven Corinn Carluk

"It's not the same," he said, wiping at his eyes. "I smell her on my pillow. Can't take care of myself. Don't know what to do with myself." He looked up, grief etched on his face. "Please, take me to her."

Reapers could take any soul to any afterlife. Sionnan had personally reunited parted couples, had taken parents to their children. "Let's go," she said, taking his hand.

She whisked them from his room to one of fire and screams. His eyes widened. "She went to Hell?"

Sionnan cackled. "No, but wife beaters do." The Reaper left him to burn.

Raven Corinn Carluk writes dark fantasy, paranormal romance, and anything else that catches her interest. She's authored five novels, where she explores themes of love and acceptance. Her shorter pieces, usually from her darker side, can be found in Black Hare Press anthologies, at Detritus Online, and through Alban Lake Publishers.
Twitter: @ravencorinn
Website: RavenCorinnCarluk.Blogspot.Com

Another World
by S. John Davis

I believe in God.

I believe in life eternal and in a world beyond death. The reflection of that place is caught only in a glimpse in our world of dreams, but one day we all return.

Today, I will see that light.

I will close my eyes for one last time, and I will enter that glorious dream wherein shall I be with my ancestors and creator.

With hope in my heart, I close my eyes each time for a little bit longer. Soon I will see. Soon I will be at peace.

So, why is it so dark?

S. John Davis is an author based in Gippsland, Victoria, Australia.
Facebook: sjohndavis

One Last Man
by J.M. Meyer

"He owes me fifty-bucks," said the skinny man with smoker's teeth and dirty clothes at the wake.

"Excuse me?" Uncle Charlie, a retired cop, asked. "Who owes you money?"

The man points to my grandfather in his open casket.

I met my grandfather alive, once. My mom whispered, "Don't be alone with him."

"Go ask him for it," Uncle Charlie said as he grabbed the guy by the back of the neck and pushed him towards grandpa's face. The man whimpered apologies before gramp's hand tightened around the front of his neck, squeezing the life out of one last man.

J.M. Meyer is writer, artist and small business owner living in New York., where she received her master's degree from Teacher's College, Columbia University. Jacqueline loves the science fiction and horror genres. Reading Ray Bradbury was a mind-blowing experience for her in 8th grade. Alfred Hitchcock and Rod Serling were the horror heroes of her youth. Mercedes M. Yardley is her current horror writing hero. Jacqueline also enjoys the company of her husband Bruce and their three children, Julia, Emma and Lauren. Jacqueline's mantra: The only time it's too late to try something new is when you are dead.
Website: jmoranmeyer.net
Twitter: @moran_meyer

The Touch of Fury
by Andreas Hort

He told me I was the only one. I believed him. Now here I am, in our bedroom, two days after my funeral, watching him fuck his "co-worker." How naïve I was.

I turn away, my eyes falling on their faces smiling at me from the picture on the table. Our own picture is already gone. Our love forgotten.

I scream, swing my hand, expecting nothing, yet feeling the edge of the frame against my palm. The picture hits the floor. The glass breaks.

Her moans stop. "What was that?"

Closing my hands into fists, I start toward the bed.

Andreas Hort resides in a small town in the northern part of the Czech Republic. When he is not earning his daily bread working various, usually physically oriented jobs, he writes and takes steps toward his goal to move to an English-speaking country. He was never published in English before. In his free time, he works out, studies the investment business, and, of course, reads.
Facebook: andreas.hort.71
Twitter: @Ondrej_Hort

Footprints
by Alanna Robertson-Webb

Pitter-patter.

Squish-shlup.

These are the sounds my footsteps make when I have to get laundry out of my flooded basement, and my basement floods almost every time it rains. I always leave a single trail of footprints behind me as I come up the steps, but today there was a child-sized set next to mine.

I live alone, and my security cameras didn't catch any children around. Even now, as I'm sitting at my table writing, I can hear someone moving about down there.

Pitter-patter.

Squish-shlup.

Each time I check, there's nothing I can see, just more tiny, little footprints.

Alanna Robertson-Webb is a sales support member by day, and a writer and editor by night. She loves VT, and lives in NY. She has been writing since she was five years old, and writing well since she was seventeen years old. She lives with a fiance and a cat, both of whom take up most of her bed space. She loves to L.A.R.P., and one day she aspired to write a horrifyingly fantastic novel. Her short horror stories have been published before, but she still enjoys remaining mysterious.

Reddit: MythologyLovesHorror

The Crossing
by Eddie D. Moore

The light came again, and another soul left the mortal realm. That light sang to him with sweet promises of a new life, but he just couldn't reach it. The heart monitor beeped steadily, and the breathing machine forced his chest to rise and fall. Each time the light appeared, he fought to break free and join the others, but the machines held him tight.

Relief filled him when a doctor stepped into the room and unplugged the machines. He waited anxiously for the light to come for him, but terror gripped him as the floor darkened and he fell.

Eddie D. Moore travels hundreds of hours a year, and he fills that time by listening to audiobooks. When he isn't playing with his grandchildren, he writes his own stories. You can find a list of his publications on his blog or by visiting his Amazon Author Page. While you're there, be sure to pick up a copy of his mini-anthology Misfits & Oddities. Website: eddiedmoore.wordpress.com Amazon: amazon.com/author/eddiedmoore

Remain
by Umair Mirxa

Rebekah tried and failed to stop the tears flowing down her cheeks as her twin dragged her outside by the arm.

"Why are you doing this?" she asked. "How are you even here?"

"It matters not," said Romilda, her voice colder than her presence.

"Rom, where are you taking me?"

Romilda did not reply. Nor, it seemed, had she listened to a word. Instead, she dragged a kicking and screaming Rebekah to their family's plot in the local cemetery and threw her inside a freshly carved-open grave.

"The only way I remain, sis," said Romilda, "is for you to go."

Umair Mirxa lives in Karachi, Pakistan. His first published story, 'Awareness', appeared on Spillwords Press. He has also had stories accepted for anthologies from Zombie Pirate Publishing, Blood Song Books, Fantasia Divinity Magazine and Publishing, and Iron Faerie Publishing. He is a massive J.R.R. Tolkien fan, and loves everything to do with fantasy and mythology. He enjoys football, history, music, movies, TV shows, and comic books, and wishes with all his heart that dragons were real.
Website: www.umairmirxa.com
Facebook: UMirxa12

The New Black
by Lynne Lumsden Green

Everyone was so excited when they developed the transporter technology that could send living things from one end of the solar system to the other. How convenient. So much like Science Fiction.

Except, the first time you use the transporter beam is the first time you die. Your body is destroyed and your soul escapes into the great beyond.

As it is a brand-new technology, it is very expensive to use the transporters; only the rich, fabulous, fashionable, and famous get the chance to use them. Any fashionista can tell you what happened next. Being soulless is the New Black.

Lynne Lumsden Green has twin bachelor's degrees in both Science and the Arts, giving her the balance between rationality and creativity. She spent fifteen years as the Science Queen for HarperCollins Voyager Online and has written science articles for other online magazines. Currently, she captains the Writing Race for the Australian Writers Marketplace on Facebook. She has had speculative fiction flash fiction and short stories published in anthologies and websites.
Website: cogpunksteamscribe.wordpress.com

A Penny for the Ferryman
by Rowanne S. Carberry

The Underworld. A place where we're all sent when we die. Where we never rest.

"Take me back," a woman screams, banging on the gates, voice going hoarse from her cries.

I would have gone over in my early days, but I've learnt since then.

There is no helping.

Looking around, I see others ignoring her, making their way to me, or else fading into the frozen images on the walls.

Stepping onto the ferry, I pick up my oar and wait for the new souls to come onboard.

A penny for the ferryman; their ticket to the other side.

Rowanne S. Carberry was born in England in 1990, where she stills lives now with her cat Wolverine. Rowanne has always loved writing, and her first poem was published at the age of 15, but her ambition has always been to help people. Rowanne studied at the University of Sunderland where she completed combined honours of Psychology with Drama. Rowanne writes to offer others an escape. Although Rowanne writes in varied genres each story or poem she writes will often have a darkness to it, which helped coin her brand, Poisoned Quill Writing – Wicked words from a poisoned quill.
Facebook: PoisonedQuillWriting
Instagram: @poisoned_quill_writing

Calling Her Back
by Alexander Pyles

We gathered in a circle, clasping hands. The candle flames flickered with our collective deep breaths as we began. Soft prayers were offered at first, but our voices grew louder.

Was the wind picking up through the window? A hair bow among the candles flickered ever so slightly. Was that just the breeze?

We encouraged one another to continue our chants, the petitions hailing through an ethereal ceiling. We were to be a beacon. A guiding light.

Our voices raised further until the window slammed shut and the candles blew out. In the darkness, we heard a whisper.

"Hi, Dad."

Alexander Pyles resides in IL with his wife and children. He holds an MA in Philosophy and an MFA in Writing Popular Fiction. His short story chapbook titled, "Milo (01001101 01101001 01101100 01101111)," from Radix Media, is due out fall 2019. His other short fiction has appeared on 101fiction.org, River and South Review, and other venues. Website: www.pylesofbooks.com Twitter: @Pylesofbooks

The Bell Tolls
by J.W. Garrett

Relaxing?

No.

Church bells. Again. Her mouth twisted. *Why am I here?* Christine bowed, feigning prayer, her thoughts turning toward her cash in overseas accounts as the offering plate passed. A man tapped her. Lights dimmed.

"Where is everybody?"

"Just you and me now. Like you've desired… Like I'd planned… Some are mine. Some I lose to him." The man pointed toward the picture above the altar.

She blinked. "I'm dead?"

A sinister chuckle left the stranger. "Indeed."

A flaming pit opened below. Christine clawed the edge. "Please!"

"Your TV, cash, drinks… All await." A scream echoed. "No begging needed."

J.W. Garrett has been writing in one form or another since she was a teenager. She currently lives in Florida with her family but loves the mountains of Virginia where she was born. Her writings include YA fantasy as well as short stories. Since completing Remeon's Quest-Earth Year 1930, the prequel in her YA fantasy series, Realms of Chaos, she has been hard at work on the next in the series, scheduled to release June 2020. When she's not hanging out with her characters, her favourite activities are reading, running and spending time with family.

Website: www.jwgarrett.com
BHC Press: www.bhcpress.com/Author_JW_Garrett.html

The Haunted House
by Jacek Wilkos

A family bought a house on a hill. It was beautiful, well maintained, not too expensive and, as it turned out later, haunted. Nothing worked; psychics, spiritualist seances, exorcisms. Previous residents just didn't want to leave.

The family chose to stay. It wasn't that bad as it seemed at first. You can get used to creaking floors, opening doors and moving furniture.

One day it all ended. The people were so happy that they didn't even wonder why.

The spirits felt something evil was coming their way and left quickly. When the family found out, it was already too late.

Jacek Wilkos is an engineer from Poland. He lives with his wife and daughter in a beautiful city of Cracow. He is addicted to buying books, he loves coffee, dark ambient music and riding his bike. He writes mostly horror drabbles. His fiction in Polish can be read on Szortal, Niedobre literki, Horror Online. In English his work was published in Drablr, Rune Bear, Sirens Call eZine.
Facebook: Jacek.W.Wilkos

In the Here and Now
by Chitra Gopalakrishnan

The casting away of the *preta*, the apparition from beyond, begins as a gyrating dance of sorts.

At Mehandipur temple in Rajasthan, where multitudes of evil spirits are exorcised, a 'possessed' woman swirls in a floor length skirt, her eyeballs revolving, her hair pirouetting.

Men bind her feet, spinning her upside down over a pit, not stopping till her tormented screams stop.

Her silence signals her freedom within, the melting away of the invasion from beyond.

It's the god of punishment, Mahakal Bhairav's victory.

Winds hurl loops of gritty sand and ravens circle around like flying ash in his honour.

Chitra Gopalakrishnan is a journalist by training, a social development communications consultant by profession and a creative writer by choice. Chitra's focus is on issues of gender, environment and health. Chitra dabbles in poetry on the sly and literary creations openly on the web using social media.
Website: unpublishedplatform.weebly.com/chitra-gopalakrishnan

The Afterlife of Lizards Run Over by Electric Golf Carts
by Joshua D. Taylor

The last thing Atomic Rex remembered was getting hit over the head with a golf cart by Superior Simian. He awoke in darkness and squirming. Hundreds of thousands of tiny lizards filled every space around him. He flexed and felt the confines of their afterlife strain under the pressure.

The spirits of crushed lizards panicked in the presence of their gargantuan cousin. They wanted nothing more than to escape. To lay in the sun once again. Rex wanted the same. He threw back his head and let out an atomic roar that shattered the thin borders of their spectral prison.

Joshua D. Taylor is an amateur writer who started writing a few years ago when he realised he was too old to play make-believe. He lives in southeastern Pennsylvania with his wife and a one-eared cat. He enjoys gardening, comic books, ska-punk music, Disney World, and travelling with his wife. Raised during weirdness that was the late 20th century Josh's eclectic interests produce eclectic works. He loves to mix-n-match things from different genres and stories elements to achieve a madcap hodgepodge of the truly unexpected. His short story 'the Obelisk' appears in Salty Tales by Stormy Island Publishing.
Facebook: authorjoshuadtaylor

Come Play
by Jodi Jensen

Phoebe woke in the darkness, moist grass beneath her. Leaves rustled nearby and she squinted into the bushes.

"Shh, she'll hear you," a child's voice drifted through the air.

"Who's there?" Phoebe scrambled to her feet and backed away as two children emerged from the shadows.

A girl in a calico print dress with a pinafore held hands with a toddler in overalls. "Come play with us."

"Play? Where're your parents?" Glancing around, Phoebe frowned. "What's going on here?"

The girl pointed to a headstone.

Phoebe Anne Baker

Phoebe crumpled to the ground.

"You're one of us now. Come play."

Jodi Jensen *grew up moving from California, to Massachusetts, and a few other places in between, before finally settling in Utah at the ripe old age of nine. The nomadic life fed her sense of adventure as a child and the wanderlust continues to this day. With a passion for old cemeteries, historical buildings and sweeping sagas of days gone by, it was only natural she'd dream of time traveling to all the places that sparked her imagination.*

Precognition
by G. Allen Wilbanks

"I see the future. Not clearly, and not a lot of it. It's more like flashes and flickers of what is about to happen. Most of the things I see are bad. I get visions of people that are about to do terrible things to me or to others."

"Some people call what I have, a gift. I'm not so sure about that. I think I might be much happier if I couldn't see anything."

"Why are you telling me this," he asks.

"I guess I'm just trying to explain. I'm sorry."

I raise the gun and pull the trigger.

G. Allen Wilbanks is a member of the Horror Writers Association (HWA) and has published over 50 short stories in various magazines and on-line venues. He is the author of two short story collections, and the novel, When Darkness Comes.
Website: www.gallenwilbanks.com
Blog: DeepDarkThoughts.com

An Inorganic Spring
by Jonathan Inbody

Android 485A stood silently in the haunted house, watching the horrible melodrama play out. She had already watched it thirty-six times, but no matter how many times it looped she never found it any less interesting. The last moments of Anthony St. Clair and his wife Agatha were forever preserved; the infidelity, the discovery, the confrontation, the push from the top of the stairs, the hard ground. Love and jealousy were not emotions Android 485A felt, though she was fascinated by them.

But then again, organic life always did leave behind some residue, and *someone* had to do the cleaning.

Jonathan Inbody is a filmmaker, author, and podcaster from Buffalo, New York. He enjoys B-movies, pen and paper RPGs, and New Wave Science Fiction novels. His short story "Dying Feels Like Slowly Sinking" is due to be published in the anthology Deteriorate from Whimsically Dark Publishing. Jon can be heard every other week on his improvisational movie pitch podcast X Meets Y.
Website: xmeetsy.libsyn.com

Double Take
by Kevin Hopson

A shiver escaped Sheryl, and her mouth hung agape. The sight of her daughter, Ellen, in the doorway made her take pause. Sheryl felt a gentle hand on her shoulder. It was her husband, Tony. He stood next to her, his awestruck face mirroring her own. It had been five years since they had last seen Ellen and, despite the shock, Sheryl noticed a few delicate wrinkles around Ellen's eyes.

How was it possible?

Sheryl and Tony had watched her die. They witnessed her burial. They knew better than anyone that she couldn't be alive.

After all, they murdered her.

*Prior to hitting the fiction scene in 2009, **Kevin Hopson** was a freelance writer for several years, covering everything from finance to sports. His debut work, World of Ash, was released by MuseItUp Publishing in the fall of 2010. Since then, Kevin has released over a dozen books through MuseItUp, and he has also been published in various magazines and anthology books. Kevin's writing covers many genres, including dark fiction and horror, science fiction and fantasy, and crime fiction.*
Website: www.kmhopson.com

A Flask of Guilt
by C.L. Steele

The deafening silence—separation—had once made the pain of her loss easier. But now, silent disconnection broke her.

The drunken accident had taken her family. Only she'd survived.

She stood on the tracks; to give death a second chance. Shiny, sun-heated steel burned hot even through her shoes. The rumble jarred her. Opening the flask of rum, she drank for the first time since swearing to never drink and drive again. Would rum's warmth free her from feeling? The screeching grew, the sorrowful whistle sounded. She closed her eyes, threw the flask away, screamed against the all-powerful—inevitable—death.

C.L. Steele creates new worlds and mystical places filled with complex characters on exciting journeys. Her typical genre is Sci-Fi/Fantasy, where she concentrates on writing in the sub-genres of Magical Realism, Near Future, and Futuristic worlds. Published in numerous anthologies, she looks forward to the release of her debut novel. In the interim, she works on other novels and continues to write short stories, novellas, and poetry. She is featured as one of five international authors in ICWG Magazine through Clarendon Publishing House and is a contributing author to Blood Puddles Literary Journal.
Facebook: author.CLSteele
Instagram: @clsteele.author

The Conduit
by Terry Miller

"What if I told you that Jemma isn't troubled?" Dr. Mullins inquired. "I believe that she is a conduit."

Mrs. Rodriguez looked puzzled. "I'm not sure I'm following."

"These voices, personalities. They're all real."

Mrs. Rodriguez shook her head.

"Bear with me a moment. These voices are trying to communicate with us, Mrs. Rodriguez; through your daughter."

She stood, clearly agitated. "I think you're off your rocker!"

Jemma stood in the doorway. "Elizabeth, listen to her doctor, please," she said with a voice familiar yet not her own. Mrs. Rodriguez recognised her dead husband's voice. "It's so cold out there!"

Terry Miller is an author and 2017 Rhysling Award-nominated poet residing in Portsmouth, OH, USA. He has self-published a dark poetry collection on Amazon and one short story to date. His work has also appeared in Sanitarium, Devolution Z, Jitter Press, Poetry Quarterly, O Unholy Night in Deathlehem, and the 2017 Rhysling Anthology from the Science Fiction and Fantasy Poetry Association.
Facebook: tmiller2015

Thirteen
by Joel R. Hunt

When Death arrived, scythe in hand, the child was ready for it.

"You're here to collect me, right?" she asked, straddling her own limp corpse, "Let's go then."

She started to move towards the billowing portal, but Death stopped her with a skeletal hand. It looked down at her body, where the scars lined her wrists. It looked up to her soul, where the scars choked her heart.

"What are we waiting for?" the child snapped, "I'm ready to go!"

Death shook its head.

"Not a chance," it said.

As paramedics kicked down the door, the child's eyes fluttered open.

Joel R. Hunt *is a writer from the UK who dabbles in the darker aspects of life, particularly through horror, science fiction and the supernatural. He has been published here and there (though likely nowhere you've heard of) and hopes to have released his first anthology of short stories later this year.*
Twitter: @JoelRHunt1
Reddit: JRHEvilInc

Journey to Death
by C.L. Williams

I travel this world and others as I give people their passage to the other side. Many go with me willingly as others struggle and I am forced to touch them, killing them instantly. My most recent journey involves getting someone who doesn't know their time is up. The person is even quite young. I know the colour will flush from their face the second I make myself visible to them. This person will try and argue and plead with me. But there is a painful truth to this, once I'm seen, time is up, and nothing can be done

C.L. Williams is an independent author from central Virginia. He has written eight poetry books, four novellas, one novel, and a contributor to multiple anthologies, with the most recent appearance being an all-ages anthology titled Temoli from Thazbook. His most recent poetry book, The Paradox Complex, features the poem "Sad Crying Clown" that is now a video on YouTube directed by Matthew Mark Hunter of MMH Productions. C.L. Williams is currently working on his first sci-fi book, an all-ages book titled Novo: Away from Earth. When not writing, C.L. Williams is reading and sharing the work of other independent authors.
Facebook: writer434
Twitter: @writer_434

Lady of the House
by A.R. Johnston

I was sitting in bed, in the back room of the house. All was quiet and still. No one else was in the house except the dogs downstairs. Locked up tight for the summer night. A chill raced up my spine, the room getting that little bit colder, my breath like a puff on a cold winter's day, and instantly I know.

I look up, there she is in my doorway. The lady of the house. She gives me a knowing smile. I smile back. Then I hear a whisper as she fades away.

"I'll keep you safe, goodnight, love."

A.R. Johnston is a small-town girl from Nova Scotia, Canada. Her style of writing is considered Urban Fantasy. Her first major publication is part of an anthology called First Love and she has several more titles lined up. She is a lover of coffee, good tv shows, horror flicks, and reader of books. She pretends to be a writer when real life doesn't get in the way. Pesky full-time job and adulting!

Asphodel Fields
by Chris Bannor

She watched the moment it happened, the moment of movement in the soul where body and spirit separated. The aura of rainbow hues and sparkling gold rose from the body and began to ascend.

These were not hallowed grounds, though, and as she blew the ash of asphodel from her palm, it swirled in the air around her. The haunted breeze of the underworld stung her nostrils for a moment before ash took form and imprisoned the last embers of the light. A haze of purple and red pulsed, and she watched, enraptured by the death of a human soul.

Chris Bannor is a science fiction and fantasy writer who lives in Southern California. Chris learned her love of genre stories from her mother at an early age and has never veered far from that path. She also enjoys musical theater and road trips with her family, but is a general homebody otherwise. Twitter: @BannorChris

Anchored
by Patrick Winters

"Bind him well," the captain had said. "I want his bones down there 'til judgment day comes."

That'd been twenty years back, and here he remained, without a reckoning in sight.

In all that time, there'd been nothing to keep him company in these silent depths, save the darting sea-life— and his old, skeletal self, still held in its chains, the cannon they'd been lashed about long-since buried under the seabed.

He'd been left to float in undulating darkness, freed of body, yet trapped all the same.

The ocean—which had once freed his soul—would now keep it, forevermore.

Patrick Winters is a graduate of Illinois College in Jacksonville, IL, where he earned a Bachelor of Arts degree in English Literature and Creative Writing and achieved membership into Sigma Tau Delta, an international English honors society. Winters is now a proud member of the Horror Writers Association, and his work has been published in the likes of Sanitarium Magazine, Deadman's Tome, Trysts of Fate, and other such titles. A full list of his previous publications may be found at his author's site. Website: wintersauthor.azurewebsites.net/Publications/List

Glass Eye
by Pamela Jeffs

The glass eye the ocularist gave me is defective. I see things with it. On Main Street, against the outlines of modern cars, there is an old man cussing a team of horses that draw a ghostly wagon filled with ale barrels.

And outside Subway, two dead gunslingers are duelling in the street. I watch and eat lunch as they shoot each other down—again.

My doctor tells me it is PTSD; that hallucinations are common for soldiers that have returned from active duty. But I don't buy it. It's the eye. It's haunted. I'm bloody well sure if it.

Pamela Jeffs is a speculative fiction author living in Queensland, Australia with her husband and two daughters. She is a member of the Queensland Writers' Centre and has had numerous short fiction pieces published in recent national and international anthologies. In 2017 and again in 2018, Pamela was nominated for an Australian Aurealis Award in the category of 'Best Science Fiction Short Story'. Her debut collection titled 'Red Hour and Other Strange Tales' was released in March 2018.
Website: www.pamelajeffs.com
Facebook: pamelajeffsauthor

Michael
by Sinister Sweetheart

Lorna's death was quick and peaceful, fading gently away in her sleep. Her last conscious moments of cognition were spent remembering her late Husband's face.

Michael married Lorna young, and he'd died young. Lorna spent her life trying to earn a place next to him in Heaven. She went to church every week. She also donated her time, money and food to anyone in need.

At the hour of her death, Lorna saw a white light. Her soul was enveloped in the warm embrace of peace. Millions of beautiful souls were there to greet her.

Michael wasn't one of them.

*Since **Sinister Sweetheart** made her first post to a popular Internet forum, she's taken the horror community by storm. Her ability to create, terrify, and drive home her stories is insurmountable. Sinister Sweetheart's published works can be found in multiple anthologies for all to read, but be forewarned, if you do... you may want to call your therapist after, her stories are terrifying, disturbing and devilishly unsettling. She is not only a fright visually, but also has a creepy tentacle in horror podcasting as well. Sinister Sweetheart writes, voice acts and is the media director of the Scarecrow Tales podcast.*
Website: Sinistersweetheart.wixsite.com/sinistersweetheart
Facebook: NMBrownStories

Goodbyes are Never Easy
by Nerisha Kemraj

Her parents sat in the hospital room, holding onto her tiny hands. They looked on hopefully, although they knew it would come to this.

Sarah's spirit lifted from her body as the glowing lady with fairy wings reached out to take her hands. The many machines attached to Sarah's little body beeped, simultaneously. Doctors rushed in.

Six-year-old Sarah looked at her parents, sadness in her eyes. She stopped, as if forgetting something. The angel-lady nodded, understanding. Sarah sailed across the room and planted a tiny forehead kiss on each of them. And with that, a sudden calmness filled them both.

*Multi-genre (short-fiction) author, and poet, **Nerisha Kemraj**, resides in South Africa with her husband and two, mischievous daughters. She has work traditionally published/accepted in 30 publications, thus far, both print and online. She holds a BA in Communication Science from UNISA and is currently busy with a Post-Graduate Certificate in Education.*
Facebook: Nerishakemrajwriter

Cold Flashes
by Beth W. Patterson

I shivered when I heard his story, for there is cold, and then there is Scottish winter cold.

He told the audience about the Battle of Culloden, and how he would drive across the former battlefield to get to his home in Inverness. A hazy glow would appear across the moor where so many Jacobites had been slaughtered, and the heat would suddenly be sucked from his car.

As we sang 'Ye Jacobites By Name' together, I had cold flashes. They say I had a heart attack onstage because nobody could explain the chest wound made by an invisible broadsword.

Beth W. Patterson was a full-time musician for over two decades before diving into the world of writing, a process she describes as "fleeing the circus to join the zoo". She is the author of the books Mongrels and Misfits, and The Wild Harmonic, and a contributing writer to thirty anthologies. Patterson has performed in eighteen countries, expanding her perspective as she goes. Her playing appears on over a hundred and seventy albums, soundtracks, videos, commercials, and voice-overs (including seven solo albums of her own). She lives in New Orleans, Louisiana with her husband Josh Paxton, jazz pianist extraordinaire.
Website: www.bethpattersonmusic.com
Facebook: bethodist

The Psychopomp in Spring
by Blake Jessop

Things grow inside you, blooming. It's hard not to think of yourself as infected, but that's wrong; it's you destroying you. Your own cells deciding to become something else, your breath getting lost in the breeze.

So, you lie in the chair and let the poison drip into you and hope the smaller deaths will eclipse the larger one, and the things you say to yourself will drown out silence.

"Just breathe," she says, brushing dark hair from blue eyes. You do. And don't. And as you fade, she puts a cool, light hand on the skin above your lungs.

Blake Jessop is a Canadian author of science fiction, fantasy and horror stories with a master's degree in creative writing from the University of Adelaide. You can read more of his speculative fiction in "I Didn't Break the Lamp: Historical Accounts of Imaginary Acquaintances" from DefCon One, or follow him on Twitter.
Twitter: @everydayjisei
Amazon: www.amazon.com/default/e/B07BB7Z73N

Psychopomp Winter
by Blake Jessop

"Come back!" she cried, her voice whipping on an icy wind. The campfire was distant as the morning.

"I'm not going," Zinaida said. Her feet were bare, her lips blue. She sat down in the snow.

Igor staggered on.

He heard the girl call again, saw the outlines of figures strewn over the snow amidst shredded tent canvas at her feet. She was a black silhouette against a black world, red handed in red firelight, her blue eyes as cold and distant as the stars. He fell.

"Close enough," she said, smiling, and strode across the snow to meet him.

Blake Jessop is a Canadian author of science fiction, fantasy and horror stories with a master's degree in creative writing from the University of Adelaide. You can read more of his speculative fiction in "I Didn't Break the Lamp: Historical Accounts of Imaginary Acquaintances" from DefCon One, or follow him on Twitter.
Twitter: @everydayjisei
Amazon: www.amazon.com/default/e/B07BB7Z73N

The Psychopomp Falls
by Blake Jessop

He stood frozen, wind whipping under his tie. Both hands gripped the bridge rail behind him, and concrete flaked under his heels. Beneath the toes of his shoes was nothing but air.

"I can't do it," he whispered.

The voice, when it came, almost made his jump.

"Are you sure?"

He looked up. Blue eyes and dark hair. He shook his head.

"You could always come with me," the girl said, and put her hands on his. Her touch was as light as a leaf skimming the wind, just about to touch the water, unwrapping his fingers from the world.

Blake Jessop is a Canadian author of science fiction, fantasy and horror stories with a master's degree in creative writing from the University of Adelaide. You can read more of his speculative fiction in "I Didn't Break the Lamp: Historical Accounts of Imaginary Acquaintances" from DefCon One, or follow him on Twitter.

Twitter: @everydayjisei

Amazon: www.amazon.com/default/e/B07BB7Z73N

The Psychopomp in Summer
by Blake Jessop

Her skin was pale, even under the sun, and the salt water had done nothing to bleach her hair. Life was like a long summer's day sometimes. Seagulls chided the air and the murmuring waves washed against sand. Like there wasn't a care anywhere in the world.

She swished up the beach and no one noticed, though her bikini didn't leave much to the imagination.

"You're pretty," a little boy said to her.

"And you're a sweetheart," the pale lady replied. "Do you like to swim?"

He nodded. She smiled, took his hand, and together they waded into the sea.

Blake Jessop is a Canadian author of science fiction, fantasy and horror stories with a master's degree in creative writing from the University of Adelaide. You can read more of his speculative fiction in "I Didn't Break the Lamp: Historical Accounts of Imaginary Acquaintances" from DefCon One, or follow him on Twitter.
Twitter: @everydayjisei
Amazon: www.amazon.com/default/e/B07BB7Z73N

The Exorcist Diet
by Shawn M. Klimek

Apart from the prominent cross around her neck, the woman at the door in the red pantsuit might have been a realtor selling door-to-door cosmetics.

"I'm Milona, ze exorcist," she said, in a thick Slavic accent. "You have ze ghosts?"

We led her upstairs to the remote bedroom with the ice-cold doorknob. My husband donned his glove before twisting it open and then bidding her enter.

Milona shrugged and then walked inside. The door slammed behind her.

Relieved, I smiled at my husband. We should be able to sleep again for another month. But feeding the house was becoming expensive.

Shawn M. Klimek is the middle child of seven creative siblings, a globetrotting, U.S. military spouse, an internationally best-selling short-story writer, a poet, and butler to a Maltese. Almost one hundred of his stories or poems have been published in digital magazines or anthologies, including BHP's Deep Space and the first six books in the Dark Drabbles series.
Website: jotinthedark.blogspot.com
Facebook: shawnmklimekauthor

Gone
by E.L. Giles

"Sofia? Honey?" I said, turning around. The crowd was thick, and there was no sign of her. "Sofia, where are you?"

I picked my phone from my pocket, pressing a button to activate the screen.

"Have you seen my girlfriend?" I asked an old man next to me, showing him her picture.

"My baby's gone!" a woman near me suddenly shouted. "She's not in her stroller anymore!"

The woman stopped passersby, pointing at the stroller, acting like a madwoman.

Voices all around elevated, shrieking and yelling, calling for friends and family. They were all gone, like they had never existed.

E.L. Giles is a dreamer, passionate about art, a restless worker and a bit of a weird human. He started his artistic journey as a music composer until the need to put his thoughts and stories down on paper grew too strong for him to resist it any longer. He lives in the French Province of Quebec, Canada, with his girlfriend and two boys.
Facebook: elgilesauthor
Website: www.elgilesauthor.com

The Curse
by K.T. Tate

We run light-footed through the house. Curtains billow, doors slam, the ancient wood writhing as we flee. It'd started subtle—items misplaced, messages in steam—but now it was at full force; the house alive with malevolence.

Once in, I bolt the door. He begs for me to open up. I scream that it's jammed, blaming the supernatural monstrosity. Then the wailing, that signature banshee howl. Ear to the door, I hear a struggle, a scream, a thud!

It's over. They'll see an accident, but they don't know about the family curse.

Another new husband broken, my financial future secured.

K.T. Tate lives in Cambridgeshire in the UK. She writes mainly weird fiction, cosmic horror and strange monster stories.
Website: eldritchhollow.wordpress.com
Tumblr: eldritch-hollow.tumblr.com

A Hand as Dark as Sin
by Shelly Jarvis

"It moved! It fucking moved!"

"You're full of shit," I say. "You moved it yourself."

Eda is shaking her head, just a tiny bit, over and over like she can't stop. She's holding her hand against her chest, massaging it with the other. She looks so frail, unlike the fiery girl I know.

"Okay, we can stop if you want," I say. I reach forward and place my hand on hers, but she rips it back from me, howling.

The dim light hits it and I see the black, burned skin that wasn't there before. It matches her new eyes.

Shelly Jarvis is a speculative fiction author from West Virginia, US. She found a life-long love of sci-fi and fantasy in the 3rd grade when she found Madeleine L'Engle's "A Wrinkle in Time." Shelly is an avid reader, a Whovian, the ideal viewer of dog rescue videos, and undoubtedly Ravenclaw. She currently has two YA sci-fi books available for purchase on Amazon.
Website: www.ShellyJarvis.com

The Footsteps
by James Turnbow

The footsteps would always follow beside me when I walked in the woods. But today they stopped.

As a child it frightened me until I sought the advice of a tribal elder.

"That's your guardian," he told me. "He walks with you to protect you from the ancient one."

I felt an invisible hand squeeze mine tight then go limp.

"It's okay old friend." I said. "I know that you tried."

The trees all around me began to weep and I joined them.

A shadow hissed and slithered around my body then began to squeeze.

"I know that you tried."

James Turnbow is a graduate from the University of Central Oklahoma with a degree in Strategic Communications. He is a proud member of the Seminole Nation of Oklahoma and works with tribal youth to empower them to pursue higher education as an Education Advisor for the Muscogee Creek Nation. He is a curator of Seminole culture and language and works to preserve the stories and words of his ancestors.

B E Y O N D
Home
by K.S. Nikakis

They were pleased when I died, despite the false trails of moisture on their cheeks. They covered the mirrors, but I knew my face and lingered, so they took me to the cross-roads and buried me there at midnight, but I followed them home. The next grave they dug was beyond the churchyard wall, the unconsecrated ground of the poor, murderers, and worshippers of the wrong gods, but still they felt my cold breath as they slept. The last grave was deeper, the tomb stone twice as heavy, but it made no difference. To leave, first you must truly belong.

K.S. Nikakis is fascinated by the hero's psychological quest (as well as physical quest) which she explores through Deep Fantasy. She is the author of The Kira Chronicles trilogy (Allen and Unwin - rights reverted), since augmented and relaunched as a six book series. She is the author of nine other novels, including the five book Angel Caste series. She holds a M.Ed (Hons) on the purposes of dragons in literature, and a Ph.D in the application of Campbell's Hero Myth to the female hero.
Website: www.ksnikakis.com
Amazon: www.amazon.com/dp/B01MXBVFRI

Diapers, Formula, Straight Punches, and Ammo
by Carole de Monclin

"Do you have experience taking care of infants, miss?"

"I started babysitting at age fourteen. I love babies."

"Are you available 24/7?"

"Yes."

"You understand the position requires total secrecy?"

"Affirmative."

"Any martial arts training?"

"Krav Maga."

"What weapons can you handle?"

"Favourite handgun, Glock 43. I enjoy the occasional AR45."

"You're hired."

"Can I ask why a baby requires several bodyguards? High profile parents afraid of kidnapping?"

"No, matter of national security. He can't fall into the wrong hands. Nobody can fathom what this child, raised with today's knowledge, will devise."

"Why so special?"

"He's Leonardo Da Vinci reincarnated."

Carole de Monclin *has lived in France and Australia, but for the moment the USA is home. She finds inspiration from her travels. She loves Science Fiction because it explores the human mind in a way no other genre can. Plus, who doesn't love spaceships and lasers? Her stories appear in the Exoplanet Magazine and Angels - A Dark Drabbles Anthology.*
Website: CaroledeMonclin.com
Twitter: @CaroledeMonclin

The Gardeners
by Nicola Currie

Beware hazel eyes. Circles of gold around black hint at darkness masked by sunshine.

Such golden eyes captivated me and led me across the city into fields of wild sunflowers. There, he told me:

"Only beauty can make beauty."

He plunged his knife into me and my blood watered the soil. He gave me a choice.

When I woke, he was pleased. I had not chosen to blossom like the thousand innocents before me, that decorated the field. Instead, my eyes changed as I took the blade.

To gold around black. To darkness hiding in the black of bright sunflowers.

Nicola Currie is 34, from Cambridge, UK where she works in educational publishing. She has published poetry in literary magazines, including Mslexia and Sarasvati, and has also completed her first novel, which was longlisted for the Bath Children's Novel Award.
Website: writeitandweep.home.blog

Another Presence
by Adam S. Furman

I'm free. Weightless. Euphoric. My astral form soars, leaves my troubles behind.

I fly above town, winding through houses and workshops. In the air, I'm my true self. There're others. Angels and spirits. They teach me and my aura grows. I round another level in my form, but halt. Someone's watching. Leering. Fear engulfs me.

I retreat home, mould back into my body. I'm anchored to skin and bone. The weight returns and materiality comes into focus. But I'm constricted. I can't move. I open my eyes. A dark figure sits on my chest, leans forward, and enters my body.

Adam S. Furman lives in rural Illinois with his family which includes a lot of kids (like...a lot). He generally writes science fiction.
Twitter: @AdamSFurman

Before
by Jack Wolfe Frost

I was there before. I remember now, it is clear. For so long I never even knew, but now I know. I was there before.

How long was I there? Always. I cannot think of a time when I was not there. Not like here, where I can count the years. The years of hell.

You were there, though I doubt you remember. We are not supposed to remember, because if we do, we realise we live in hell. Compared to there—before.

The knife bites into my flesh, and blood spurts. The pain is irrelevant now.

I'm going home.

Jack Wolfe Frost is the Eternal Rebel; he rebels against everything which may have the word "rules" or "behave" within it. Born in Sheffield, UK, in 1956; he first started writing in 1982, as a hobby - Now older and wiser, he has had several poems and short stories published.
Website: jackjfrost.wordpress.com
Twitter: @JackWolfeWriter

Beyond the Veil
by Cindar Harrell

Everything was hazy beyond the veil, like a thick fog over my eyes.

My sister beckoned me with her sobs. She was in pain and crying out. The death of a twin is a hard thing to grasp. No one could understand. Candles surrounded us on both sides of our mystic barrier between life and death.

I placed my hand on it, rippling like liquid silver, and I knew she did the same.

"I would give anything to see you again," she whispered.

I forced my hand through and grabbed her throat.

As she fell, I smiled. "So would I."

Cindar Harrell loves fairy tales, especially ones with a dark twist. Her stories are often fairy tale inspired, but she is also working on a mystery series. Her stories can be found on Amazon and in various anthologies. You can follow her on Facebook and visit her blog, which she promises to try and update more often,
Website: cindarharrell.wordpress.com
Facebook: CindarHarrell

The Walk
by Chris Bannor

Ghosts walked the halls beside him and reached for a taste of what life clung desperately to his body. His boots echoed heavily off empty halls and metal steps, his head high and shoulders squared, towards this inevitable end. There was no fear in his eyes. He felt only immense relief as he finally atoned for his directing hand in their demise.

Death enticed him forward but it was no friend. It had been an ally though, for a simple man with too much ambition and too great a vision. It was finally time to pay the ferryman his due.

Chris Bannor is a science fiction and fantasy writer who lives in Southern California. Chris learned her love of genre stories from her mother at an early age and has never veered far from that path. She also enjoys musical theater and road trips with her family, but is a general homebody otherwise. Twitter: @BannorChris

The Bleeding Girl
by Karen Heslop

Kevin struggles not to wipe his mom's kiss from his forehead.

"Have a good day at school."

"What if I see her again?"

"The bleeding girl isn't real, Kevin. Just count to five and repeat what we told you."

"Ok."

Hours into the day, Kevin can't hold it in anymore. He has to use the bathroom. He uses it quickly and rushes hand washing. She's there when he turns. Blank sockets stare at him as blood from her wrists pool on the floor.

He looks away and repeats, "It's not real."

A voice whispers, "Ask your Mommy about Auntie Jane."

Karen Heslop writes from Kingston, Jamaica. Her stories can be found in The Drabbledark Anthology, Soft Cartel and The Weird and Whatnot among others.

Bloody Mackenzie
by Matt Lucas

Mackenzie spent his life mercilessly persecuting Scotland. Unremorsefully, he sentenced heretics to heinous torture. A smile slithered across his face when strolling through Greyfriar's Cemetery, seeing his enemies filling mass graves.

He believed in the same God as his victims. However, pretentious Mackenzie deemed himself superior. Then he died.

Mackenzie's spirit accompanied his body as it was laid in Greyfriar's. In the otherworldly realm he saw spirits hovering above mass graves. Angelic hosts arrived, ushering them into paradise.

When Mackenzie's guide arrived, the bloody monstrosity grasped his neck, plunging him to hell where there was weeping and gnashing of teeth.

Matt Lucas is a drone, who still remembers life before corporate mind control. Desperately, his soul yearns to burst forth from his cubicle- shaped imprisonment and write riveting fiction wrought with action and twists. Now, having secured an agent and actively pitching for publication, he's undertaking submitting to smaller publication to gauge interest in new ideas in sci-fi, fantasy, and other genres. Writing is his passion and he hopes to spend his days cultivating captivating stories with impactful messages.

The Boy Who Drowned
by Derek Dunn

Even on the coldest winter days, the small pond in Black Ridge Forest remained unfrozen. It had sparked many rumours. Some thought it was a hot spring. Others claimed the water was salty. And then there were tales of the boy who drowned, his spirit trapped, keeping the water warm, keeping it alive.

Like many before, Donny's curiosity drew him to the pond. He waded into the water, its warmth inviting him further. Before he knew it, he'd been pulled underneath.

A boy's face appeared; and then another. Dozens of boys reached out, pulling him down to his new home.

Derek Dunn lives in the American Northwest with his family. He's a film enthusiast and musician who writes primarily horror and mystery stories.
Twitter: @DerekTDunn

Like Smoke
by Cecilia Dockins

You spoon the soup into your husband's bowl. Napkin to the left. Iced tea to the right. Try not to flinch. Stomach sucked in. Stand straight. Be attentive. He's always had a temper.

Your body is a eulogy. Purple black blue verses, he's authored.

What are you?

A good southern woman.

One sip. He coughs. Body convulses. Blood everywhere. It's been so long since you've smiled, you mistake the tightness for tears.

Vapor rises and curls and blooms from his chest like fume from a lover's cigarette. You retrieve the new nail hidden in your bra.

What are you?

Prepared.

Cecilia Dockins *grew up fishing in the creeks and rivers deep in the backwoods of Tennessee. She earned her B.A. in English from Middle Tennessee State University in 2010 and is a graduate of the Odyssey Writing Workshop. She has passed instruments in surgical suites and slung drinks in bars. When not writing, she spends her free time digging through decaying boxes at local bookstores or the occasional barn for the forgotten, the lost, and the bizarre. Cecilia lives with her husband, two parrots, and boxer pup in a lovely subdivision. On rainy nights, she can hear the river calling.*

Exodus
by C.L. Williams

I wake up and I try to talk to others as I see people in mourning. I go by them and they keep crying and move along. I am uncertain what is going on as I try and speak to them. I walk over and cannot believe what I'm seeing. Everyone here is crying because I am dead! I did not realize that I wasn't waking up from a nap. I am a ghost, I just exited my body. I see that everyone is mourning my death. If only I could find out how I am one of the deceased.

C.L. Williams is an independent author from central Virginia. He has written eight poetry books, four novellas, one novel, and a contributor to multiple anthologies, with the most recent appearance being an all-ages anthology titled Temoli from Thazbook. His most recent poetry book, The Paradox Complex, features the poem "Sad Crying Clown" that is now a video on YouTube directed by Matthew Mark Hunter of MMH Productions. C.L. Williams is currently working on his first sci-fi book, an all-ages book titled Novo: Away from Earth. When not writing, C.L. Williams is reading and sharing the work of other independent authors.
Facebook: writer434
Twitter: @writer_434

Ten Minutes
by Stuart Conover

When he was a teenager, James swore spirit boards were real.

He thought it had been a joke, but the planchette had moved by itself.

Occasionally, it would move when his friends joined; it was always some joker messing around.

Not that first time.

He'd been alone.

Ever since, he'd been trying to make contact again.

The spirit had tried to warn him.

To tell him when he'd die.

James had to know.

Had to try and stop it.

Yet the planchette refused to move.

Until just now.

When it spelled out that he only had ten minutes to live.

Stuart Conover is a father, husband, rescue dog owner, published author, blogger, journalist, horror enthusiast, comic book geek, science fiction junkie, and IT professional. With all of that to cram in daily, we have no idea if or when he sleeps or how he gets writing done! (We suspect it has to do with having evil clones.) Stuart is a Chicago native and runs the author resource Horror Tree.

The Voices
by S. John Davis

I first spoke to them through a board at a party.

Listening, they spoke back. The more I payed attention, the more I could hear. Soon I could understand. They would tell me things I had never known, about those long passed, and things yet to be. They shared immense joys and each time they spoke, I better learned to hear.

Until the day came when I couldn't stop hearing. Their wisdom became chaos, millions of voices, crying, screaming. I bore their weight for days until I couldn't.

I stepped from the ledge and became a part of the chorus.

S. John Davis is an author based in Gippsland, Victoria, Australia.
Facebook: sjohndavis

St. Elmo's Fire
by Dawn DeBraal

The ship was lost at sea for thirty days. Now out of food, their fresh water depleted, the crew faced certain death. The conditions were right for the electrical charged weather phenomenon known as St. Elmo's fire a coronal discharge. It hovered over the mast of the ship lighting up the night sky. Truly a sign they would be saved. Another ship nearby seeing the lights, made their way to the *Bradigan*. Sailors were transported onto the rescue ship, knelt down thanking St. Elmo the patron saint of the sailors, for delivering them from certain death with a guiding light.

Dawn DeBraal lives in rural Wisconsin with her husband, two rat terriers, and a cat. She successfully raised two children (meaning they didn't return to the nest!) After many years serving the government at the Federal and County level, she recently retired. Having extra time on her hands she started to write after a paralyzed vocal cord took her ability to speak for two months. Not finding her voice, she discovered that her love of telling a good story could be written. Her works have been published in Palm-sized press, Spillwords, Mercurial Stories, Potato Soup Journal, and Blood Song Books.

Soul Eater
by Jo Seysener

"Ohhh," whispered the soul, drifting forward.

The Angel nodded. *Yes, just a little further now…*

The soul surged forward, ready to follow him anywhere. He smiled benevolently, slipping his lasso around the soul's wrist, tightening it. The soul smiled back, and he nodded, jerking with all his essence.

A maelstrom gaped beneath them, tearing at the soul's visage, but not touching his own; as agreed, of course. Signed with some poor soul's blood.

"But you…you're the Angel of Death, angel!" the soul muttered, feet disappearing into the void.

The angel smiled, revealing pointed incisors, and whispered a word.

"Reaper."

Jo Seysener is a mum of three crazies, a scatter of chickens, a decrepit kelpie and a rambunctious GSD. She lives with her husband near Brisbane, Australia. When she is not exposing her kids to cult story books from her childhood, she can be found in the kitchen experimenting with new flavours and pairings. She adores alpacas.
Facebook: joseysener
Website: www.joseysener.com

The Invasion
by J. Farrington

I can still hear the sirens filling the night sky across the city. People rushing from their houses, filling their cars, fighting for supplies. A city in chaos. The sirens were meant for natural disasters, but we had nothing in place for this kind of emergency.

The spirits of the dead were rising, and they were angry.

Lashing out at all living things, laying waste to everything in their path.

We never stood a chance.

The government struck back, dropping bombs across the city…

With each explosion, their ranks grew.

How do you kill an enemy who is already dead?

J. Farrington *is an aspiring author from the West Midlands, UK. His genre of choice is horror; whether that be psychological, suspense, supernatural or straight up weird, he'll give it a shot! He has loved writing from a young age but has only publicly been spreading his darker thoughts and sinister imagination via social platforms since 2018. If you would like to view his previous work, or merely lurk in the shadows...watching, you can keep up to date with future projects by spirit board or alternatively, the following;*
Twitter: @SurvivorTrench
Reddit: TrenchChronicles

Faulty Directions
by John H. Dromey

Warren's new home was haunted. Unliveable. He consulted a witch.

"Can you provide me with a protection spell that will prevent spirits from passing through the walls of my house?"

"Yes. At a price."

Warren wrote her a large cheque.

A few days later he demanded his money back. "Your spell failed."

"No, it didn't. You got what you paid for."

"What do you mean?"

"No ghosts, friendly or otherwise, can pass through the walls of your house, but that doesn't mean they can't pop up through the floor or pass down through the ceiling."

Warren reached for his chequebook.

John H. Dromey was born in northeast Missouri, USA. He enjoys reading—mysteries in particular—and writing in a variety of genres. He's had short fiction published in Alfred Hitchcock's Mystery Magazine, Martian Magazine, Stupefying Stories Showcase, Thriller Magazine, Unfit Magazine, and elsewhere, as well as in a number of anthologies, including Chilling Horror Short Stories (Flame Tree Publishing, 2015).

The Other Place
by Gregg Cunningham

Life's twists can be real bitch slaps.

Death's twists on the other hand, are dealt by a size ten straight between your legs.

Take today for instance. Today was meant to be a happy occasion for all the family. A day for us to celebrate.

I gathered everybody that could make the journey to be there for his arrival.

Even Grannie Bess was making a rare appearance.

But instead of celebrating his passing, I find out I won't be reunited with my son after all. I just got the news he isn't coming here...

He's going to *the other place*.

Gregg Cunningham is a short story writer from Western Australia. He has had several short stories publishing by Zombie Pirate Publishing in Relationship add Vice, Full Metal Horror, Phuket Tattoo, World War four and Flash Fiction Addiction, with GBH due later in the year. Most recently, his work has been accepted into Black Hare Press Drabbles set including Monsters, Angels, Worlds, Unravel, Beyond, and Apocalypse, with his latest short story included in Black Hare Press soon to be released fine Deep Space anthology.
Website: cortlandsdogs.wordpress.com

Fetch
by Vonnie Winslow Crist

Dressed in jeans, sweater, and fringed boots, the woman standing in the salon's doorway was a dead ringer for Ella's best friend, Toni.

"Can I help you?" asked Ella.

The woman tapped her chest, hugged herself, then pointed at the hairdresser.

She's having a heart attack, thought Ella as she grabbed her phone from between hair styling products.

"Do you need help?"

Toni's double smiled faintly, shook her head.

Suddenly, Ella's phone rang. She answered.

"Are you sitting down?" asked her mother.

"Why?"

"There was an accident on the interstate. Toni was killed."

Ella turned around—Toni's fetch was gone.

Vonnie Winslow Crist is author of *The Enchanted Dagger, Owl Light, The Greener Forest, Murder on Marawa Prime,* and other award-winning books. Her fiction is included in *"Amazing Stories," "Cast of Wonders," "Outposts of Beyond," Killing It Softly 2, Defending the Future - Dogs of War, Midnight Masquerade, Chaos of Hard Clay,* and elsewhere. A cloverhand who has found so many four-leafed clovers she keeps them in jars, Vonnie strives to celebrate the power of myth in her writing.
Website: www.vonniewinslowcrist.com

Text from my Ex
by R.J. Hunt

There is a graveyard we cannot visit.

Online profiles of the dead, frozen in time, from the moment they passed. Sometimes flowers are laid on their graves; messages from friends and family on social media, final photos posted in fond memory. Beyond that, they remain still.

A timestamp keeps track. Last seen: 3 days ago. 10 days ago. A month. A year.

My wife's account said 2 years. Until today. Now the timestamp says 'Active'.

It must be a malfunction. Hackers, maybe. Kids, playing games.

It wasn't her typing.

It wasn't her who sent the message, "Help me."

…was it?

R.J. Hunt is a Civil Engineer from Nottingham who loves creating worlds and writing stories in his spare time. Whilst he has a roughly infinite supply of half-finished stories, he's currently working on the second draft of his debut novel, 'The Final Carnivore' - a story about horrible people being granted immortality and mind-control powers, causing misfits with hidden abilities of their own to rise in an effort stop them.
Twitter: @RJHuntWrites
Reddit: RJHuntWrites

A Home Without My Heart
by Shelly Jarvis

He wouldn't take my hand. I could've pulled him to safety, but he refused. Now I lay at the edge of Heaven, alone, numb.

I see pearly gates in the distance and there's a sweet melody on the air. My heart feels ready to leap from my chest and run to the golden city on its own. But it doesn't. Just keeps pounding away the seconds as if time still matters in this place.

Tears stream as I force myself to look at my new home. But it's a home without Joseph. I turn, stare into the abyss, and jump.

Shelly Jarvis is a speculative fiction author from West Virginia, US. She found a life-long love of sci-fi and fantasy in the 3rd grade when she found Madeleine L'Engle's "A Wrinkle in Time." Shelly is an avid reader, a Whovian, the ideal viewer of dog rescue videos, and undoubtedly Ravenclaw. She currently has two YA sci-fi books available for purchase on Amazon.
Website: www.ShellyJarvis.com

Partying with Josephine
by Ximena Escobar

Josephine's blue eyes glassed into transparency.

She had that photogenic beauty, an alluring dead-like expression, that stirred darker than lighter appetites; but the only shots today had been served with lime.

None believed in spirit-boards, but the planchette quivered instantly at the sound of Jo's voice, travelling decisively towards her as it began to shoot frantically in all directions across the board; like Jo was pulling it magnetically with her stiff doll eyes. Everyone's pupils followed in awe; and Jo looked up suddenly, veiled by whiteness.

A fountain of blood emerged in her chest.

I AM JOSEPHINE, spelled the planchette.

Ximena Escobar is an emerging author of literary fiction and poetry. Originally from Chile, she is the author of a translation into Spanish of the Broadway Musical "The Wizard of Oz", and of an original adaptation of the same, "Navidad en Oz". Clarendon House Publications published her first short story in the UK, "The Persistence of Memory", and Literally Stories her first online publication with "The Green Light". She has since had several acceptances from other publishers and is working very hard exploring new exciting avenues in her writing.
She lives in Nottingham with her family.
Facebook: Ximenautora

Death and Taxes
by Crystal L. Kirkham

"Mr. Petrokovich?"

"Who's asking?" the old man grumbled as he glared through his coke bottle glasses at the dark hooded figure.

"A friend."

"Somehow I doubt that." Petrokovich waved his hand at the figure. "Go away."

"I can't. It's time."

"Time for what?"

"Your inevitable end." The figure swung an item that Petrokovich only recognised as a scythe when it entered his body. He laughed.

Death stared in amazement as the old man became young again. "How?"

"I've managed to avoid paying taxes my entire life, do you really think I wouldn't find a way to avoid death as well?"

Crystal L. Kirkham *resides in a small hamlet west of Red Deer, Alberta. She's an avid outdoors person, unrepentant coffee addict, part-time foodie, servant to a wonderful feline, and companion to two delightfully hilarious canines. She will neither confirm nor deny the rumours regarding the heart in a jar on her desk and the bottle of reader's tears right next to it. Her paranormal urban fantasy series, Saints and Sinners, is available on Amazon and her YA Fantasy, Feathers and Fae will be released October 11, 2019, from Kyanite Publishing.*
Website: www.crystallkirkham.com

Madness
by Jodi Jensen

The sound of a woman screaming jolted Mallory from a restless sleep. She got out of bed, slipped quietly from her room and padded barefoot down the hallway.

At the end of the corridor, behind a closed door, the racket grew louder.

She stood, hands pressed to the wood, listening to the wails until she couldn't stand it a second longer.

Someone's gotta help that poor woman.

Mallory cracked the door and peeked inside. Her mind shattered when she saw herself lying there, vacant stare, sobs racking her body.

"Come rest, dear," a voice whispered behind her. "You've gone mad."

Jodi Jensen grew up moving from California, to Massachusetts, and a few other places in between, before finally settling in Utah at the ripe old age of nine. The nomadic life fed her sense of adventure as a child and the wanderlust continues to this day. With a passion for old cemeteries, historical buildings and sweeping sagas of days gone by, it was only natural she'd dream of time traveling to all the places that sparked her imagination.

Eyes
by Jasmine Jarvis

A whisper stirs me from my slumber. It is dark in my bedroom except for a shard of silver light from the moon that slips through the gap between the bedroom window curtains. In the corner of my room, a pair of opaque eyes emerge from the darkness, I know it is staring straight at me. The temperature in the room drops. I try to move, but my body is paralysed in complete terror. I watch as a ghostly white withered hand reaches out from the dark corner, touching the shard of moonlight, extinguishing it.

Leaving us in the darkness.

Jasmine Jarvis is a teller of tales and scribbler of scribbles. She lives in Brisbane, Australia with her husband Michael, their two children, Tilly and Mish; Ripley, their German Shepherd; indoor fat cat, Dwight K. Shrute; and grumpy old guinea pig, Doctor Who.

Bedtime Blues
by Lynne Lumsden Green

Your heart is the hourglass of your life. Each heartbeat is another grain of sand slipping down into the pit of time.

What happens afterwards? What happens when the clock stops?

I've been having trouble going to sleep lately. I hear 'time's winged chariots drawing near' much too loud to rest. Every time you go to sleep, it is a little death—even Shakespeare knew that. If this is it, if this life is the only tiny portion of eternity that I get to experience, why should I sleep it away?

I want to stay up past my bedtime.

Lynne Lumsden Green has twin bachelor's degrees in both Science and the Arts, giving her the balance between rationality and creativity. She spent fifteen years as the Science Queen for HarperCollins Voyager Online and has written science articles for other online magazines. Currently, she captains the Writing Race for the Australian Writers Marketplace on Facebook. She has had speculative fiction flash fiction and short stories published in anthologies and websites.
Website: cogpunksteamscribe.wordpress.com

Medium
by David Bowmore

"Switch the lights off. Good, now we can commune with the spirit world. Place your hands on the top of the table and hold the hand of the person next to you. No matter what happens, do not break the circle. I will now go in to a trance."

The medium's breathing deepened. A painting crashed to the floor.

"Who is it that dares to disturb my rest?"

"It is I. Do you have a message, spirit?"

"Yes? Do not disturb the dark man." The lights flared revealing a hooded figure behind the medium.

A blade fell.

A head rolled.

David Bowmore *has lived here, there and everywhere, but now lives in Yorkshire with his wonderful wife and a small white poodle. He has worn many hats in his time; head chef, teacher and landscape gardener. His first collection of short stories 'The Magic of Deben Market' is available from Clarendon House.*
Website: davidbowmore.co.uk
Facebook: davidbowmoreauthor

The Devil Is Not a Harry Potter Fan
by Jacob Baugher

Dylan's mom threw my Harry Potter books in the fireplace.

"No devil books in *my* house!"

I got out my chalk and drew a circle on the yellow linoleum. I put a plastic wand, goat's cheese, a photo of Justin Bieber, and an Algebra test at the cardinal points before saying the summons.

Satan popped into existence and handed the ashy books back. He wore an "I Love NY" bro-tank. He grinned at Dylan's mom with cockroach teeth.

"I knew it!" she screamed. "Those devil books!" She grabbed Dylan and ran.

"Actually," he called after her, "I prefer erotic romance."

Jacob Baugher teaches Creative Writing at Franciscan University of Steubenville. When he's not teaching or coaching the track team, he can be found in the Cuyahoga Valley hiking with his wife and son or brewing beer on his front porch. He's received honourable mentions for his work in the Writers of the Future contest and he co-edits a series of Fantasy and Science Fiction anthologies titled Continuum.

Graveyard Whispers
by Cindar Harrell

Ever since she died, I have come to this graveyard, hoping to hear her voice again. I bring something new every time, things that psychics recommend for communicating with the dead. I've tried it all, still she remains silent.

Tonight, I have brought the necklace she was wearing when she died, along with the knife found at the scene. A witch imbued them with her magic so that they would draw her spirit back.

I sit at her grave, the items around me.

A voice whispers in the wind.

I look up and see the ghostly face of her killer.

Cindar Harrell loves fairy tales, especially ones with a dark twist. Her stories are often fairy tale inspired, but she is also working on a mystery series. Her stories can be found on Amazon and in various anthologies. You can follow her on Facebook and visit her blog, which she promises to try and update more often,
Website: cindarharrell.wordpress.com
Facebook: CindarHarrell

Simple Reminders
by Wendy Roberts

All she wants is his attention. Just a small sign that he knows she is still here and not just a body rotting in the ground. So, she doesn't see any harm in tipping a vase over or breathing into his ear when he isn't paying attention. She misses him and knows he misses her. It's when he dismisses her as a breeze through the house and packs her stuff away that she grows angry.

Decides that a scratch here and there would be more of a gentle reminder that he is never alone. That she'll forever be with him.

*Writing short stories and novels started as a past time for **Wendy Roberts** and has now become a fully fledged passion. She posts short stories on her website at flippinscribbler.wordpress.com and can be found most days on twitter @_WARoberts*

Cryptids Spelled Out
by Carole de Monclin

Creatures every child dream to encounter one day,

Recluse, elusive, fantastic, sometimes feral, but always fascinating.

You live and prosper in the human mind, some say. But others believe you're as real as the sun,

Prowling at the edge of imagination and reality, only waiting to come into the light,

To claim your rightful place alongside us. No longer chimeras.

Imaginary or genuine? With a planet so vast and mysterious, who can hold certitudes?

Denying your existence feels like killing the last trace of magic in the world.

So next time a sceptic notices a strange dark silhouette, don't hide.

Carole de Monclin has lived in France and Australia, but for the moment the USA is home. She finds inspiration from her travels. She loves Science Fiction because it explores the human mind in a way no other genre can. Plus, who doesn't love spaceships and lasers? Her stories appear in the Exoplanet Magazine and Angels - A Dark Drabbles Anthology.
Website: CaroledeMonclin.com
Twitter: @CaroledeMonclin

Lend a Hand
by Paul Warmerdam

According to the article, the girl had been around the same age when she was drowned. Nina looked over the edge of the pier and saw what no one else could. Thirty years had passed, but the victim still stared up at her from below the water's surface.

Their eyes met. Something in that gaze was pleading for help. Nina crouched down and reached. The dead girl mirrored the gesture. Their hands met in the reflection.

The next thing Nina knew, she was drowning. She looked up through the murky water at a face that was no longer her own.

Paul Warmerdam is a Dutch-American with decades of experience writing stories, who only recently decided to start submitting them. He lives in the Netherlands, where there's plenty of rainy hours shut indoors with a story in mind.

Family Ties
by J.U. Menon

"I see dead people," Peter said softly.

I looked up from my book at my little brother. He was sitting cross-legged on the floor, playing with his toy train.

Mum's eyes widened, but she composed herself and knelt down beside him. "Why do you say that, sweetie?"

"Don't listen to him, mum. He's making stuff up again," I scoffed, returning to my book.

Mum ignored me. "Peter?"

Peter slowly raised a pudgy finger and pointed at me. "I can see Robert. He's sitting right there," Peter sobbed. I gasped and looked down as my body began to fade to nothing.

J.U. Menon is a scientist living in Rhode Island, USA, and is currently working on her young adult novel. She writes fantasy and science fiction while occasionally dabbling in dark fiction and poetry.
Twitter: @ju_menon
Instagram: @iam_jumenon

Confessions
by Cameron Marcoux

They say that all dogs go to heaven. But then how do you explain the hounds of hell?

When I was six, I watched my wheaten terrier slaughter a litter of kittens. I was too scared to stop it. Clumps of white fur and viscera were scattered around the cardboard box. It seemed a ritual disembowelment. I had learned of demons in my Sunday School. In the Bible they once entered swine. I knew they were in Clemens. One night, I snuck from bed and killed him while he slept.

I still hear him. At night. Clicking across the floor.

Cameron Marcoux is a writer of stories, which, considering where you are reading this, makes a lot of sense. He also teaches English to the lovely and terrifying creatures we call teenagers. He lives in the quiet, northern reaches of New England in the U.S. with his girlfriend and scaredy dog.

I Used to Love Her
by Stephen Herczeg

Last night, she stood there again, at the foot of my bed all night, staring. I could feel her cold eyes through the blankets.

She hates me. I don't really blame her.

At first, things were brilliant. We treasured each other's company and did everything together.

I'm the first to admit, I used to love her.

Then it went sour. The love faded, replaced with that constant nagging about any little thing.

After a while, I just couldn't put up with it any more.

I just wish she'd leave me alone.

Maybe I shouldn't have buried her in the backyard.

Stephen Herczeg is an IT Geek based in Canberra Australia. He has been writing for over twenty years and has completed a couple of dodgy novels, sixteen feature length screenplays and numerous short stories and scripts. His horror work has featured in Sproutlings, Hells Bells, Below the Stairs, Trickster's Treats #1 and #2, Shades of Santa, Behind the Mask, Beyond the Infinite; The Body Horror Book, Anemone Enemy, Petrified Punks and Beginnings. He has also had numerous Sherlock Holmes stories published through the Belanger Books - Sherlock Holmes anthologies.

An Exchange of Souls
by Alexander Pyles

The souls swirled by. Silvery wisps confined to a river, they reached for me. I watched the poor things slip past and attempt to beckon me in. Was it him?

I left the bank and headed towards the gate and the large, obsidian guardian.

"What do you have to offer?" The rumble of its voice reverberated through my body.

I held out a pocket watch. The hands were frozen, dead like him.

"That is not enough." The heavy spear continued to block the gate.

"Then I offer myself." His life was cut short, mine was too long.

"A fair trade."

Alexander Pyles *resides in IL with his wife and children. He holds an MA in Philosophy and an MFA in Writing Popular Fiction. His short story chapbook titled, "Milo (01001101 01101001 01101100 01101111)," from Radix Media, is due out fall 2019. His other short fiction has appeared on 101fiction.org, River and South Review, and other venues.*
Website: www.pylesofbooks.com
Twitter: @Pylesofbooks

The Lonely Ghost
by Zoey Xolton

Silently, she waited. No one had called for…how long? She wasn't sure. She wasn't even sure how to be sure. Time seemed to have lost all meaning. There were just moments that turned into days, months and years. She'd lost count.

In the distance, she heard the sound of footfalls echoing up the stone halls. Her face lit up and she smiled from ear to ear. *Company!* She blinked in and out of existence, appearing before a young girl with a torch.

"Hello!" she sang excitedly.

The girl screamed.

An eyeless spectre with a gaping maw howled at her.

*Zoey Xolton is an Australian Speculative Fiction writer, primarily of Dark Fantasy, Paranormal Romance and Horror. She is also a proud mother of two and is married to her soul mate. Outside of her family, writing is her greatest passion. She is especially fond of short fiction and is working on releasing her own themed collections in future.
Website: www.zoeyxolton.com*

Memory
by Jem McCusker

The kitchen is a place of warmth, of memories made, and memories shared. The microwave dings and my husband removes the once frozen meal. The kids groan and trudge to the table.

"But it's Friday, dad. It's spaghetti night," my youngest says.

"I know." My husband puts their plates in front of them.

"So why are we eating—"

"Just eat it." My daughter hunches over and eats with feigned enthusiasm.

"No. It's spaghetti night. I'm not eating it." He swipes the plate from the table. It crashes to the floor.

I turn to comfort him; my hand passes through him.

Jem McCusker is a middle grade fiction author, living near Brisbane with her two sons and husband. Her first book Stone Guardians the Rise of Eden was released in 2018 and she is working on the sequel. She is releasing a Novella for the Four Quills writing group, A Storm of Wind and Rain series in July, 2019. She longs to be a full-time author, won't wear yellow and loves rabbits. Follow Jem on Twitter, Facebook and Instagram. Details on her website.
Website: www.jemmccusker.com

Beyond the Grave
by Cecelia Hopkins-Drewer

It was Mother's Day, and Evelyn was visiting the cemetery with a bunch of carnations. She fell on her knees before the grave and sobbed.

"I've been so lonely since you died."

The marble plaque did not move, but the sky became ominously darkened.

"So faithful, always visiting me!"

Evelyn seemed to hear a raspy whisper. She longed for the voice of her mother, but instead she heard the nasal falsetto of her stepfather. That evil man who had beaten her mother daily and crept into Evelyn's bedroom at night.

A hand reached out from the grass. "Come here, daughter."

Cecelia Hopkins-Drewer is a speculative fiction writer, poet and scholar, who lives in Adelaide, South Australia. She has also written a Masters paper on H.P. Lovecraft, and a teenage vampire series that commences with "Mystic Evermore". Her science fiction poetry has been published in "The Mentor" a fanzine edited by Ron Clarke.
Amazon: amazon.com/Cecelia-Hopkins-Drewer/e/B071G968NM

Beyond War
by Cecelia Hopkins-Drewer

Vanth shuddered as she landed on the river bank. This mission was one of mercy, but even the experienced psychopomp was shocked by what she found. The bomb had shattered the bodies of men, women and children alike. Blood and gore stained the muddy bank, and body parts rolled down the slope.

There was an order, even in death. A tiny hand reached out, begging for comfort and the release from pain. Vanth hardened her heart, as she had to gather the most damaged souls first. Those who were only incurably injured would have to suffer until their time came.

Cecelia Hopkins-Drewer is a speculative fiction writer, poet and scholar, who lives in Adelaide, South Australia. She has also written a Masters paper on H.P. Lovecraft, and a teenage vampire series that commences with "Mystic Evermore". Her science fiction poetry has been published in "The Mentor" a fanzine edited by Ron Clarke.
Amazon: amazon.com/Cecelia-Hopkins-Drewer/e/B071G968NM

Beyond Proof
by Cecelia Hopkins-Drewer

Monty had been investigating the paranormal for some time. So far, he had only uncovered hoaxes and quirks of nature. He required a real documented manifestation.

The cameras and sensors were set facing the ancient altar. Monty quaked with excitement as he read the inscription out loud, wondering vaguely why supernatural creatures always spoke Latin. "Mortuos surgere, et loquor vobis".

Monty was about to repeat the phrase, when the alarms sounded. Foul breath blew into his face as the creature spoke. "Why couldn't you just believe?"

The bony hand grabbed him from behind and rotten teeth sank into his throat.

Cecelia Hopkins-Drewer is a speculative fiction writer, poet and scholar, who lives in Adelaide, South Australia. She has also written a Masters paper on H.P. Lovecraft, and a teenage vampire series that commences with "Mystic Evermore". Her science fiction poetry has been published in "The Mentor" a fanzine edited by Ron Clarke.
Amazon: amazon.com/Cecelia-Hopkins-Drewer/e/B071G968NM

Beyond Murder
by Cecelia Hopkins-Drewer

When Mattie rose up out of her body, she knew that she was dead. She was glad. The killer knelt over her inert form, doing obscene things to it, but she could no longer feel pain.

It was weird to watch a pattern being carved in her stomach and her eyes being gouged out. The psycho was grinning fiendishly, and she wished she could wipe the smile off his face.

Her mobile phone dropped, and Mattie attempted to send an electronic impulse.

"Emergency, can I help you?" an Operator asked.

"I want to report a murder," the stricken soul whispered.

Cecelia Hopkins-Drewer is a speculative fiction writer, poet and scholar, who lives in Adelaide, South Australia. She has also written a Masters paper on H.P. Lovecraft, and a teenage vampire series that commences with "Mystic Evermore". Her science fiction poetry has been published in "The Mentor" a fanzine edited by Ron Clarke.
Amazon: amazon.com/Cecelia-Hopkins-Drewer/e/B071G968NM

Beyond Death
by Cecelia Hopkins-Drewer

Megaine stepped through the portal into death. It was dark and echoed with dripping water. The sentry was a stone dog.

"What do you want?" asked Dog.

"My Grandmother," Megaine said.

"Would you exchange places with her?" Dog asked, indicating a shadowy figure.

Megaine hesitated, but all the grandchildren adored her. "Yes!"

"Bargain accepted," Dog said.

Megaine felt her life exit her body and pass into the elderly woman. The woman grinned cruelly and stepped out the portal into life.

"That is not my Grandmother," Megaine cried.

The dog barked with callous disregard. "Too late to tell me," it said.

Cecelia Hopkins-Drewer is a speculative fiction writer, poet and scholar, who lives in Adelaide, South Australia. She has also written a Masters paper on H.P. Lovecraft, and a teenage vampire series that commences with "Mystic Evermore". Her science fiction poetry has been published in "The Mentor" a fanzine edited by Ron Clarke.
Amazon: amazon.com/Cecelia-Hopkins-Drewer/e/B071G968NM

Mary Marrin
by Pamela Jeffs

Her fingers are pale sticks in the moonlight. Her face forms, blurs and forms again. Her gown is transparent, so much that I can see her name etched in the gravestone behind her.

Mary Marrin.

"I miss you, my dear," she whispers in a voice that sounds hollow and cold.

I shudder as her fingertips brush my cheek. I miss her likewise, and so endure the touch. Then she fades away. I curl my tail around my legs and drop to the ground. Then I wait for tomorrow evening when she will appear again. A hound never abandons his mistress.

Pamela Jeffs is a speculative fiction author living in Queensland, Australia with her husband and two daughters. She is a member of the Queensland Writers' Centre and has had numerous short fiction pieces published in recent national and international anthologies. In 2017 and again in 2018, Pamela was nominated for an Australian Aurealis Award in the category of 'Best Science Fiction Short Story'. Her debut collection titled 'Red Hour and Other Strange Tales' was released in March 2018.
Website: www.pamelajeffs.com
Facebook: pamelajeffsauthor

Auras

by Alanna Robertson-Webb

Even the dead have auras. While the living generally have bright shades—like sky blues, berry reds and grass greens—the dead tend to show darker colours.

Greys, olives, and browns are common among the departed. I didn't know a bright colour could linger on a corpse, but the man I watched get hit by a truck three days ago is still showing yellow.

My father always promised me that, if he died too early, he would keep his spirit tethered so I would never be without him. That must be why my aura is both yellow and blue now.

Alanna Robertson-Webb is a sales support member by day, and a writer and editor by night. She loves VT, and lives in NY. She has been writing since she was five years old, and writing well since she was seventeen years old. She lives with a fiance and a cat, both of whom take up most of her bed space. She loves to L.A.R.P., and one day she aspired to write a horrifyingly fantastic novel. Her short horror stories have been published before, but she still enjoys remaining mysterious.
Reddit: MythologyLovesHorror

The Forgotten
by Derek Dunn

Margaret's son had been gone for two years now. She passed his room less and less these days. She used to sit on the edge of his bed and sing the nursery rhymes he once loved.

After the first year, she would only stop in the doorway and look at his drawings. He was so talented. He'd even won some competitions. The blue ribbons still hung over his desk.

Now, she kept the door closed.

Tim missed his mother. He used to sing along with her every night. He'd watch her admire his art. But now, she'd shut him out.

Derek Dunn *lives in the American Northwest with his family. He's a film enthusiast and musician who writes primarily horror and mystery stories.*
Twitter: @DerekTDunn

Perfection
by A.R. Dean

She died too young. A tragic twist of fate. I just couldn't continue life without her. I took my shovel and freed her from her grave.

It looks like she is sleeping, lying next to me in bed. So peaceful and so sweet, she's finally the perfect wife. I hold her tight and kiss her rotting flesh.

Her spirit tries to beg for peace. She haunts me like an annoying fly. All day long she wails and moves things, trying to scare me. I suppose if you kill a woman and dig her up; it tends to annoy her ghost.

A.R. Dean is a dark and twisted soul. Dean has spent their whole life spreading fear with the tales from their head. Best known for stories that terrify and show the evilest side of human nature. So, look for Dean haunting your local cemetery or under your bed, because they're here to spread the fear. Turn off your lights and enjoy a scare. Keep a lookout for more stories from this master of terror.
Facebook: ghoul.demon.orghost.a.r.dean

Phantom Requiem
by Becky Benishek

Angel of Music? Ha.

In hiding once more—yes, I lived!—from teenage ingenues screeching note after note as they practice "singing" in their rooms.

The same unholy pact that created my disfigured existence also gifted me with wretched immortality.

The pages turn, and I speak again. The music plays, and I sing again. And it's not just confined to these sanctioned articles. Every new reference, recitation, or swooning diary entry sparks my life anew.

My triumph. My defeat.

But I've composed my next piece. One day, someone will manifest me properly.

And this time I won't be so kind.

Becky Benishek is the author of the children's books "The Squeezor is Coming!", "What's At the End of Your Nose?", "Dr. Guinea Pig George," and "Hush, Mouse!" She loves to create stories that help children believe in themselves and find the magic in ordinary things. Becky also manages online communities that connect people with resources to help people with special needs thrive. She has an extensive Lego collection, a working Commodore 64, and a tendency to stick googly eyes on objects minding their own business. Becky is married with guinea pigs.
Website: beckybenishek.com
Amazon: www.amazon.com/author/beckybenishek

River Lethe
by Raven Corinn Carluk

I would remember this time. I'd barely drunk the water, refusing to let them wipe my memories.

The rules were simple; live a mortal life, bring those experiences back. Each life was different, but the more active I was, the more time I got to spend in Elysium.

But I wasn't allowed to remember. I had to drink, have my memories wiped. Supposedly for my own good, to protect my sanity.

Not this time. I would have memories, would share my knowledge.

I settled into my new body to wait, soft and warm within the womb. Clinging to fading memories.

Raven Corinn Carluk *writes dark fantasy, paranormal romance, and anything else that catches her interest. She's authored five novels, where she explores themes of love and acceptance. Her shorter pieces, usually from her darker side, can be found in Black Hare Press anthologies, at Detritus Online, and through Alban Lake Publishers.*
Twitter: @ravencorinn
Website: RavenCorinnCarluk.Blogspot.Com

Portals
by R.A. Goli

The dark matter was hypnotic. Vivid purple and blue with flecks of silver swirled and twisted as they watched, their wrinkled hands clasped together. The portals were a mystery, all they knew is that once you went through, there was no coming back. Eliza squeezed her husband's hand. Forty years they'd been together, and she couldn't imagine going through with anyone else.

"Ready?"

"Ready as I'll ever be." His voice trembled, betraying his fears.

As she stepped through, Brent's hand slipped from her grasp.

She turned, shocked as he mouthed the words 'I'm sorry', right before the portal shimmered closed.

R.A. Goli is an Australian writer of horror, fantasy, and speculative short stories. In addition to writing, her interests include reading, gaming, the occasional walk, and annoying her dog, two cats, and husband. Check out her numerous publications including her fantasy novella, The Eighth Dwarf, and her collection of short stories, Unfettered;
Website: ragoliauthor.wordpress.com
Facebook: RAGoliAuthor

The Switch
by Donna Cuttress

I don't care what you had for your last meal, or if you cry or piss your pants. I'm waiting. I'm serving my time, and you will take my place. You'll watch through the glass the faces of those you angered and destroyed, spit your name.

I wait for the lights to dim and for a brief moment, you'll see my face before you as your heart stops beating in your chest. That's when I'll scream at you. "I'm your nightmare! Your sentence ain't over yet, bud! You gotta take my spot. I'm moving on to hell. You're death now."

Donna Cuttress *is a short story writer from Liverpool, U.K. Her work has been published by Crooked Cat, FOF publishing and Latchkey Tales. She has had work published by Sirens Call as part of Women in Horror Month and been included in Flame Tree Publishings, Chilling Ghost Short Stories anthology. Her work for the Patchwork Raven's 'Twelve Days' is available as an art book. She has also been a speaker at the London Book Fair.*
Twitter: @Hederah

To the Bone
by Jonathan Inbody

Professor Baker steadied the pickaxe in his hand, then wiped the sweat and sand from his forehead. He had come too far to turn back now, but the fear still rose in his chest. He called for the priest to begin the exorcism, then sat back and loaded his pistol in case it failed. He had been digging all day under the boiling sun, but the worst was yet to come. Phantom claws and spectral teeth awaited him, and if he was unlucky then ectoplasmic stomach acid too.

Palaeontology had become much more complicated after the discovery of dinosaur ghosts.

Jonathan Inbody is a filmmaker, author, and podcaster from Buffalo, New York. He enjoys B-movies, pen and paper RPGs, and New Wave Science Fiction novels. His short story "Dying Feels Like Slowly Sinking" is due to be published in the anthology Deteriorate from Whimsically Dark Publishing. Jon can be heard every other week on his improvisational movie pitch podcast X Meets Y.
Website: xmeetsy.libsyn.com

Weight
by Phil Dyer

At first, an apple was enough to put the damn thing back in the dirt. A fly, scooped from the windowsill. A goldfish. A rabbit. But here it comes again, scratching and whimpering, flyblown and stinking, and a trip to the pet store won't do the trick this time, oh no. It's very clear about what it wants.

It says it can't go far enough without. It tries. It just needs weight, a little ballast on its soul. The waters are wild, it says, though we buried it a hundred miles from the sea. They keep on throwing it back.

Phil Dyer does medical research in Liverpool and writes spec fic on the side. His stories have appeared in Unfit Magazine, 101 Words and The Drabble. He retweets animal videos.
Twitter: @ez_ozel

Pendle Hill
by Elizabeth Montague

"It's just a hill," she says as they reach the summit, "It's cold, I'm not staying."

"You promised," he answers, retrieving the skinny tent from his backpack.

She frowns but helps him, then glares at him as he sleeps soundly whilst the wind howls outside. He doesn't wake when the scratching starts, when the darkness swallows them, when something takes hold of her hand, the grip so cold it freezes her breath and her scream.

"It's just a hill," she says the next morning as they leave, rubbing the scratch on her arm that won't stop bleeding. "Just a hill."

Elizabeth Montague is a multi-genre author from Hertfordshire, England. Her short story collection, Dust and Glitter, was released by Clarendon House Publications in May 2019. She has previously featured in nine anthologies from the same publisher alongside publications from Scout Media, Black Hare Press and Iron Faerie Publishing. She is currently working on her first novel alongside continuing to produce short stories in several genres.
Website: elizabethmontagueauthor.wordpress.com
Facebook: elizabethmontaguewrites

Heaven or Hell
by Melissa Neubert

Thunder boomed, the lights began to flicker. She sensed it was time. She had lived a long life. She was ready. She had to face what was next.

She had stopped the abuse—she killed her own father—she and her mother lived in peace. But murder was a sin. They never found out who did it, but she had to live with it and now die with it.

Another flash of light and she saw him; illuminated wings glowed in the dark room showing the angel of death.

The only question is; would she go to Heaven or Hell.

Melissa Neubert was born in the Pacific Northwest and currently lives in Illinois with her husband, three children and two dogs. Melissa has been a daycare provider, veterinary assistant, teacher/library aide, and administrative assistant. Melissa travels extensively both domestically and internationally where she finds inspiration for her writing in beautiful and unique locations. When she is not writing she enjoys music, reading, concert and wildlife photography, football and camping. Although Melissa has been writing since grade school, she has only recently begun pursuing the craft seriously. She writes mostly in the genres of Suspense/Thriller and Adult Paranormal Romance.

Visitor
by R.J. Meldrum

"You really doing this?" asked John.

"Yup," replied Eric.

"You're going to sit by the bedside until Death arrives, then interview him?"

"Yup."

"But, Death isn't a person."

"He is."

Eric entered the bedroom. His grandad lay in the bed. He was close to the end.

The next morning, John returned to the room, expecting to find Eric either bored or grieving. He opened the door. The old man lay in the bed, clearly deceased. Eric lay on the floor; deaf, dumb, blind and insane. Whoever he'd met that night, whatever had been said, the secret stayed with him forever.

R. J. Meldrum is an author and academic. Born in Scotland, he moved to Ontario, Canada in 2010. He has had stories published by Horrified Press, the Infernal Clock, Trembling with Fear, Darkhouse Books, Smoking Pen Press, and James Ward Kirk Fiction. He also has had stories published in The Sirens Call e-zine, the Horror Zine and Drabblez Magazine. He is an Affiliate Member of the Horror Writers Association.
Twitter: @RichardJMeldru1
Facebook: richard.meldrum.79

Rebirth
by Sinister Sweetheart

Crimson pools spread from beneath my fallen frame. I feel heaviness tug my soul, attempting to lure it from my corporeal form. Once I stop fighting, I know life will be over. Every fibre of my being struggles to stay focused on living.

I fade to black. There is no feeling, no sight, no sound… Just nothing. The bottoms of my feet are planted on a floor that I cannot see.

Suddenly, there's a blinding light. My body falls down a narrow path, out into a frigid room. A giant woman holds me, and I cannot speak.

I am…reborn.

*Since **Sinister Sweetheart** made her first post to a popular Internet forum, she's taken the horror community by storm. Her ability to create, terrify, and drive home her stories is insurmountable. Sinister Sweetheart's published works can be found in multiple anthologies for all to read, but be forewarned, if you do… you may want to call your therapist after, her stories are terrifying, disturbing and devilishly unsettling. She is not only a fright visually, but also has a creepy tentacle in horror podcasting as well. Sinister Sweetheart writes, voice acts and is the media director of the Scarecrow Tales podcast.*
Website: Sinistersweetheart.wixsite.com/sinistersweetheart
Facebook: NMBrownStories

Balloon
by Phil Dyer

"Doesn't it hurt?" I ask, reaching out a finger. The medium's ballooning skin is taut, translucent, filled with lights and turbulent ectoplasm.

"Well, don't *poke* it," she says, batting my hand away. "But no, not really. Tickles sometimes." She adjusts a curl of hair, trailed down from atop her distended cranium. Her face seems very small beneath the mass.

"Looks scary," I say.

"They're just babies," she shrugs. "Little unborn children, looking for a place to grow. They'll pass on when they're ready."

There are faces in there, moving under her skin. They don't look like anyone's children to me.

Phil Dyer does medical research in Liverpool and writes spec fic on the side. His stories have appeared in Unfit Magazine, 101 Words and The Drabble. He retweets animal videos.
Twitter: @ez_ozel

Singled Out for Jeopardy
by John H. Dromey

Lou Trottelmeier trembled with fear when he saw a man who looked exactly like him get out of a taxicab. The two men of identical height and build parted their thinning hair on the same side. Even Lou's shock of recognition was mirrored by the other man's face.

Scared to death, Lou hired a paranormal investigator, then holed up in his flat.

Later, the PI showed his client a newspaper clipping with a gruesome photo. "This freak accident victim could be your twin."

"What's does it mean?" Lou asked.

"It's simple really. That man wasn't your doppelgänger—you were his."

First published in *Flashshot*, 2011

John H. Dromey was born in northeast Missouri, USA. He enjoys reading—mysteries in particular—and writing in a variety of genres. He's had short fiction published in Alfred Hitchcock's Mystery Magazine, Martian Magazine, Stupefying Stories Showcase, Thriller Magazine, Unfit Magazine, and elsewhere, as well as in a number of anthologies, including Chilling Horror Short Stories (Flame Tree Publishing, 2015).

Frequency
by Beth W. Patterson

Even in the age of satellite radio and pre-recorded podcasts, you can still sometimes hear it: the jumble of static for a second or two. And in the midst of that entropic scramble, you might even hear the sounds of screaming and cries for help.

Some of you might even recognise them as the morning deejays Ted and Kari, who died mysteriously.

I'm not saying that this is the sort of thing that typically happens to radio personalities who prank call sleep deprived people and taunt them for the world to hear. But it's ill-advised to do to voodoo practitioners.

Beth W. Patterson was a full-time musician for over two decades before diving into the world of writing, a process she describes as "fleeing the circus to join the zoo". She is the author of the books Mongrels and Misfits, and The Wild Harmonic, and a contributing writer to thirty anthologies. Patterson has performed in eighteen countries, expanding her perspective as she goes. Her playing appears on over a hundred and seventy albums, soundtracks, videos, commercials, and voice-overs (including seven solo albums of her own). She lives in New Orleans, Louisiana with her husband Josh Paxton, jazz pianist extraordinaire.
Website: www.bethpattersonmusic.com
Facebook: bethodist

Reaching Out
by Patrick Winters

I stand beside her, silent and unseen, giving her all the answers she needs to hear.

Now, with teary eyes and a quivering voice, she asks: "Do you still love me?"

I urge the planchette to slide to "YES," but something's wrong. Now there's…resistance. Then, to her shock and mine, it shoots over to "NO."

She jumps, pulling her hands away. She looks pale, crushed; and it hurts my soul.

"What—?"

Before she can finish, the planchette darts about on its own, spelling out "H-A-T-E," over and over again.

She starts crying harder—and something chuckles over my shoulder…

Patrick Winters is a graduate of Illinois College in Jacksonville, IL, where he earned a Bachelor of Arts degree in English Literature and Creative Writing and achieved membership into Sigma Tau Delta, an international English honors society. Winters is now a proud member of the Horror Writers Association, and his work has been published in the likes of Sanitarium Magazine, Deadman's Tome, Trysts of Fate, and other such titles. A full list of his previous publications may be found at his author's site. Website: wintersauthor.azurewebsites.net/Publications/List

Tether
by Umair Mirxa

Tristan backed away, wild-eyed and frantic, until his back hit the wall.

"Come now, darling," said the demon, moving ever closer. "All I want is for you to tether me to this world."

The demon took another step forward, and slowly they merged.

Tristan laughed deep and loud, flexing his newfound strength.

We shall rule this world together, you and I, said the demon inside his head.

Their shared delight transformed into horror the next moment as the room's door crashed open.

"Sorry I'm late, son," said the Angel of Death to Tristan, even as he took his head off.

Umair Mirxa lives in Karachi, Pakistan. His first published story, 'Awareness', appeared on Spillwords Press. He has also had stories accepted for anthologies from Zombie Pirate Publishing, Blood Song Books, Fantasia Divinity Magazine and Publishing, and Iron Faerie Publishing. He is a massive J.R.R. Tolkien fan, and loves everything to do with fantasy and mythology. He enjoys football, history, music, movies, TV shows, and comic books, and wishes with all his heart that dragons were real.
Website: www.umairmirxa.com
Facebook: UMirxa12

The Tower
by Chris Bannor

Cards spread over the table and with each turn, a darker path was revealed. "The spirits watch over us all," she whispered into the hushed room, "But some of us more than others. Some are just a flicker in their sphere of existence, but others call to them, beacons of light in a land of never-ending dark. Some see the future. Some see the past. Some see death itself. There is always a price though, always a reckoning. Would you pay it?"

The small party at her table gasped, but even as they prayed, the Darkest One found his mark.

Chris Bannor is a science fiction and fantasy writer who lives in Southern California. Chris learned her love of genre stories from her mother at an early age and has never veered far from that path. She also enjoys musical theater and road trips with her family, but is a general homebody otherwise. Twitter: @BannorChris

Barstool Called Earth
by Rennie St. James

I read the human body is seventy percent water. That doesn't seem right to me. I think it's a more deadly cocktail of needs, flaws, dreams, and fears. Some are pretty, frothy drinks meant for colourful umbrellas and beaches. The majority are watered down, weak. A few are potent and clear like vodka.

I was more of straight, dark whiskey. A mixture of golden goodness swirling in darker hues. Few understood my complexity—I wasn't one of them.

That's probably why I can't transcend, move on, whatever. I'm stuck on this barstool called Earth haunting myself more than anyone else.

Rennie St. James *shares several similarities with her fictional characters (heroes and villains alike) including a love of chocolate, horror movies, martial arts, history, yoga, and travel. She doesn't have a pet mountain lion but is proudly owned by three rescue kitties. They live in relative harmony in beautiful southwestern Virginia (United States). The first three books of Rennie's urban fantasy series, The Rahki Chronicles, are available now. A new series and several standalone stories are already in the works as future releases.*
Website: writerRSJ.com

Stalker
by Nicole Little

He sent letters, because he knew where I lived. Flowers delivered to my work. *Thinking of you,* said the card. Somehow, he always found my new number. *Hey U up?* said every 2am text.

The police can do nothing unless he hurts me or kills me. So, there is euphoric relief at news that he's died. Freak accident, I'm told.

Two years later, Halloween party. There're chips, dip and a spirit board. Our fingers barely touch the planchette; it's careening around the board and we're trying our best to decipher the message. I gasp; *h e y u u p*...

Nicole Little is an award winning short story writer who lives in St. John's, Newfoundland, Canada. Her publishing credits to date include Sweet Sixteen (Kit Sora: The Artobiography, 2019), The Market (Dystopia from the Rock, 2019) and Last One Standing (Dystopia from the Rock, 2019). Her short story Doxxed placed favorably in the Writers Alliance of Newfoundland and Labrador's "A Nightmare on Water Street: Scary Story Reading". In her spare time, Nicole can be found with either a pen in her hand or her nose in a book. She is married with two daughters.

Feeling of Peace
by A.R. Johnston

Everything is like a fog, shadowy even. I can't seem to move though, speech wasn't even an option. I felt my heart race faster. Why didn't anything work?

A light started to appear to my right, getting brighter and brighter. It wasn't my time, was it? How had this happened? I don't remember.

"It's alright. It's best not to remember. Just let it go."

"But I need to know."

"Let's walk, I'll tell you all about it."

"You will?"

"Of course."

I take the hand of the figure that looks like my grandmother, someone I've never met. I feel peace.

A.R. Johnston is a small-town girl from Nova Scotia, Canada. Her style of writing is considered Urban Fantasy. Her first major publication is part of an anthology called First Love and she has several more titles lined up. She is a lover of coffee, good tv shows, horror flicks, and reader of books. She pretends to be a writer when real life doesn't get in the way. Pesky full-time job and adulting!

Paving
by Annie Percik

The path stretches out before me. Individual stones amidst a sea of empty darkness. A cold wind blows, chilling me as I walk. I step neither left nor right, my feet drawn inexorably along this path I have built out of my own weakness. I'll do it tomorrow... I thought you'd like it... I never imagined that would happen... I didn't think it through... It seemed like a good idea at the time... The voices whisper in my ear, spirits of my past mistakes haunting my progress, adding stones to the path ahead. Paving the road to my final destination.

Annie Percik lives in London with her husband, Dave, where she is revising her first novel, whilst working as a University Complaints Officer. She writes a blog about writing and posts short fiction on her website. She also publishes a photo-story blog, recording the adventures of her teddy bear. He is much more popular online than she is. She likes to run away from zombies in her spare time.
Website: www.alobear.co.uk
Website: aloysius-bear.dreamwidth.org

Reunited
by Stephanie Scissom

I sat on the grass, listening to my four-year-old chatter as he played in the sandbox.

A low-flying plane startled us, and Alex hurried over to climb in my lap. As we watched it, he said, "When the bad men flew into my building, no one came to help. It was hot, and me and Mike couldn't breathe, so we walked into the air. I saw the sky between my feet and we fell really fast."

He smiled, then patted my stomach. "I'm glad he found me."

Stunned, I gaped at him. I hadn't yet told him I was pregnant.

Stephanie Scissom hails from Tennessee, where she lives with her two children, inspects tires by night and plots murder by day. She has four full-length romantic suspense titles and is published in both flash and short story anthologies. Her story, Dandelions, garnered her a Sweek Star recognition and placed first in the international short story competition. Her current project and obsession is an apocalyptic trilogy starring Lucifer, his insane wife, and his deadly, power-hungry siblings
Facebook: Stephanie Scissom, Author
Twitter: @chell22_7

Cheers
by Brian Rosenberger

Friends since middle school. Vacationing parents. Fully stocked bar. Their only teenage child, Abe, unsupervised. Abe, Justin and me.

A drinking game.

Drink every time you see the murder's weapon, hear a scream, or view tits.

Justin didn't survive to witness the fourth kill. Just me and Abe going drink for drink, kill for kill.

Abe never woke up. The coroner ruled his death accidental. Alcohol poisoning.

His parents blamed us, themselves too.

Cemetery séance. Burnt candles. Sacrificed parakeet. Blood and feathers.

No response.

I said, "Let's go, Justin."

Justin said in a familiar voice, "Justin has left the building."

Brian Rosenberger lives in a cellar in Marietta, GA (USA) and writes by the light of captured fireflies. He is the author of As the Worms Turns and three poetry collections. He is also a featured contributor to the Pro-Wrestling literary collection, Three-Way Dance, available from Gimmick Press.
Facebook: HeWhoSuffers

Mother
by Rhiannon Bird

My mother was sitting in her chair, her favourite chair. She was just knitting, the same jumper that she had been working on for three years now. The concentration on her face as her needles clacked together was a look I knew well.

She turned towards me and gave me a big grin. Different than usual, more dangerous. "Sit, we have a lot to talk about." She gestured to the couch.

The movement shifted out of focus. But I was frozen. My brain had slowed to sludge, and I wrapped my hands tighter around the urn containing my mother's ashes.

Rhiannon Bird is a young aspiring author. She has a passion for words and storytelling. Rhiannon has her own quotes blog; Thoughts of a Writer. She has had 4 works published. This includes 3 short stories and 2 poems. These are published on Eskimo pie, Literary yard, Down in the Dirt Magazine and Short break fiction. She can be found on Facebook, Instagram, and Pinterest.

Thirteen Months
by Jefferson Retallack

I am thirteen months old when it first visits, paces outside my crib, snarling.

It puffs from its nose—like Buster. It must be three feet tall!

Its muzzle bends the bars, reaching, breaching. Spittle hits me and I'm paralysed with fear, can't move my pacifier if I try.

Dad! I'm saved. He's watching, trying not to be too obvious. Mustn't wake baby.

No. He can't see it. He leaves.

It backs off. Sickness emanating from where it was.

Lips peel back, revealing tiny teeth—thousands.

It's voice, vile, only I hear.

This. Every night.

Then it watches till sunrise.

Jefferson Retallack is an Australian writer of speculative fiction. He is based in Adelaide. His work draws influence from linguistic science fiction, the new weird and Australia's big things. Outside of the literary world, he skateboards on the weekends and spends afternoons on the beach with his partner, their son, and their Pomeranian, Tofu.
Website: jwretallack.wordpress.com
Twitter: @JWRetallack

Four and Three Quarters
by Jefferson Retallack

I had almost learned to live with it. But, enthralled by chicken pox induced fever on New Year's Day—three months before my fifth birthday—the beast that's haunted me nightly evolves.

As my brain overheats, it sees opportunity. Not even night, it moves in the walls—it is the walls.

It breaks forth, stretching the brick like it's a balloon. Myriad teeth pockmark my skin.

I'm within you.

"Get out!" I scream.

Night. And day.

Both parents to my rescue, flannel refreshed, they apply much needed hugs.

But the hugs don't stop it from scarring. Or the insatiable hunger.

Jefferson Retallack is an Australian writer of speculative fiction. He is based in Adelaide. His work draws influence from linguistic science fiction, the new weird and Australia's big things. Outside of the literary world, he skateboards on the weekends and spends afternoons on the beach with his partner, their son, and their Pomeranian, Tofu.
Website: jwretallack.wordpress.com
Twitter: @JWRetallack

Thirteenth Birthday

by Jefferson Retallack

My thirteenth birthday party. My first attack.

Mum's on barbecue duties, so Granddad sneaks me a whiskey.

I feel woozy.

Mark is here. He's taller than the other boys. I wonder if he likes me.

I eat some bacon, raw. Dad hates that I do this, but he's not here.

Drunkenly courageous, I give Mark a single 'come here' with my index finger. The boys egg him on. I disappear inside my childhood cubby.

He smells incredible. I kiss his neck.

Eat.

Inhibitions lowered, my phantasm seizes control. Mark can't escape. The thousand teeth—my teeth—tear out his throat.

Jefferson Retallack is an Australian writer of speculative fiction. He is based in Adelaide. His work draws influence from linguistic science fiction, the new weird and Australia's big things. Outside of the literary world, he skateboards on the weekends and spends afternoons on the beach with his partner, their son, and their Pomeranian, Tofu.
Website: jwretallack.wordpress.com
Twitter: @JWRetallack

On the Eve of Eighteen
by Jefferson Retallack

March thirty-first. My psychiatrist says I'm cured. But I know I'm only muted. There's no medication for what ails me.

I wish her correct and pray my release is not simply of bureaucracy—no adults reside within this facility.

Both parents pick me up.

Silence.

It's late. We're driving home, sole movers on the highway.

Freedom envelops me.

The medication? Placebo.

No...

It's stronger now.

Our maw gaping, lips peeling back to reveal not teeth, but a blossoming explosion of ghostly fangs, we devour everything within the car.

Then we fold back together. I'm alone again.

Just me.

For now...

Jefferson Retallack is an Australian writer of speculative fiction. He is based in Adelaide. His work draws influence from linguistic science fiction, the new weird and Australia's big things. Outside of the literary world, he skateboards on the weekends and spends afternoons on the beach with his partner, their son, and their Pomeranian, Tofu.

Website: jwretallack.wordpress.com

Twitter: @JWRetallack

Thirteen Decades
by Jefferson Retallack

I was barely a toddler when the phantasm introduced itself. Thirteen decades later, somehow both frail and hale, it holds these aching bones together.

All I want? Rest.

All it wants? *Eat.*

It's grown insatiable, tentatively maintaining self-control—just enough to mask its presence.

I've tired of warning them. But, food never listens.

It must've consumed an ark-worth of life in sustaining itself—us...me. These dried up buds lust for a morsel of *real* food, but the teeth—sabres—leave me longing.

* * *

The dock is quiet.

Another vessel berths.

I pray for them. They'll not have time in the bedlam.

Jefferson Retallack is an Australian writer of speculative fiction. He is based in Adelaide. His work draws influence from linguistic science fiction, the new weird and Australia's big things. Outside of the literary world, he skateboards on the weekends and spends afternoons on the beach with his partner, their son, and their Pomeranian, Tofu.
Website: jwretallack.wordpress.com
Twitter: @JWRetallack

Haunted
by C.L. Williams

I shoot the man, wanting to get his wallet. His body falls and I go for his pockets and grab his wallet. I go for his cash, his cards, and look for anything that could indicate his PIN number. I don't see any indications, but I do see his social security card. I grab it, and I have access to a number to call. Before leaving, I hear a voice yell out, "HEY! That's mine! Give it back!" I turn around and see no one other than the guy I shot. I then turn back and I see his ghost.

C.L. Williams is an independent author from central Virginia. He has written eight poetry books, four novellas, one novel, and a contributor to multiple anthologies, with the most recent appearance being an all-ages anthology titled Temoli from Thazbook. His most recent poetry book, The Paradox Complex, features the poem "Sad Crying Clown" that is now a video on YouTube directed by Matthew Mark Hunter of MMH Productions. C.L. Williams is currently working on his first sci-fi book, an all-ages book titled Novo: Away from Earth. When not writing, C.L. Williams is reading and sharing the work of other independent authors. Facebook: writer434
Twitter: @writer_434

The Old Haunt
by J. Farrington

We have a poltergeist in our house.

Mom and Dad don't believe me but, trust me, old Mrs Winters is real. I remember when she first showed up; I was nine when she wrote on my chalkboard 'I'm not here to harm you, my husband is coming'. She went on to warn me that he was an evil man, a man not to be trusted, he's the one who killed her. She's written that message every day for three years.

Until today.

We just had a knock at the door.

And a simple message left on the chalkboard

He's here.

J. Farrington is an aspiring author from the West Midlands, UK. His genre of choice is horror; whether that be psychological, suspense, supernatural or straight up weird, he'll give it a shot! He has loved writing from a young age but has only publicly been spreading his darker thoughts and sinister imagination via social platforms since 2018. If you would like to view his previous work, or merely lurk in the shadows...watching, you can keep up to date with future projects by spirit board or alternatively, the following;
Twitter: @SurvivorTrench
Reddit: TrenchChronicles

Will it End?
by Hunter LaCross

Sometimes I can hear my own screams resonate through the cold night air. The haunting memory of that night will play on repeat evermore. The frigid feel of the knife impaling me in the abdomen. The visions of my family torn apart from the demons lurking in the shadow.

Will it ever end?

Will that night even leave my blurred vision as I rot in a work unknown?

The answer to these questions, I will never know. It seems, for all the wrong I've done, I will be forced to watch this night for all eternity, screaming from the shadows.

Hunter LaCross, known on Reddit as XxAtroticusxX, is a customer service representative by day and a story teller by night. He lives in PA. He has been writing for just over a year. He lives with a fiance and a cat, both of whom take up most of his free time. He loves to L.A.R.P., and one day he aspires to create his own L.A.R.P game. His short horror stories have been published before, but he still enjoys remaining in the shadows.

Retribution
by Isabella Fox

Basketball practice finished late, so Jay took a shortcut through the cemetery. Cemeteries gave him the creeps, but the night was cold, and he was eager to get to his warm bed.

As he passed a newly filled grave, a black mass emerged from the dirt mound, swirling and morphing into an old woman. Her long bony hand pointed at him in accusation. She said, "You!"

"Oh, my God!" Jay exclaimed. "Mrs. McAdams, I swear it was an accident. I didn't mean to kill you."

The black mass engulfed him leaving only his basketball to be found the next day.

Isabella Fox teaches primary aged students to love writing by making it challenging. In her spare time she reads, goes for long walks with her husband and works hard on her farm.

Desolation
by Terry Miller

When I flatlined, I felt free. I watched as they pulled the cover over my head, relieved that I had requested my DNR. I turned to exit the room, then I crossed over.

I saw no light, no long tunnel. Instead, it was simply dark; not pitch-black, just dark. It was like a place where the Sun had never shined. No trees, no grass, nothing but barren land.

"Hello," I called out. Nothing.

I must've walked for miles. I walked, I ran, I screamed for someone, anyone. Was I truly alone in this desolate place?

I walked, ran, and wept.

Terry Miller is an author and 2017 Rhysling Award-nominated poet residing in Portsmouth, OH, USA. He has self-published a dark poetry collection on Amazon and one short story to date. His work has also appeared in Sanitarium, Devolution Z, Jitter Press, Poetry Quarterly, O Unholy Night in Deathlehem, and the 2017 Rhysling Anthology from the Science Fiction and Fantasy Poetry Association.
Facebook: tmiller2015

The Significance of the Spiritualist's Sentence
by Steven Holding

We slipped through the crowd towards a distant tent; a chalkboard sign declared "FORTUNE TELLER".

"It'll be fun!" he whispered.

Inside, the usual props were present. Flickering candles. Glass orb upon the table.

A withered crone draped in silk.

We took our seats.

With silver coin clutched in palm, the gypsy began to moan.

"Donnie still loves you!" she hissed at my husband. "He watches over you… Always…"

Suddenly, sobbing, he dragged me back into the daylight.

I held him tightly.

Then gasped, remembering tales of dead Uncle Donald.

And those terrible things he did to him as a child.

BEYOND

Steven Holding lives with his family in the United Kingdom. His stories have been published by TREMBLING WITH FEAR, FRIDAY FLASH FICTION, THEATRE CLOUD, AD HOC FICTION and MASSACRE MAGAZINE. Most recently, his story THREE CHORDS AND THE TRUTH received first place in the INKTEARS 2018 FLASH FICTION COMPETITION, while another of his pieces WALK WITH ME THROUGH THE LONG GRASS AND I SHALL HOLD YOUR HAND was runner up in the annual WRITING MAGAZINE 500 WORD SHORT STORY COMPETITION. He is currently working upon further short fiction and a novel.
Website: www.stevenholding.co.uk

327

Evil Intent
by Nicola Currie

The spirit follows as Marco walks me home from our first date.

All week the spirit cruelly mocked me, ridiculing old griefs, changing faces between those I've lost. I gave Marco my number last Saturday at the club, but it was the spirit who came home with me and stayed.

"Can I come in?" Marco asks.

I decline, turning towards my door. The spirit stands inches away, my dead brother's face contorted into murderous rage. I flinch as his arm shoots towards me.

It passes my shoulder. Brother spirit smiles and fades.

Marco clutches his chest, falls, drops his knife.

Nicola Currie is 34, from Cambridge, UK where she works in educational publishing. She has published poetry in literary magazines, including Mslexia and Sarasvati, and has also completed her first novel, which was longlisted for the Bath Children's Novel Award.
Website: writeitandweep.home.blog

Death in the Mirror
by Monica Schultz

The mirror reflects everything. Her pimpled face. The rolls of her stomach. Her vibrating phone with another anonymous text. But not Death.

Death stands shoulder-to-shoulder with Penny. *Pudgy Penny*. The name her mother screeches. Death wishes Penny could see herself through empty eye-sockets. The pits of Death's skull are kinder than a mirror.

Penny sheds the tears Death cannot. They dribble down her chin. *Drip*. Another smudge on the note. A million reasons to hurt.

Penny's hand trembles, but she has resolved. Razor to the vein. *Blood*. It pools around her feet. Death catches her as she falls. If only.

Monica Schultz writes young adult fantasy novels for anyone who needs an escape from reality. She can often be found reading novels, with a cat curled on her lap, to hide from her own mundane life.
*Twitter: @MonicaSchultz_*
Instagram: @miss.schultz

Death Crossing
by Shawn M. Klimek

Bernie Hedge pressed his Gucci soles onto the accelerator of his red, BMW convertible and made the hazy, blue mountain on the horizon rush to meet him. A triangular yellow sign warned of winding roads ahead. The wealthy financier zoomed confidently up the steep gradient and around sharp corners with scarcely a squeal. This mountain, too, would be his.

Soon, a second triangular yellow sign displayed an unlikely pedestrian crossing—one featuring a silhouetted hooded figure wielding a scythe.

Bernie laughed, rubbed his eyes, and reached for his designer sunglasses, fatally diverting his attention just as Death entered the crosswalk.

Shawn M. Klimek is the middle child of seven creative siblings, a globetrotting, U.S. military spouse, an internationally best-selling short-story writer, a poet, and butler to a Maltese. Almost one hundred of his stories or poems have been published in digital magazines or anthologies, including BHP's Deep Space and the first six books in the Dark Drabbles series.
Website: jotinthedark.blogspot.com
Facebook: shawnmklimekauthor

The End of the Line
by David Bowmore

I have been travelling for a long time.

Before I manned the train, I was in charge of a wagon and before that, a hand pulled cart. At some point in the far distant past, it had been just me.

This locomotive, with elegant trimmings, has served the souls well. I've enjoyed being the engineer. She and I have collected the souls of man and beast, bringing them to the afterlife they deserve, with a touch of grandeur.

Now, there's no one left to collect.

This is my final journey, and then it will be time for Death to retire.

David Bowmore has lived here, there and everywhere, but now lives in Yorkshire with his wonderful wife and a small white poodle. He has worn many hats in his time; head chef, teacher and landscape gardener. His first collection of short stories 'The Magic of Deben Market' is available from Clarendon House.
Website: davidbowmore.co.uk
Facebook: davidbowmoreauthor

Emily

by Andrew Anderson

John was snoozing. He was startled awake by his daughter, Jess, hysterically screaming.

"Go away, Emily!"

John bolted upstairs two at a time. He could hear a voice, a deafening whisper. Bursting into Jess' room without knocking, the noise abruptly stopped.

The cloying room smelled of rotted flowers.

He saw the figure sitting cross-legged before the vanity table, staring into the mirror.

Jess' long auburn hair was now bone white. She turned in instalments towards him. Her green eyes had each been replaced by a glistening black void.

"Jess isn't here now. It's Emily's turn. She doesn't play so nice."

Andrew Anderson is a full-time civil servant, dabbling in writing music, poetry, screenplays and short stories in his limited spare time, when not working on building himself a fort made out of second-hand books. He lives in Bathgate, Scotland with his wife, two children and his dog.
Twitter: @soorploom

From the Mists Beyond Time
by Chitra Gopalakrishnan

Mists, white shadows with teeth, close in on us.

It is midnight in the abandoned hilly Swala village in Uttrakhand, the December air so cold it hurts to breathe.

Sheltered within a crumbling, empty temple—the result of a car stall—we hear screams from within.

When we seek them, a rain of stones assails us.

Neighbouring villagers tell us of soldiers robbed and left to die by villagers when their truck fell into a trench in 1952.

And now they come here, from the mists beyond time, choosing to stay on and chase everyone who tries to gather roots.

Chitra Gopalakrishnan is a journalist by training, a social development communications consultant by profession and a creative writer by choice. Chitra's focus is on issues of gender, environment and health. Chitra dabbles in poetry on the sly and literary creations openly on the web using social media.

Website: unpublishedplatform.weebly.com/chitra-gopalakrishnan

Tapper
by Joachim Heijndermans

Tap tap tap!

I tap against the wall. One of them hears it. She just shrugs it off.

Tap tap tap!

Now they all hear me. They shiver. They jump. They look but do not see anything. One suggests it was a mouse. They relax. For now.

Tap tap tap!

One shrieks. One swears. The last wants to leave the house. They don't.

I could tap again, but I might lose them. And I would be alone again, trapped in the wall my Da holed me in all those years ago. I could tap, but I'll hold off.

For now.

Joachim Heijndermans writes, draws, and paints nearly every waking hour. Originally from the Netherlands, he's been all over the world, boring people by spouting random trivia. His work has been featured in a number of anthologies and publications, such as Mad Scientist Journal, Asymmetry Fiction, Hinnom Magazine, Ahoy Comics's Edgar Allan Poe's Snifter of Terror, Metaphorosis and The Gallery of Curiosities, and he's currently in the midst of completing his first children's book.
Website: www.joachimheijndermans.com
Twitter: @jheijndermans

Sorry
by Belinda Brady

The room is silent as the girls place their shaky fingers on the glass on the spirit board.

"Are you there, Ebony? I'm sorry. I was drunk…careless. I'd never have driven us home if I knew…" Sadie whispers.

The glass stays still.

"This is stupid," Sadie declares, jumping up from the table. "I'm going."

Sadie rushes from the house in tears, ignoring her friend's pleas to stay.

"I'm sorry, Ebony," she sobs, driving the familiar road home.

Ebony appears in the passenger seat, bloody and broken, just as the car makes a sharp turn towards a tree.

"Apology accepted."

Belinda Brady is passionate about stories and after years of procrastinating, has finally turned her hand to writing them, with a preference for supernatural and thriller themes; her love of both often competing for her attention. She has had several stories published in a variety of publications, both online and in anthologies. Belinda lives in Australia with her family and has been known to enjoy the company of cats over people.

A Soul Adrift
by Jo Seysener

"Which one are you?" the soul, who used to be a man, stuttered.

The angel shrugged indifferently.

"I wasn't aware there was more than one of me," he replied, idly flicking a squishy blob of ectoplasm from his holy visage.

The soul reached for the angel who shied away, flapping fastidiously at his robes.

"But...you *are* here to take me to the good place, aren't you?"

The angel sighed. The recently dead had *so* many questions, until they entered their destination. Then the questions stopped.

He flicked a hand, and just for giggles, changed his glowing robes to darkest black.

Jo Seysener is a mum of three crazies, a scatter of chickens, a decrepit kelpie and a rambunctious GSD. She lives with her husband near Brisbane, Australia. When she is not exposing her kids to cult story books from her childhood, she can be found in the kitchen experimenting with new flavours and pairings. She adores alpacas.
Facebook: joseysener
Website: www.joseysener.com

Widowmaker
by Peter J. Foote

The storm had been a harsh one, even the old oak at the park dubbed "Gallows Tree" had suffered.

A large limb had broken, and gotten caught, and the oak waited for its perfect victim.

Murders, thieves, and rapists had all hung from its strong boughs, it knew a twisted soul when it saw one, and didn't wait long.

"Old Dickie" Misner slunk out and hid behind the trunk to watch the children playing, his leering eyes, and heavy breathing betraying his nature.

The oak allowed the wind to dislodge its broken branch, the fall ending in a wet smack.

Peter J. Foote is a bestselling speculative fiction writer from Nova Scotia. Outside of writing, he runs a used bookstore specialising in fantasy & sci-fi, cosplays, and alternates between red wine and coffee as the mood demands. His short stories can be found in both print and in ebook form, with his story "Sea Monkeys" winning the inaugural "Engen Books/Kit Sora, Flash Fiction/Flash Photography" contest in March of 2018. As the founder of the group "Genre Writers of Atlantic Canada", Peter believes that the writing community is stronger when it works together.
Twitter: @PeterJFoote1
Website: peterjfooteauthor.wordpress.com

White Spectre
by E.L. Giles

"Can we go?" asked Samantha.

"Aw, c'mon, Sam. Don't be such a wimp."

Matthew took Samantha closer to the lake in which he had once seen her, the White Spectre.

"I want to go... I'm afraid."

"It's a bloody ghost, Sam. Nothing else."

Matthew smirked and approached the lake with a cocky swagger.

"See? Nothing happens to—"

A glacial draught silenced him. He tried to turn around but remained stuck, petrified.

"Matthew, it's right behind you!" screamed Sam.

A white, vaporous mass materialised behind Matthew, enveloping him in a shroud of icy shards.

"Run," a ghostly voice resonated. "Run."

E.L. Giles is a dreamer, passionate about art, a restless worker and a bit of a weird human. He started his artistic journey as a music composer until the need to put his thoughts and stories down on paper grew too strong for him to resist it any longer. He lives in the French Province of Quebec, Canada, with his girlfriend and two boys.
Facebook: elgilesauthor
Website: www.elgilesauthor.com

Homecoming
by Jonathan Inbody

Joey sat alone underneath the bleachers, clutching the plastic planchet and homemade spirit board. It had only taken him a half-hour to make, and that was including the five minutes he spent on the internet researching it. Tonight's dance would be starting soon, and all of his least-favourite classmates would be there smiling. Since he didn't have a date, Joey figured the night would be much improved by the return of his high school's championship-winning football team, even if they had died in that fiery bus crash nearly forty-five years ago.

"Let's see how they'd like some real school spirit."

Jonathan Inbody is a filmmaker, author, and podcaster from Buffalo, New York. He enjoys B-movies, pen and paper RPGs, and New Wave Science Fiction novels. His short story "Dying Feels Like Slowly Sinking" is due to be published in the anthology Deteriorate from Whimsically Dark Publishing. Jon can be heard every other week on his improvisational movie pitch podcast X Meets Y.
Website: xmeetsy.libsyn.com

It's Time
by Stuart Conover

Gary watched his son playing in the backyard.

He felt like it was only yesterday when he was still crawling.

It would be nice if they could spend more time together.

He'd love to play catch with his son, maybe take him for some ice cream.

"Tim," he called out.

His son didn't respond.

He hadn't in a very long time.

"ITS TIME," came the voice.

Gary slowly nodded.

The air shimmered around him as he stepped back into the ether.

He waved goodbye to his child.

Though he would never see it, Tim's father would always watch over him.

Stuart Conover is a father, husband, rescue dog owner, published author, blogger, journalist, horror enthusiast, comic book geek, science fiction junkie, and IT professional. With all of that to cram in daily, we have no idea if or when he sleeps or how he gets writing done! (We suspect it has to do with having evil clones.) Stuart is a Chicago native and runs the author resource Horror Tree.

A Strange Beauty
by Austin P. Sheehan

I knew this day would come, but I'm not ready.

They say it's meant to be beautiful, that I should be honoured, but I'm terrified.

I can feel them now, squirming under my skin, burrowing through my flesh.

Is it meant to hurt like this?

My arms are covered in bulging red spots. This is horrible. This is agony. Every inch of my flesh is being eaten from the inside. I can't last much longer.

***

Bellies full, our wings dry in the sun.

We honour our birthing mound before taking off as one, our beautiful turquoise wings filling the sky.

Austin P. Sheehan is a writer of speculative fiction, a lover of language, literature and '90s TV. Armed with a psychology degree, he went into the world to study humanity, and now prefers the company of his wife and their greyhounds. He grew up in the valleys of Victoria's high country, and despite living in Melbourne, always feels at home amongst the mountains. You'll often find mountains in his stories, whether they're sci-fi, fantasy or alternative history.
Website: austinpsheehan.com
Twitter: @AustinPSheehan

The Futility of Scrying
by Jonathan Ficke

The tea leaves remained silent, and I marked another failure in my journal. Mirrors, cards, tossed bones, all failures.

"Why won't you listen?"

The ephemeral whisper of a voice long since devoid of lips to speak danced in my ears. "If you'd speak to the dead, you know the price."

I ran my fingers along the crinkled corners of my eyes and tried to avert my gaze from the knife that lay on the edge of the table.

"Don't you want to hold me again?"

"I do." I took up the blade and laid it against my flesh. "I will."

Jonathan Ficke lives outside of Milwaukee, WI with his beautiful wife. His fiction has appeared in "Writers of the Future, Vol 34" and he muses online at;
Website: jonficke.com
Twitter: @jonficke

Ethereal Prey
by Alexander Pyles

"We can't let this one get away." The ectoplasm was scattered all around the woods. The green glowed like living emeralds. The spectre was wounded, but dangerous.

Nate came up behind me, panting. "It's not going to get away." He patted his holstered spectral pistol.

No time to lose. I began to run when a searing flash burned through my leg. I screamed as I fell. I twisted in the dirt to see who or what shot me.

Nate stood over me, his face slack. I noticed the small smear of green on his neck as he raised his gun.

Alexander Pyles resides in IL with his wife and children. He holds an MA in Philosophy and an MFA in Writing Popular Fiction. His short story chapbook titled, "Milo (01001101 01101001 01101100 01101111)," from Radix Media, is due out fall 2019. His other short fiction has appeared on 101fiction.org, River and South Review, and other venues. Website: www.pylesofbooks.com
Twitter: @Pylesofbooks

See No Evil
by Joel R. Hunt

For his entire life, Callum had been plagued by visions of the dead. They appeared before him, screamed at him, begged him to resolve their unfinished business in this world. After years of suffering, Callum finally met a doctor whose invasive—and expensive—surgery could set him free.

The implant was a success. Callum's ability to see and hear ghosts was entirely inhibited. At last, he could sleep undisturbed.

Until he felt them—a thousand cold, ethereal fingers clawing through his brain, trying to wrench the implant free. The spirits would stop at nothing to be seen.

Joel R. Hunt is a writer from the UK who dabbles in the darker aspects of life, particularly through horror, science fiction and the supernatural. He has been published here and there (though likely nowhere you've heard of) and hopes to have released his first anthology of short stories later this year.
Twitter: @JoelRHunt1
Reddit: JRHEvilInc

Payment
by Jodi Jensen

"Please, save her." Abner cradled his sickly newborn while his wife's hand stroked the downy, fuzz-covered head.

The cloaked being drew closer, red eyes glowing as its gnarled hand reached for the infant. "What'll you give for her life?" it whispered.

Abner glanced at his wife and nodded. Though she'd done the summoning, he'd offer himself as payment. The baby whimpered in his arms. "Anything you want."

A clawed finger touched the infant's forehead. "She'll live." Red eyes flashed under the hood as it snatched his wife.

The last thing Abner saw before they vanished, was the being's twisted smile.

Jodi Jensen grew up moving from California, to Massachusetts, and a few other places in between, before finally settling in Utah at the ripe old age of nine. The nomadic life fed her sense of adventure as a child and the wanderlust continues to this day. With a passion for old cemeteries, historical buildings and sweeping sagas of days gone by, it was only natural she'd dream of time traveling to all the places that sparked her imagination.

Alone
by Stephen Herczeg

Another Christmas alone.

I remember that night. My family beside me. Too much speed. Too many beers. Too many screams.

Then I was alone.

For so long I wallowed in my despair. Friends. Job. Relatives. All left me alone.

Last Christmas eve. I sought solace at the bottom of a bottle.

Looking up through bleary eyes, my family appeared before me. I ran to them. Hugged them. Overjoyed at their return, but by morning they were gone.

This year will be different. The cold steel feels heavy.

I'm ready to join them.

A simple squeeze and it will be over.

Stephen Herczeg is an IT Geek based in Canberra Australia. He has been writing for over twenty years and has completed a couple of dodgy novels, sixteen feature length screenplays and numerous short stories and scripts. His horror work has featured in Sproutlings, Hells Bells, Below the Stairs, Trickster's Treats #1 and #2, Shades of Santa, Behind the Mask, Beyond the Infinite; The Body Horror Book, Anemone Enemy, Petrified Punks and Beginnings. He has also had numerous Sherlock Holmes stories published through the Belanger Books - Sherlock Holmes anthologies.

Souls of Restless Women
by Matthew Wilson

Nans are not nice people. Not after I stole her money, and then she swore to haunt me.

I thought her cancer would end my problems, but some souls do not pass on.

My wife screamed when our house burned. I did when my newborn girl inherited my nan's eyes. Nothing good came of the old hag's money; the food I bought with it soured in my mouth.

Her footsteps still resonate in the attic and lightning illuminates her smile at the window.

Nans aren't nice. It was her that killed my family, but no one believes me.

Matthew Wilson has been published over 200 times in such places as Horror Zine, Star*Line, Zimbell House Publishing and many more. He is currently editing his first novel.

Reflections
by Jem McCusker

I hang from the ceiling, my surface pristine and void of touch. Below me, I reflect on the long white sheet, billowing out in its attempt to conceal its deepest secrets. The soft glow of candle light illuminates me and provides warmth to my cold sterility.

I gravitate toward the warmth. I see her. My body lays before me. A shell prone to vanity. The Keeper looks through me.

"I sense you. Leave now, fallen spirit." He holds his precious plant over the candle.

Ignoring him, I lay across my body, ready to return.

Then it hits: he burnt sage.

Jem McCusker is a middle grade fiction author, living near Brisbane with her two sons and husband. Her first book Stone Guardians the Rise of Eden was released in 2018 and she is working on the sequel. She is releasing a Novella for the Four Quills writing group, A Storm of Wind and Rain series in July, 2019. She longs to be a full-time author, won't wear yellow and loves rabbits. Follow Jem on Twitter, Facebook and Instagram. Details on her website. Website: www.jemmccusker.com

On the Other Side of the Dark Entry Gate

by Sara L. Uckelman

Don't slam the gate—you'll wake the monsters on the other side. There's a reason we keep it open, just a crack, so that we do not disturb their slumber. Keep the hinges well oiled, too, so that they do not hear the grind of metal upon metal. You needn't be afraid; I've crossed beyond many a time. The monsters leave you alone if you leave them alone. What, you ask, *aren't the monsters lonely?* Yes, sometimes they get lonely. Sometimes they put on a kind face and try to find a friend. Me? Of course I'm not a monster.

Sara L. Uckelman is an assistant professor of logic and philosophy of language at Durham University by day and a writer of speculative fiction by night. Her short stories are published or forthcoming in Manawaker Studio Flash Fiction Podcast, Pilcrow & Dagger, Story Seed Vault, and The Martian Wave, and anthologies published by Exterus, Flame Tree Publishing, Hic Dragones, Jayhenge Publications, QueerSciFi, and WolfSinger Publications. She is also the co-founder of the reviews site SFFReviews.com.

Tuned In
by A.R. Johnston

If there was anything that she hated more, it was people who didn't pay attention. The veil really was thin, everyone should be able to see her. She could run down the hallway naked if she wanted, it wouldn't matter. No one seemed to notice her anymore. No one was 'tuned in' enough. She strolled back to her attic room, completely starkers. She giggled, sticking out her tongue at the cat who hissed.

She entered her room, the door shutting as if by phantom breeze.

"Can you put some clothes on, please?" He stood there staring at her.

She gasped.

A.R. Johnston is a small-town girl from Nova Scotia, Canada. Her style of writing is considered Urban Fantasy. Her first major publication is part of an anthology called First Love and she has several more titles lined up. She is a lover of coffee, good tv shows, horror flicks, and reader of books. She pretends to be a writer when real life doesn't get in the way. Pesky full-time job and adulting!

One Last Time
by K.T. Tate

Urgent pounding on our hotel door wakes me. Scrambling up I open it. The bellboy fidgets awkwardly as he speaks.

"Sorry to disturb you, sir, but you're needed at reception."

"It's 2am," I growl, tired.

"Sir, it's about your wife."

"Did she complain already? Good for her. You're meant to be the country's most haunted hotel but we've not experienced anything all weekend. But surely this can wait till morning?"

The bellboy pales, "But, sir, you've been here alone."

"What?" I mutter, turning to my unexpectedly empty bed.

"The police are downstairs, there was an accident, she never made it."

K.T. Tate lives in Cambridgeshire in the UK. She writes mainly weird fiction, cosmic horror and strange monster stories.
Website: eldritchhollow.wordpress.com
Tumblr: eldritch-hollow.tumblr.com

Board and Bodies
by Will Shadbolt

"I," read Ben, staring at the spirit board. "W."

Marcus sat cross-legged with rapt attention, while John looked on with a half-amused smile.

"A."

They had asked, "Why do you haunt Earth?" Some good intentions were involved—"Maybe we can help"—but it was mostly just teenagers' curiosity in the occult.

"Can we play videogames or something after?" asked John, failing to suppress a yawn.

Neither Ben nor Marcus paid him any mind. "N."

"Guys..."

"T." Ben and Marcus gazed at each other, wondering what the spirit wanted.

Then John spoke with a deep voice: "I wanted a new body."

Will Shadbolt has lived across the world, including in Germany and China. He currently works in NYC. His fiction has appeared in Daily Science Fiction and numerous drabble anthologies.

Death's Door
by Crystal L. Kirkham

A young boy stood amid the chaos of shattered glass and twisted metal, his eyes wide with fear.

"Are you looking for your mom?" a woman asked, and held out her hand to him. He stared at it in silence, unsure of what to do.

"It'll take you to her, I promise." She smiled kindly.

He hesitated for a moment and then took her skeletal hand. As soon as he did, a door opened behind her. His mother waited on the other side and he ran to her, laughing and happy.

The door closed, and she wiped away a tear.

Crystal L. Kirkham *resides in a small hamlet west of Red Deer, Alberta. She's an avid outdoors person, unrepentant coffee addict, part-time foodie, servant to a wonderful feline, and companion to two delightfully hilarious canines. She will neither confirm nor deny the rumours regarding the heart in a jar on her desk and the bottle of reader's tears right next to it. Her paranormal urban fantasy series, Saints and Sinners, is available on Amazon and her YA Fantasy, Feathers and Fae will be released October 11, 2019, from Kyanite Publishing.*
Website: www.crystallkirkham.com

Universe
by Pamela Jeffs

The beeping of the heart monitor fades. As does the touch of the hand tightly holding mine. My desire to linger pervades, but my time is due.

My family weeps as I pass.

I will be missed.

That last thought weighs heavy in me as the darkness creeps in. I feel afraid, as I am set adrift. Sorrowful heaviness fills my soul.

But I have no voice to ease it.

And then I begin to forget.

The darkness around me lightens revealing a vast infinite dotted with stars.

The Universe.

Then I understand. Death is the door to the infinite.

Pamela Jeffs is a speculative fiction author living in Queensland, Australia with her husband and two daughters. She is a member of the Queensland Writers' Centre and has had numerous short fiction pieces published in recent national and international anthologies. In 2017 and again in 2018, Pamela was nominated for an Australian Aurealis Award in the category of 'Best Science Fiction Short Story'. Her debut collection titled 'Red Hour and Other Strange Tales' was released in March 2018.
Website: www.pamelajeffs.com
Facebook: pamelajeffsauthor

Antique Beauty
by Matthew M. Montelione

Dustin entered the nineteenth-century house and shut the door. He shivered, excited to be the only one in the historic Long Island home. He relished the antique air until the floorboards creaked above him.

He ascended the staircase and peered into a dusty room. A portrait of a young woman adorned the wall.

"God," he said as he stared at the painting, "you're beautiful."

The armoire's door opened and touched his shoulder. Dustin backed up into the hallway. The door to the room creaked towards him but did not shut.

Dustin nervously left; his body yearned for one long dead.

Matthew M. Montelione is a horror writer born and raised on Long Island in New York. His stories have been published in Quoth the Raven: A Contemporary Reimagining of the Works of Edgar Allan Poe, Thuggish Itch: Devilish, MONSTERS: A Horror Microfiction Anthology, Eerie Christmas, and other titles. Matthew is also an American Revolution historian who focuses on the local experiences of Loyalists on Long Island. His work on the subject has been published in Long Island History Journal and Journal of the American Revolution. Matthew lives with his wife in New York.
Website: maybeevils.com
Twitter: @maybeevils

Naïve
by Rich Rurshell

"What in the blazes is this ritual?"

Seth stared scornfully at his younger brother's friends. They stood naked around a pentagram marked out in parcel tape on the living room floor.

"We're Satanists," replied Richard. "We're raising the devil."

"Have you even read The Satanic Bible?" asked Seth.

"My sister has it," replied a girl with dozens of piercings in her face.

"I asked if you'd read it."

The following silence answered his question. Seth shook his head and left the room.

Upstairs, he meditated. Soon enough, he felt the presence of the higher being.

"Forgive them…they are naïve."

Rich Rurshell *is a short story writer from Suffolk, England. Rich writes Horror, Sci-Fi, and Fantasy, and his stories can be found in various short story anthologies and magazines. Most recently, his story "Subject: Galilee" was published in World War Four from Zombie Pirate Publishing, and "Life Choices" was published in Salty Tales from Stormy Island Publishing. When Rich is not writing stories, he likes to write and perform music.*
Facebook: richrurshellauthor

The End of Time
by Carole de Monclin

Harbinger of destruction, the sun looms enormous and blinding in the sky.

Soon, I'll follow the others and let myself drift into space. Last respects must be paid first. Centuries ago, Earth saw me live and die.

Sadly, nothing remains of the green expanses that covered her but scorched dust. The oceans boiled. Life vanished without a trace.

If only I could keep a handful of soil as a memento.

We ghosts are granted eternity to wander, explore, and contemplate. Earth was by nature ephemeral.

As I float into the unknown, I wonder if eternity ends when the Universe does.

Carole de Monclin *has lived in France and Australia, but for the moment the USA is home. She finds inspiration from her travels. She loves Science Fiction because it explores the human mind in a way no other genre can. Plus, who doesn't love spaceships and lasers? Her stories appear in the Exoplanet Magazine and Angels - A Dark Drabbles Anthology.*
Website: CaroledeMonclin.com
Twitter: @CaroledeMonclin

Do Something
by Gabriella Balcom

"I *have* to know why my husband is acting differently," Marion stressed. "I'm afraid he's sick or dying."

"My crystal ball will reveal the truth," Leetha replied. "But understand I don't control what you'll see."

After staring into the ball, Marion wailed, "He's *cheating* on me with another woman. Please *do* something!"

"All right. I can help you, but I need to know exactly what you want. For example, I can make her hair fall out, or her teeth. He can become impotent, or I can cause them to sicken and die."

Marion demanded, "Can you do all of that?"

Gabriella Balcom lives in Texas with her family, loves reading and writing, and thinks she was born with a book in her hands. She works in a mental health field, and writes fantasy, horror/thriller, romance, children's stories, and sci-fi. She likes travelling, music, good shows, photography, history, interesting tales, and animals. Gabriella says she's a sucker for a great story and loves forests, mountains, and back roads which might lead who knows where. She has a weakness for lasagne, garlic bread, tacos, cheese, and chocolate, but not necessarily in that order.
Facebook: GabriellaBalcom.lonestarauthor

River of Memory
by Zoey Xolton

The river churned and swirled, the current strong. Hidden treasures tumbled beneath the waves, revealed by the shifting silt. A locket, tarnished by time and rusted by the waters, caught on a hook that withdrew swiftly from the river's depths.

The fisherman reeled in his unlikely prize, turning it over in wizened hands. With effort, he opened it. His voice caught in his throat and tears welled in his eyes. It was her. It'd been forty long years since his wife drowned.

Blinking back the tears, he glanced across to the opposite bank. She smiled, and then she was gone.

Zoey Xolton is an Australian Speculative Fiction writer, primarily of Dark Fantasy, Paranormal Romance and Horror. She is also a proud mother of two and is married to her soul mate. Outside of her family, writing is her greatest passion. She is especially fond of short fiction and is working on releasing her own themed collections in future.
Website: www.zoeyxolton.com

An Old Man's Best Friend
by Glenn R. Wilson

"How have you lived to be a hundred?"

At this, the old man held up an old shotgun that he carefully placed back at his side.

Perplexed, I couldn't help but ask him why—.

"Just sit there and wait."

Roused from a deep sleep hours later, I cleared my eyes quick enough to see the vision of a misty figure with scythe in hand approach the old man. Fast as a cat, he grabbed his weapon and fired. The figure disintegrated.

"How did you do that?"

"Rock salt and holy water," he said, while patting its handle with a smile.

.

Glenn R. Wilson has come full circle. Making a point to mature, like fine wine, before diving head-first into his long list of writing projects, he's approaching them with a plan. That strategy is to build with one brick at a time. He's accumulated a few bricks already and is adding more. Over time, with persistence and determination, he'll have a home. But for now, a solid foundation is the goal. Please, enjoy the process with him.

Compunction
by David Shakes

She stares at him through the steamed cafe window. She's anguished. Pressing grey finger to cold glass, she writes:

It was...

Two women bustle past, one asks the other if she's heard about the suicide girl. They don't see her.

Her slow scribing continues, and though her finger remains poised, the accusation is complete:

It was you.

But both those women and the coroner say otherwise.

She uses her other hand to raise a small bundle from her lap. There's a foetal shape nestled within. Impossibly, it moves.

Her finger traces the final letters of her message:

It was yours.

David Shakes is a writer and artist residing in Birmingham, England. He has been writing since he turned forty, predominantly in the flash fiction forums. He was a founding 'Flashdog' – an international group of flash fiction writers with several anthologies and Twitter competitions to their name. He is co-editor of 'The Infernal Clock' – a series of time themed horror anthologies. David's work has featured in numerous anthologies and publications, including being one of the few fiction writers to be published in The Birmingham Mail. The horror genre is David's first passion, alongside amateur photography and folklore. He also likes beer.
Twitter: @TheShakes72

Kalma's Decision
by Vonnie Winslow Crist

What is that putrid smell? wondered Viktor. *And why am I being subjected to it after death?*

The answer drifted toward him: a woman riding a cloud of stench.

"Who are you?" he asked.

"Kalma, Goddess of Decomposition."

Viktor noticed her eyes were white.

"I decide your afterlife destination," she explained.

"What if I'm happy here?"

"Then, you become one of the Old Folk—flesh gone, moss growing on bones. You'll be summoned by shamans to fight witches and goblins."

"Seriously?" Viktor realised she wasn't joking. "Wait!"

"Decision made," said Kalma as Viktor's shadow rejoined his corpse to await reanimation.

Vonnie Winslow Crist is author of The Enchanted Dagger, Owl Light, The Greener Forest, Murder on Marawa Prime, and other award-winning books. Her fiction is included in "Amazing Stories," "Cast of Wonders," "Outposts of Beyond," Killing It Softly 2, Defending the Future - Dogs of War, Midnight Masquerade, Chaos of Hard Clay, and elsewhere. A cloverhand who has found so many four-leafed clovers she keeps them in jars, Vonnie strives to celebrate the power of myth in her writing.
Website: www.vonniewinslowcrist.com

Date Auction
by Mark Mackey

Miranda Davenport, in desperate need of some cash, came up with a perfect idea on how she would get it. She'd auction a date with herself on Ebay.

Perfect, that was, until the winning bidder showed up at her doorstep for their date.

Who he was made her frown. His hooded cloak and scythe gripped in his hand, held across his chest, revealed him to be the one and only Grim Reaper, his bone white skull gleaming out from underneath his hood.

"Let's go, we have reservations at a fancy steakhouse at eight sharp. Right before I claim your soul."

Mark Mackey is the author of various self-published books and has had various short stories published in charity anthologies. They include such captivating titles such as Christmas Lites, No Sleeves and Short Dresses: A Summer Anthology, Painted Mayhem, and Grynn Anthology, among others. A long-time resident of Chicago, when not writing, he spends time reading various genres of books.

Spectre
by Brandy Bonifas

I see him each night at the edge of the woods, a transparent spectre. We're no longer of the same world, but I'd loved him, and he still comes to visit.

I follow him through the woods…back to our house. Standing over the bed we once shared, I watch him sleep. He wakes in a cold sweat screaming my name, his hands clutching his throat the same way he wrapped them around my neck, choking the life from me.

I return to the woods until tomorrow night…when his guilty conscience will come again to haunt my unmarked grave.

Brandy Bonifas lives in Ohio with her husband and son. Her work has appeared or is forthcoming in anthologies by Clarendon House Publications, Pixie Forest Publishing, Zombie Pirate Publishing, and Blood Song Books, as well as the online publications CafeLit and Spillwords Press.
Website: www.brandybonifas.com
Facebook: brandybonifasauthor

Beyond
by Alanna Robertson-Webb

My finger brushed across the well-worn planchette, and I wished for the millionth time that my mother reach out to me from the *Beyond*.

I focused my energy on the piece of wood, as though I could move it by sheer willpower. I was about to give up when suddenly the word 'garden' was rapidly spelled out.

"Thank you, Mother dearest."

She was always so loving, so compassionate, up until she married that man. I need to know where he's buried so I can attempt to salt and burn his bones.

Then, just maybe, the spirit haunting me will stop.

Alanna Robertson-Webb is a sales support member by day, and a writer and editor by night. She loves VT, and lives in NY. She has been writing since she was five years old, and writing well since she was seventeen years old. She lives with a fiance and a cat, both of whom take up most of her bed space. She loves to L.A.R.P., and one day she aspired to write a horrifyingly fantastic novel. Her short horror stories have been published before, but she still enjoys remaining mysterious.
Reddit: MythologyLovesHorror

When the Lights Go Out
by Rowanne S. Carberry

Skin writhing, fingers curling, eyes rolling, mouth foaming, Jack convulses off the bed.

A hand pushes against his stomach from the inside, those around the bed recoil.

The priest gulps and crosses himself before stepping forwards.

Unstopping the Holy water, he finds the words he needs.

"Demon, I repel you," the priest shouts, throwing Holy water on the writhing body. Skin rippling, a head presses through the chest cavity, an eerie scream followed by black smoke.

Jack awakens.

"Where am I?"

Sighs of relief echo through the room. Untying him, no one notices the flash of black in his eyes.

BEYOND

Rowanne S. Carberry was born in England in 1990, where she stills lives now with her cat Wolverine. Rowanne has always loved writing, and her first poem was published at the age of 15, but her ambition has always been to help people. Rowanne studied at the University of Sunderland where she completed combined honours of Psychology with Drama. Rowanne writes to offer others an escape. Although Rowanne writes in varied genres each story or poem she writes will often have a darkness to it, which helped coin her brand, Poisoned Quill Writing – Wicked words from a poisoned quill.
Facebook: PoisonedQuillWriting
Instagram: @poisoned_quill_writing

Sunrise Awaits
by Cindar Harrell

The flesh between my teeth was tender, the blood sweet. So young. I dropped the corpse, letting my fangs slide out with a pop. The girl was dead. My girl.

What was left of my humanity screamed in terror from inside the demon's vessel, my old body. I wanted to break free, but my soul was in chains.

How did this happen? Why me? Why *her*?

Warmth ghosted over my skin and a whisper reached my ear. It was her; my Emmaline. Her spectral shade beckoned me as the sky lightened, turning crimson.

"This way, Mommy. Sunrise awaits."

I followed.

Cindar Harrell loves fairy tales, especially ones with a dark twist. Her stories are often fairy tale inspired, but she is also working on a mystery series. Her stories can be found on Amazon and in various anthologies. You can follow her on Facebook and visit her blog, which she promises to try and update more often,
Website: cindarharrell.wordpress.com
Facebook: CindarHarrell

Resurrection
by Raven Corinn Carluk

I stepped inside and was met by the scent of death. Breathing deep, I smiled at the distraught man. "You've made the right decision," I said.

He wrung his hands. "Wife keeps crying. I had to...the digging."

"I know," I crooned. "The coffin is always so hard when it's so small."

"Will she remember...?"

"No." I followed my nose to the girl's bedroom. "It will be like she was having a bad dream."

Except she won't be your little girl. Souls never come back. She'll be my minion, waiting for my orders. Grief makes people trust anyone who offers help.

Raven Corinn Carluk *writes dark fantasy, paranormal romance, and anything else that catches her interest. She's authored five novels, where she explores themes of love and acceptance. Her shorter pieces, usually from her darker side, can be found in Black Hare Press anthologies, at Detritus Online, and through Alban Lake Publishers.*
Twitter: @ravencorinn
Website: RavenCorinnCarluk.Blogspot.Com

A Wasted Gift
by Sinister Sweetheart

The pain's been too much, for as long as I can remember. Since then, my mind's been plagued with voices, most of them mine. But then there are...others. *You'll never be enough. The high will never last. Everything is meaningless.*

Give up.

The noose tight around my throat; I jump. The jolt of my weight is temporary; as if the rope's elongating. My breath never falters.

I crash into a sea of nothing; my body and senses fading. The other voices are here, along with their owners. God and Satan argue omnisciently, furious to have both lost a soul.

*Since **Sinister Sweetheart** made her first post to a popular Internet forum, she's taken the horror community by storm. Her ability to create, terrify, and drive home her stories is insurmountable. Sinister Sweetheart's published works can be found in multiple anthologies for all to read, but be forewarned, if you do... you may want to call your therapist after, her stories are terrifying, disturbing and devilishly unsettling. She is not only a fright visually, but also has a creepy tentacle in horror podcasting as well. Sinister Sweetheart writes, voice acts and is the media director of the Scarecrow Tales podcast.*
Website: Sinistersweetheart.wixsite.com/sinistersweetheart
Facebook: NMBrownStories

Survivor
by Eddie D. Moore

Suzan spread a blanket beside the freshly turned dirt of a too-small grave. Hot tears fell from her cheeks as she laid down and used her jacket as a pillow. The sun slowly slipped behind the trees, and darkness fell around her. A gentle breeze rustled the leaves, and a wind chime rang soft soothing tones in the distance.

She ran her fingers through the loose dirt and softly whispered, "This isn't the way things were supposed to happen. We were supposed to die together."

Small, cold arms wrapped around her neck, and she heard a familiar voice say, "Mommy."

Eddie D. Moore *travels hundreds of hours a year, and he fills that time by listening to audiobooks. When he isn't playing with his grandchildren, he writes his own stories. You can find a list of his publications on his blog or by visiting his Amazon Author Page. While you're there, be sure to pick up a copy of his mini-anthology Misfits & Oddities. Website: eddiedmoore.wordpress.com Amazon: amazon.com/author/eddiedmoore*

Sparkles
by J.M. Meyer

"I have a grandma-like figure here asking for her granddaughter, Lauren," the medium, Sparkles, tells the crowd.

Samantha nudges her sceptical sister, Lisa. "That's Mom, she means my youngest daughter, Lori."

Lisa rolls her eyes.

"This woman tells me she passed from an accident late last year."

"See how she says general things? It's a hustle," Lisa whispers to Samantha.

Samantha calls out, "It's my mom."

Sparkles walks over to the sisters and closes her eyes.

"Lisa." The medium glares accusingly into Lisa's eyes.

She knows my name, Lisa thinks, terrified.

"She's asking, 'Why did you cut my brakes, Lisa?'"

J.M. Meyer *is writer, artist and small business owner living in New York., where she received her master's degree from Teacher's College, Columbia University. Jacqueline loves the science fiction and horror genres. Reading Ray Bradbury was a mind-blowing experience for her in 8th grade. Alfred Hitchcock and Rod Serling were the horror heroes of her youth. Mercedes M. Yardley is her current horror writing hero. Jacqueline also enjoys the company of her husband Bruce and their three children, Julia, Emma and Lauren. Jacqueline's mantra: The only time it's too late to try something new is when you are dead.*
Website: jmoranmeyer.net
Twitter: @moran_meyer

Portal
by Umair Mirxa

Parisa wiped the lonely tear running down her cheek and put the framed photograph back on the desk.

"You know," said a voice behind her, one she had been most desperate to hear again. "You promised you wouldn't sit around and mope once I was gone."

She stared at him, the crooked smile and the untidy hair exactly as they'd been in life.

"H-how are you here?"

"I believe it's more pertinent to ask why I'm here," he said, as a dark portal appeared behind him.

Her screams were silenced abruptly as he dragged her into the portal with him.

Umair Mirxa lives in Karachi, Pakistan. His first published story, 'Awareness', appeared on Spillwords Press. He has also had stories accepted for anthologies from Zombie Pirate Publishing, Blood Song Books, Fantasia Divinity Magazine and Publishing, and Iron Faerie Publishing. He is a massive J.R.R. Tolkien fan, and loves everything to do with fantasy and mythology. He enjoys football, history, music, movies, TV shows, and comic books, and wishes with all his heart that dragons were real.
Website: www.umairmirxa.com
Facebook: UMirxa12

I'm Here
by Terry Miller

There was a chill in the night air. Kyle felt like someone just walked over his grave, a feeling he couldn't shake. He shivered on the long walk down Fifth Avenue, all hairs stood on end. He turned to see if someone was watching him, but no one was there.

At the apartment, Kyle turned on the shower for a quick warm up, steam quickly filling the room. The water felt great and relieved the shivers instantly. He finished, dried himself off, then was hit with another chill. He stood at the vanity, the fogged mirror read I'M HERE, KYLE.

Terry Miller is an author and 2017 Rhysling Award-nominated poet residing in Portsmouth, OH, USA. He has self-published a dark poetry collection on Amazon and one short story to date. His work has also appeared in Sanitarium, Devolution Z, Jitter Press, Poetry Quarterly, O Unholy Night in Deathlehem, and the 2017 Rhysling Anthology from the Science Fiction and Fantasy Poetry Association.
Facebook: tmiller2015

The Deal
by Stuart Conover

Kyla would give anything for one last moment with her true love.

Blood, pain, and now part of her soul.

That is what the demon demanded.

In exchange, she would be with Julie again.

One last day together.

The air shimmered.

Pain ripped through her.

She had expected that.

What she hadn't expected lay before her.

Julie.

Not how she'd been in the prime of her life.

It was at the end.

In the hospital bed.

There, but not.

Already dead.

"This wasn't the deal," she cried out.

"You only asked for a day. Not which one," the demon replied.

BEYOND

Stuart Conover *is a father, husband, rescue dog owner, published author, blogger, journalist, horror enthusiast, comic book geek, science fiction junkie, and IT professional. With all of that to cram in daily, we have no idea if or when he sleeps or how he gets writing done! (We suspect it has to do with having evil clones.) Stuart is a Chicago native and runs the author resource Horror Tree.*

Voices
by David Bowmore

It was the only option she had.

The specialists had investigated and found nothing living or dead in the pipes or wall cavities.

The paranormal investigators found nothing with spectrographs or recording devices.

But she was knew she was right. The sounds were there, when the library was empty, and she was alone. Breathing, whispering and sometimes she heard a trumpet playing a lonely tune.

Only when she was alone. But she wasn't mad, most definitely not.

As head librarian, it was her responsibility. Her duty.

The building burned for three days.

The voices thanked her for setting them free.

David Bowmore has lived here, there and everywhere, but now lives in Yorkshire with his wonderful wife and a small white poodle. He has worn many hats in his time; head chef, teacher and landscape gardener. His first collection of short stories 'The Magic of Deben Market' is available from Clarendon House.
Website: davidbowmore.co.uk
Facebook: davidbowmoreauthor

The Haunted Auction
by Shawn M. Klimek

The clerk pointed to his watch. The auctioneer nodded, and then revealed to the crowded gallery of attentive bidders, an antique, wooden spirit board and edge-worn planchette.

"Last, we present Item 56: the spirit board first owned by William Butler Yeats, then later employed by Aleister Crowley to summon the ghost of Little Lord Fauntleroy. Bidding will start at $1,000. Who will bid first for this priceless, occult relic? Anyone? Anyone?"

His breath fogged the air. The planchette levitated briefly before falling to the podium. The noise echoed through the now empty gallery.

"Too late," declared the clerk, dejectedly. "Sunrise."

Shawn M. Klimek is the middle child of seven creative siblings, a globetrotting, U.S. military spouse, an internationally best-selling short-story writer, a poet, and butler to a Maltese. Almost one hundred of his stories or poems have been published in digital magazines or anthologies, including BHP's Deep Space and the first six books in the Dark Drabbles series.
Website: jotinthedark.blogspot.com
Facebook: shawnmklimekauthor

Driving Home for Christmas
by Stevie Adler

Christmas eve, Michael should have stayed at the airport. Instead, the hire car is embedded in a snowdrift.

Should have stayed put but reckoned on a three hour hike, tops. It was now past midnight.

Scrunch, scrunch, scrunching along, Michael's mind wandered. Did little Stevie put out mince pies and brandy for Santa? He could do with a nip. With hardly a breeze, moon lit frozen whiteness continued to feather down, dampening sound, dampening spirit. In different circumstances this would be magical.

The distant beacon of a porch light twinkled into view and Michael collapsed here, like every year before.

Stevie Adler is a retired IT Professional enjoying writing and publishing short stories especially Microfiction. He concentrates his writing on his website.
Website: medium.com/stevieadlerteachandblog/steviesmicrofiction

Adopted
by Eddie D. Moore

Cara dropped a match into the bowl of incense, let three drops of her deceased husband's blood fall into the flames, and consulted the spirit board.

Children's music playing in the adjacent room bled through the walls as she spoke. "Are you there, my love?"

The planchette moved slowly without anyone touching it to the 'yes' painted on the board.

"I've found us another daughter. Can you see her?"

The planchette moved off the 'yes' and then back again.

"Does she please you?"

The planchette moved. Cara sighed, picked up her knife, blew out the flames and left the room.

Eddie D. Moore *travels hundreds of hours a year, and he fills that time by listening to audiobooks. When he isn't playing with his grandchildren, he writes his own stories. You can find a list of his publications on his blog or by visiting his Amazon Author Page. While you're there, be sure to pick up a copy of his mini-anthology* Misfits & Oddities. *Website: eddiedmoore.wordpress.com*
Amazon: amazon.com/author/eddiedmoore

Running Late
by Amber M. Simpson

I rushed into the classroom, running late as usual. And like usual, my students didn't seem to notice.

"Good morning, class," I called, but it fell on deaf ears. Again, like usual.

It wasn't until I began writing equations on the chalkboard that the cacophony of chatter abruptly stopped. They were finally paying attention!

Just then, Principal Horn walked in, a sombre look on his pale, pudgy face.

"I'm sorry to have to tell you this, class," he said, wiping his brow, "but Ms. Claymore was in a fatal car accident on her way to school this morning."

Well, shit.

Amber M. Simpson is a chronic nighttime writer with a penchant for dark fiction and fantasy. When she's not editing for Fantasia Divinity Magazine, she divides her creative time (when she's not procrastinating) between writing a mystery/horror novel, working on a medieval fantasy series, and coming up with new ideas for short stories. Above all, she enjoys being a mom to her two greatest creations, Max and Liam, who keep her feet on the ground even while her head is in the clouds.
Website: www.ambermsimpson.com

BEYOND

BLACK HARE PRESS

ACKNOWLEDGEMENTS

Thank you, once again, to all the amazing authors who submitted to our fourth Dark Drabbles anthology. As always, we had a great time reading through the hundreds of micro tales that were sent in.

There's such a vast talent pool of new and seasoned authors out there that we always have a hard time choosing which ones will appear in these publications, but we're grateful for every one we receive, and appreciative of the time taken to create them.

Thank you to everyone who has supported us, too; we hope we'll make you proud every step of our journey.

www.blackharepress.com

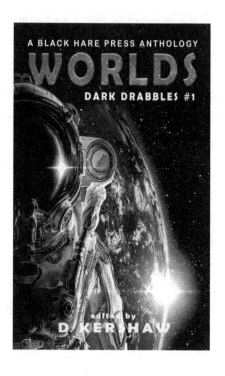

Stories of new worlds, new creatures, alien colonisation, humanity's new home, space accidents, alien snackcidents, evil planets, military mashups, alien autopsies, and much, much more.

Available 25th June 2019

Beatific angels, holy wars, kitty saviours, epic battles between good and evil, devils and demons, fallen angels and many more tantalising tiny tales.

Available 23rd July 2019

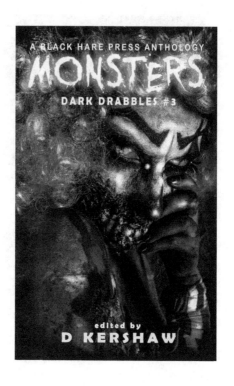

Wendigos, vampires, things that go bump in the night or hide under the bed, witches, demons, upirs, kelpies, toad people, zombies, sirens and hundreds of other tiny terrifying tales.

Available 20th August 2019

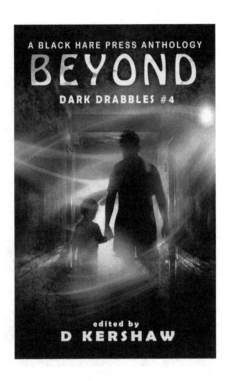

Micro myths of the paranormal;
poltergeists, spirit boards, ghosts
and ghouls, avenging apparitions
and horrifying hauntings.

Available 3rd September 2019

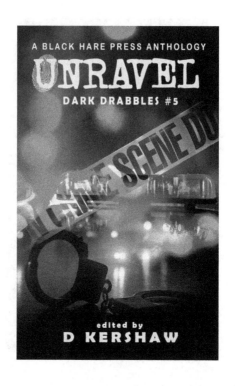

Murder mysteries, criminal chronicles, whodunnits, revenge, suspicion, mayhem, intrigue, and lots more.

Available 17th September 2019

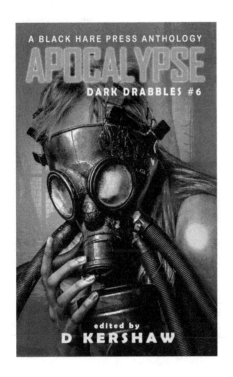

Coming soon

BEYOND

BLACK HARE PRESS

BEYOND